Follow Me West

God bless you!

Sonny

Follow Me West

THE LEGEND OF ABRAHAM

H.L. "Sonny" Jacks

1St Edit by Martha Smith

CROSSBOOKS
PUBLISHING

CrossBooks™
A Division of LifeWay
1663 Liberty Drive
Bloomington, IN 47403
www.crossbooks.com
Phone: 1-866-879-0502

First published by CrossBooks 10/17/2011

ISBN: 978-1-4627-0675-4 (sc)
ISBN: 978-1-4627-0676-1 (hc)
ISBN: 978-1-4627-1144-4 (e)

Library of Congress Control Number: 2011916574

Printed in the United States of America
This book is printed on acid-free paper.

Dedication

So, who does a small town country boy dedicate his first published book to? Well, to God. This book isn't about anything other than hopefully encouraging readers to find out more about Abraham and the life he had following God.

I have been blessed in my life to be surrounded by Christian people like my mother. My mother is a single mother that raised me and my two sisters by herself. Moving us from the city as children to a place we thought was surely hell, was the best thing she could have ever done, other than her continuous prayer. She moved us to the small town of Antlers, Oklahoma where she grew up as a child. There she worked six days a week to provide for the entire family. As I wrote this book, the events of our lives made me realize, again, just how special she really is. During this time, my elder sister, Teresa, was involved in a head on collision. She has spent the past three months in the hospital at Dallas TX. Every weekend, my mother leaves her home and travels the three hour drive to stay with Teresa from Saturday to Tuesday. She stays in her room sleeping in a chair. She returns home on Tuesday, works in her beauty shop Wednesday through Friday and returns to Teresa early Saturday morning. During all of that, I happened to have a heart attack and ended up in the Heart Hospital in Oklahoma City. I considered what I would be thinking if both of my children should knock on deaths door within weeks of each other. It would be devastating. My mother never wavered in her faith and in her prayers. She kept believing and kept on praying. Today as I write this, my sister is being brought home from the hospital to stay with my mother and as you can tell, I am fine. She is our rock.

My wife, she is as solid as they come. Trust me, I am not that easy to grow up with, and that is exactly what we have done. From the first time I talked with her at her locker in southwest hall of Jr. High, and every day since, though I have not always shown it, I have been blessed by God. We were married on July 4, 1979 at the ages of nineteen and eighteen. We have honestly grown up together. She gives all of us a beautiful example of direction and discipline in our spiritual lives. I hope as we continue to grow old together I am able to bless her life as she blesses all of ours. I love my JennyJack!

My children; Quite honestly my children are just a straight gifts from God. They are both headed for an eternity with Jesus Christ and if they did nothing else in their lives, that would be good enough for me. They are gifted with talent, compassion, discipline and understanding of what it means to be an example. Through the every day happenings in their lives they continue to impress both their mother and I. They inspire me daily. My love could not be stronger and will never grow weaker.

There are many friends and acquaintances that have guided me and helped me along my way. I will never be able to tell them all what they mean to me. God bless each of you.

As special thank you to Randy and Trina Low who have made the dream of publishing this book become a reality.

But this book, this book is dedicated to God.

Forward

Most Religions today agree that Abraham is the Patriarch of their Religion. Christianity teaches that the story of Abraham is more than the story of one man; he is the Patriarch of the Jewish nation.

Abraham's story is that Abraham enters into a covenant with God and God tells Abraham to leave his homeland and just follow Gods daily direction. We all know the story as it is written in the Bible in the book of Genesis. But, how would that same story sound if it was written in the days of the old west? What if the story has Abraham and his descendants, as God tells them to leave their homes and follow Him, starting out on a cattle drive and wagon train, and what if the story has Abraham as the trail boss who continually leads the people to trust in God as they face extreme hardships along the trail.

If you are like me, you have had times where you have had trouble personalizing the stories in the Bible. Until my wife and I traveled to the land of Israel, when I read stories about great men in the Bible like Abraham and the places where they lived, well to be honest, sometimes they were just great stories that we have always trusted by faith. But, when I got to go there and walked in all the places that the Bible talks about, the stories came alive to me, and then I could visualize those Bible stories taking place. Most of us have never been or will never be able to go to the land of Israel to see the places where the stories of the Bible were written. So it is with great honor that I get to introduce you to my friend and writer, Sonny Jacks.

Sonny has written this book in your hands which is titled "Follow Me West, The Legend of Abraham." In this wonderful story of the life of Abraham, Sonny doesn't take us to the land of Israel; He brings Abraham to the old west. I have been around stories of the old west all my life, so as I read this story I could imagine myself in every hardship and every struggle they faced. Every time Abraham taught his people to trust in God I could see my own life in a whole new perspective as God fulfills the promises He made to Abraham.

Well, I hope you are as intrigued as I am because you are about to go on a journey. You are not just going to be transported into the adventurous times of the old west but you are going to get to see the life of Abraham thru the eyes of a great story teller Sonny Jacks.

So, saddle your horse, put on your spurs, and mount up. God is about to take you on the ride of a lifetime.

Aaron Reed, Pastor
First Baptist Church, Antlers Ok.

Preface

I have had the privilege to enjoy the art of writing for many years. For the most part it has been daily devotionals that were published in our small town newspaper or to the followers that received them via internet. I have also greatly enjoyed writing songs for both praise and worship services and for specials. One of my greatest writing enjoyments was the verse by verse devotionals and studies that I have written such as "Riding through Romans" that will soon be published. However, nothing I have ever written has intrigued me as mush as Follow Me West; The Legend of Abraham. It has allowed me the chance to really look into the daily life of Abraham and his family and use my imagination and understanding of the country life to blend together the facts and experiences of the Bibles documentation of Abraham's life with the fictional background of the wild, west. Admittedly there are events in the book that are not in the Bible as well as characters, but every event that Abraham experienced is written into this western adventure. The whole purpose is to help you see how exciting the Bible can be, how hard our ancestors worked to please God and encourage you to read the word of God and give yourself a chance to experience the power, joy and peace of His righteousness. Now, quit reading this nonsense and get to the story!!!

Table of Contents

CHAPTER 1

The Ranch

As the smooth breeze makes its way through the window above the pine cabinets of the kitchen it catches Sarai's attention. She moves her hair from around her face and lifts her head for a chance to breath in the morning air. Or at least what would have been the morning air. Instead she smells the aroma of livestock in every essence of the word.

Her small rustic home sits in the middle of the cattle ranch. In every direction she can see the men and women that are putting in an honest day's work. Gazing out the window across the small fenced yard and the dry summer dirt of the cattle run, she notices that Abram and his father have stopped work and are talking by the barn.

She has been Abram's wife for many years and over that time she has learned every body motion that he has. His slumped shoulders and the occasional look toward the sky tell her that they are discussing something that neither of them is happy about. Abram's father looks to the ground and kicks away dried manure. With neither of them being able to contain their feelings, they embrace and show a father and son bond of emotion that Sarai has rarely seen on the ranch. Something is certainly wrong. Abram glances toward the house and sees Sarai looking out the window. She quickly looks back toward the dishes she had been washing and then moves away from the window. She dares not take a second glance.

Abram is a tall lean rough riding man. He has grown up on the ranch and worked for his father all his life, and life has been hard. Since he was a

boy he has had the ability to ride and rope with the best. Even when hired
hands were killed during cattle drives, young Abram never faulted on his
responsibilities. He fought his fights, winning some and losing some, but
never backing away. As time passed and Abram grew, the "losing some",
became a thing of the past. His hands are as calloused as boot leather.
His skin remains darkened by the scorching of summer sun. His clothes
are always three days worn and dusted from the fourteen hour days of
ranching. His hat settles deep on his head and without as much as a word
his expression from under the brim commands respect. Abram never had
any desire to leave or do anything other than ranch. He was born to be a
cowboy. Some men just have that in them.

The rusted hinges of the front door grind as Abram enters the house.
Sarai is still standing in front of the kitchen cabinets and does not look
back toward him as he hangs his hat on the partially rotted deer antlers
that are nailed just inside the door. Even though Sarai is no longer doing
the dishes she can tell that Abram needs a minute without words. In a few
minutes Abram cracks the door back open, spits out past the porch and
closes the door again.

He clears his throat.

"Sarai, I need ya to fix a little extra for dinner, I'm gonna call the men
in to eat."

Sarai turns and faces her husband. With her hands behind her she
grasps the cabinet and leans back against it.

She hesitates and then asks, "Abe, everything alright?"

Abram debates on whether or not he should tell her what's going on.
He turns his back to her contemplating what to say as he gets his hat right
back off the antlers. While wiping off the dust and re-adjusting the crease
of his hat, he says,

"Everything'll be good. I'll explain to ya in a bit. For now, just make
sure we got plenty to eat."

He puts on his hat, grabs the door and looks back at Sarai. With an
ornery half smile, he walks to her. Holding her close to his chest with his
arms firmly around her shoulders he attempts to settle her thoughts.

"I always give ya a wild ride of life don't I?"

She nestles closer to him wrapping her arms around his lower waist.

"Most the time," she answers.

He presses back with both calloused hands on her shoulders and being as gentle as he can he looks into the brown eyes that have been the settling factor for many years. With dust outlining every sun aged wrinkle in his face, he smiles.

"Well, get-a-hold, we're bout to ride again."

Her eyebrows lower as her mind races with curiosity.

"What does that mean?"

Abram steps to her side and lifts a tin cup of water from the cabinet. Without realizing it was full of soapy dish water he takes a swig. Apparently it tasted better than dirt because he never says a word. As he wanders back toward the door he replies,

"You'll see what I mean later this evening, for now, ya best get to cook'n."

He walks out of the house and as usual he leaves the front door just a bit open. Sarai can't begin to remain calm as she peers out the kitchen window and watches him walk back toward the corrals. She shakes her head and then moves over and closes the door. The creaking of rusted hinges catches Abram's attention and he glances back to the house with a half smile.

Earlier in the years Abram's brother had been one of the unfortunate that were killed during a month long cattle drive across the plains. The brother had left behind a son by the name of Lot. Lot is quite a character. He is as tough as a worn out saddle. If it is dangerous and requires guts or maybe just ignorance, you can count on young Lot to be the first in line. He is up at the crack of dawn and the last one down at night. He isn't tall and lean like Abram but is still in great shape, an average size man with an extra large heart and personality.

As Abram walks away from the house he's watching Lot brand a young heifer. The smell of burning cow hair is embedded into Lots gloves as he reaches out to shake Abram's hand.

"Morn'n boss!" he says as he extends his hand.

Abram looks down towards the extended glove.

"I ain't shaken that glove."

Lot smiles, spits in his glove and rubs his hands together vigorously. He then kisses the palm of his glove as to show how tough his gut is. Abram laughs, shakes his head and then looks out toward the herd.

"When ya get done I need ya to round up the boys. Tell 'em to meet me at the house tonight for dinner."

Lot shoves the hot iron into the hind quarters of another heifer.

"Really! What's up?" he asks.

Though Abram is as patient as a staring cat, sometimes he is a little annoyed with questions so he replies with sarcasm.

"I'm announcing that this is your last week." Abram answers.

Lot takes a quick glance toward Abram. Abram smiles as he watches two other hired hands burn the ranch brand into another bawling heifer.

"Just make sure ya get everybody to the house at sundown. Pa said he would have his men watch the night shift."

Lot realizes his job was still safe and answers,

"You ain't right Abe!"

He then grabs the branding iron from the hired hand and points it toward Abram. The smoke of burning cow hair is steaming off the red hot brand. Lot cocks his eyebrow up as if to say "Do ya dare me?" Abram never moved. *A patient man can show wisdom but a quick tempered man will make a mistake.

Lot lets out a grunt of laughter,

"Okay, I'll make sure they're there."

Abram pats him on the back and heads towards the barn. Between the whispering of his jeans and the singing of his spurs there is a presence about Abram that causes every man along his path to acknowledge him. Some simply nod their heads while others completely stop work and catch his eye. Abram, though standing heads above everyone he meets in both physical stature and prestige, is also the most humble of anyone he meets. This, more than any other factor, is the reason he gets respect. As Abram makes his way toward the barn, his father appears in the shadows of the main stalls. In his hands are the reins to his favorite leather bridle. Behind him comes the Bay horse.

This Bay is a prize stud who had first been noticed in a herd of wild horses about four years ago. Abram's father had immediately laid claim to this colt. He began to train the colt when it became a two year old.

"Who ya got behind ya, Pa?" Abram asks.

Pa pulls the Bay closer and feeds him a hand full of grain. Without a word, he drops the reins and walks around the hind quarters to pick up an old, worn out saddle blanket. He wipes the dust off the horse's back and lays the blanket on him.

"Ol Bay looks good, don't he Abe?"

"He still does!" Abram answers.

Pa throws the saddle onto the horse. He then walks around the flank of the horse, reaches under the girth and cinches the saddle down about three-quarters.

"Where ya headed?" Abram asks.

"I'm fixin' to go have that beautiful Sarai fix me another cup of coffee." Pa answers.

A little confused, Abram re-organizes his question as he lifts the stud's foot and checks the back hooves.

"I meant on Bay."

His Pa re-adjusts the halter, centers the saddle, gives the girth another tightening, walks over and hands the reins to Abram.

"You're gonna need the best . . . .He's the best."

He looks at Abram with a father's pride as his old shaking hands are extended.

"Go see how ya like 'em."

Abram stands in a shocked and dazed state of consciousness. For a second he denied the gift, but his Dad demanded.

"You're giving me the Bay?" Abram asks.

"He was yours all along, you just didn't know it."

Abram's father can see that he had blessed his son. Abram walks around his new prize procession at least four times. After smiling at his Pa, he mounts up, spins the Bay in a couple of circles and heads out toward the hills. Pride overwhelms Pa as he watches the silhouette of his son ride into the sun. The dust under foot of the Bay creates a larger cloud the harder the he ran until they have run out of sight.

Abram has ridden the Bay off the other side of the mountain and toward a hidden place that he had found when he was still a boy. He often rode to this area when he needed to be alone, and today, he needed to be alone. Abram climbs out of the saddle and loosens the girth from under the Bay. The Bay is tied to a weak tree hidden from the sun. Abram then climbs into an area of rocks that makes for a perfect seat. He settles in and removes his hat. He takes the rag from around his neck and wipes his face. By now most of the day has passed and the sun is headed down the backside of the horizon. He sits there for several minutes just taking in the view. For all his life he has had chances to sit and absorb everything around him and nothing is ever the same. Most of the trees have grown taller, some have passed and some have broken. The earth has moved its features through wind and storm. The animals from deer to buffalo to doves and quail to any hot natured insect have all passed through the valley that he overlooks. God's creation may be consistent but it is also ever changing. Abram lays his head back and closes his eyes to pray.

The evidence of the stressful conversation Abram had with his father is suddenly found in the words of his prayer. In the peace of the moment Abram allows his soul to be at one with God. He sits quietly and allows the Spirit of God to relax within him. Then as a whisper of wind, as from the very anthem of the clouds, the voice of God clearly speaks out,

"I want you to leave your father's place, take your herd and family and go to the new land I will show you. I am going to give you many children and many blessings."

Abram lies still, partially because of his spirit, partially in respect and most definitely in fear. He then opens one eye slowly. There is no wind, no birds, and no movement. As an unexpected mist whistles through the branches the Bay blows and quickly raises his head and perks his ears startling Abram just a bit. The wind had vanished just as quickly as it whistled by and an unusual peace comes upon the countenance of Abram. He has long been a servant to God in every aspect of his life. Anyone that knows him knows that he is driven to glorify the Lord. But now, he has witnessed, in a way that he will never be able to explain, the very presence of God. For the second time God has given him this message. He stands to his feet and stretches his back, knocks some dust off his pants with his hat, looks around to see if anyone else is with him and nods his head toward heaven. In amazement and still just a little uncertain of what had just happen he grins.

"Okay, then," he says with a sigh, "Let's go."

He pulls down on the brim of his hat, girths the Bay, settles himself into the time proven saddle of his Pa's and heads back to the ranch.

As Abram rides back to the barn he can see that all of the hired hands have already gathered in his cabin. He walks the Bay into the barn and unsaddles him taking a few extra minutes to brush him down. Many times the ranch horses are put up wet with the white foamy sweat of a day's hard work left to dry in the heat of the night, but Abram was taking a little extra time as he realizes how much effort his Pa has put into this incredible gift. He leads the Bay into the stall, feeds him some hay and grain and hangs a bucket of water over the gate.

Abram walks out of the barn and pauses to take in the view of all the men in his cabin. Through the opened shutters of the windows he can see that they are laughing and cutting up as they are gathered in several small groups shooting the bull. Sarai is working frantically to keep them settled until Abram gets home. They have come from all parts of the land and in spite of their backgrounds have managed to become one family. For as much as the men have learned to work together for the betterment of the ranch, the women may have an even closer relationship. Tonight the ladies of the ranch are joining together to help Sarai prepare the dinner. The kids are in the back roping each others legs, chasing chickens and two of the boys are wrestling. Wait, correction, a boy and girl are wrestling and right now she's got the upper hand.

As Abram stands at the front of the barn his memory runs through all the years this ranch has grown. With his hands in his pockets and his mind on God his boots drag across the dust of the ground as he makes his way to the house. He can smell the home cooking that could draw in every stranger from a hundred miles away. When he enters the cabin he catches Lot in the middle of the room holding court and he is knee deep in a surely exaggerated story.

"Seriously", Lot exclaims, "he was nine and a half foot long and had forty-three rattlers. I snatched him up by the tail, whirled 'em around and popped his head off like it was at the end of a forty foot bullwhip."

The group of men and women break out in laughter. Abram has made his way to Sarai scratching his head and hanging his hat on the antlers.

"Is that the same rattlesnake he killed last year?" He whispers in her ear.

"I believe so.", she answers as she sits out the last bowl of biscuits.

He puts his arm around her neck.

"Did I drink soap water earlier today?"

She giggles, "Yep."

"Okay everyone, gather around!" Sarai says as she is still smiling at Abram.

The other women stop what they are doing and go to join their husbands. A few of the ladies gather in the children. Abram stands patiently for several minutes as everyone bunches into the small cabin. Eventually they are all inside and waiting to hear from him.

"Let's pray. God, as I look around at my friends and family I thank You for everyone You have sent to be with us. I thank You for the blessings You have given each of us. For our health, our children, our spouses, parents, brothers and sisters. I thank You for this ranch and for the way You have blessed my father's house. I pray that You bless this food we are about to eat. In Jesus name . . . "

Everyone in the house said, "Amen."

You don't have to tell this group twice that it is time to eat. A couple of the women have already gathered up some of the food and start making plates for the children to eat outside. A line forms along the wall for a true country buffet.

"Make sure you all leave some for the person behind you". The last man in line speaks out.

The clanging of silverware against the tin plates, a few not so pleasant smackers, and an assortment of mouth filled compliments are all signs of good food. Several stories of today's events are shared among both men and women along with a few "We still need to do's." As Abram finishes his last biscuit he moves into the living area. The women in that area can tell that he is ready to hold a meeting with their husbands and they begin to move into the kitchen with Sarai. Though Abram will be speaking directly to the men, rest assured the women will hear every word.

The men begin to move into more comfortable places, some on furniture some on the floor. Some are a little slow to give up that last biscuit or pie. Abram sits beside the fire place. Other than a few dishes being stacked together in the kitchen, the house grows silent.

Scratching his head, Abram begins to speak,

"Men, I been work'n this ranch with my Pa since I was as old as Jake's boy. I have put my blood, sweat and tears into every inch of this land. I know many of ya'll have done the same. We've created someth'n here to be proud of. God has blessed. I know many of ya'll have never considered anything in your life other than grow'n old right here and watch'n your family grow with ya.", . . . he pauses . . . "I'm the same way. But the Lord has showed me that *we can make our plans, but He will guide our steps. And that's exactly what's about to happen. For the last several days I've felt the Lord speak'n to me. I have talked it over with my Pa and spent some serious time in prayer and so you'll know, I'm ah hundred percent sure of what God has said."

"What have you heard?" asks Lot.

The others nod their heads and rustle around a bit with anxious concern.

Abram stands to his feet.

"God has called me out."

He places his hand on the shoulder of Russ who is the oldest of the hired hands.

"God has told me that it is time for me to leave the ranch."

Many of the men are noticeably caught off guard. You can hear the gasp of the women in the kitchen. The look on Sarai's face tells them that this is also the first time she has heard what Abram is saying. They quickly gather around her in support.

"You're leave'n us Abe?" asks Russell.

"Well, I am leave'n the ranch, but hopefully not all of ya'll. God has said, ""Follow Me west"" and that is what I'm gonna do. But I'm kinda hope'n you guys will go with me. He has told me to take my herd, my family and those of you who'll go."

With a look of serious concern Russ asks, "Where we go'n?"

Abram walks around to the front of Russ.

"That mean you're in, ol man?"

With a slight grin Russ answers, "Where ya go'n?"

Abram moves to the other side of the room.

"Well, here is the hard part. I don't know where we're go'n. I was told to go to the place He would show me, but where that is I ain't got any idea. I do know that we'll be blessed."

In the kitchen the sniffles of sadness, worry and fear are beginning to overcome the women. The back door suddenly burst open as one of the kids run into the living area covered in mud. He freezes in his steps when he sees the angered look of his father. Without turning around he slowly backs out of the door and closes it.

"I know this is a big decision for each of you and your families. I don't expect an answer tonight." Abram remarks as he looks around the room.

One of the single young men stands to his feet.

"You know I'm in Abe, I like adventure."

"That's easy for you to say." another replies, "You ain't got children and a wife."

As Abram moves back toward the fireplace he states,

"Listen, no one is being forced to go. Pa has said that he is will'n to keep anyone on that wants to stay. I won't hold it against ya. If ya go with me it's got to be cause ya want to not cause ya feel obligated."

One of the elderly ladies appears from the huddle of concerned tears and steps out of kitchen.

"We are obligate . . . We are all obligated." She states, "Everything we have enjoyed is because Abe and his family have blessed us. They have blessed us and all of our families."

She looks toward her husband with eyes that call out for compassion and agreement.

"We're obligated and proud of it." She says as she continues looking at her husband.

For just a moment her husband looks directly into her eyes without so much as a blink, his chest rises as he takes a deep breath.

"She's right", he says, "I don't know bout the rest of ya, but I'll be honored to go where ever Abe wants to go."

One by one the men stand to their feet, "I'm in." each one says. At first they look at each other with confusion, fear and concern but as the seconds pass the mood begins to change from despair to excitement. In just moments they are all laughing and shoving each other around. The women try to show that same excitement but in all honesty, it wasn't the same.

With a huge smile on his face Abram loudly says,

"We got a lot to do to get ready. Tomorrow will be a long day. Get some rest. We leave in four days!"

The men all shout with excitement to the point of scaring the kids and aggravating the women. They spend several minutes discussing all there is that needs to be done in order to leave in four days as the women continue to help Sarai clean the kitchen and more importantly calm her nerves. Sarai is very good at putting on a hospitable smile in hopes of hiding the flood of emotions that are causing her hands to tremble. As the crowd begins to make its way out both the front and back door Abram quietly and quickly drops one more bit of information into Sarai's already overwhelmed thought process.

"By the way," he whispers in her ear, "you're gonna have a baby."

If that was to be some sort of cowboy-ish romantic advance, she was not impressed. Needless to say he didn't stick around long enough to explain and it was all she could do to keep from fainting to the floor. It takes an hour or so to get everyone out of the house and headed home. It's late when Abram gets in bed so nothing more is discussed until morning.

It has been many years since the sun has beaten Abram out of bed. For years he has made it a habit to sit on the back porch in an oak branch rocker that is tied together with woven rope. Every movement creates a different sound from all different parts of the chair but to date it has yet to fall apart. Sipping the strong, straight black coffee from his favorite tin cup he watches God paint the eastern sky as the sun dares to raise its head. There is a row of several small cabins of every shape and design that sits behind the cabins of Abram and his Pa. At this time of year most all the shutters will be open to allow the nights breeze a chance to cool the rooms. In the distance Abe can see a small herd of deer that have eased in behind the garden to eat. He remembers when the only thing he saw from his porch was open range. As the ranch has grown so has this small community. Before the sun ever rises the flickering of lanterns begin to bring life to some of the families. Mainly those who have drawn early morning herd duty. They know that there are several other hired hands that have been in the valley all night and need some rest. It's not long before the sound of a baby's cry and the smell of bacon bring the day to its beginning. At the end of the row young Jake steps out into the morning air and lets out a cowboy's call to the wild, which inevitably brings forth the barking of dogs, clucking of chickens, griping of women, and crying of babies and goats.

Abram rises from his rocker and throws the remaining portion of his coffee into the dirt and partially on the dog. The surprised dog yelps and ducks under the house.

"Sorry Pete." Abram mutters.

He turns and walks back into the house expecting to see Sarai finishing up breakfast. To his surprise, there is no breakfast. By now, on a normal morning, the hand sewn blankets are neatly laid across the bed, the dirty clothes have been moved to the porch, the furniture, what furniture there is, has been put back in place and a full breakfast awaits Abram's blessings. Today is apparently not a normal morning. When Abram makes his way into the kitchen he finds Sarai staring out the window in a mass of bewilderment. Her apron is clenched in her right hand and her left covers her mouth. It doesn't take a genius to see that she is crying. He debates for a moment on whether to let her work through this alone or see if he can make it worse by meaning one thing and saying another, because that is indeed the fear and probability. He also knows *it's better to sleep on a roof than live in a house with a mad wife. But, he is a brave man. He eases up behind her and looks out the window to see what she sees. She senses his presence and her eyes take a quick glance back.

After a few seconds he says, "You okay?"

In his mind he is praying that she says "yes".

She wipes some tears from her eyes and says, "I'm fine."

Abram has been married long enough to know that "I'm fine" means anything but that.

"Are you worried about leave'n out?"

As she ties the apron around her waist she shakes her head "no".

Still fishing he asks, "Are you sad about leave'n?"

She shrugs her shoulders and moves away to grab a skillet from under the cabinet. Then it dawns on him.

He pauses . . . "Are you pregnant?"

And there it is . . . his fear has come to light. Although he meant to be there to show compassion he has instead invoked anger from whence he has no idea. Sarai whirls in front of him, looks straight through his eyes and storms into the shadows of the bedroom. Naturally and reluctantly, he follows.

"Wait, I don't know what I've done."

Again she whirls and stares directly at him.

"You don't know! You don't know! . . . . How can you not know!? How can you be so smart bout everything that deals with this ranch or with your bible and you cain't figure out what is bother'n me!?"

If there is one form of wisdom that Abram has developed over the years it is the wisdom of a husband and using that wisdom he knows better than to answer her question. Instead, he wipes his sleeve across his mouth, and stands with nothing more to say, basically playing possum. Her disgust grows more apparent.

"Abe, what is the one thing that I've wanted more than anything in life?"

His eyebrows lower as his mind ponders, then he realizes exactly what she is referring to.

A child.

Through all the years of their life together they have never had any children. Instead, Sarai has watched torturously as all the other ladies have enjoyed the pleasures of raising children. Some have raised children who are now raising children of their own. Sarai has tried to be available for sitting and helping when the children are sick or in any way she can to be a part of the children's lives. To all the other women, she is invaluable and definitely a major part of their families. But to Sarai, that part of her life is as empty as a dry well. She has spent many nights crying out to God to bless her with a child, but Gods answer, for now, has been "no".

As Abram extends his arms and walks towards her she breaks down into an uncontrollable cry. As he hugs against her he can tell that her tears have drenched the front of her dress.

"I know you want to have a child, and you will . . . "

Sarai interrupts, "I will! My time for child bearing is passed, how am I suppose to have a child!?"

Abram knows that what would appear to be anger is instead a broken heart. Sarai is not looking for a fight.

"It ain't gonna have noth'n to do with your time, Sarai, it'll have everything to do with God's time. God promised me that you and I will have children. If I can trust Him with our lives and with the lives of the families that are about to follow us, if we can trust Him with our eternity, then surely we can trust Him to keep His promise and bless us with a child. I don't know when, and I didn't mean to upset you, but I'm tell'n ya just as sure as Jake yells ever morn'n, God will keep His promise."

Through the tears she asks, "Why does He force us to wait?"

Abram has no answer

The morning sun crests the horizon casting its light and shadow in the back door and across the cracks of the floor leaving the silhouette of a man and woman embraced in life. Lot stands at the door in silence. He has heard these cries from Sarai before and no one feels more compassion for Abe and Sarai than he does. He bows his head, offers a small prayer and quietly walks away. Sarai gently pats Abram on the chest as she moves away;

"I'm okay. I just hope your right."

She grabs the dirty jeans from the floor at the end of the bed.

"Do you still want some eggs?" she asks through her sniffles.

Abram grabs the corner of the blanket on the bed as if to think he might actually straighten it up.

"Nah, I'm good for now." he answers.

He catches her by the arm before she leaves the room and kisses her on the forehead.

"We're a blessed family with or without children, but I know what God has promised and I know you will be an even better mother than you are my wife."

Sarai, a beautiful woman even with tear swollen eyes, smiles and walks away.

Abram returns to the back porch to gather his thoughts. With everything that is on his mind, nothing bothers him more than to see Sarai upset. He's reminded of the first time he saw her. She was a petite and strong young lady. He first saw her as she walked up with a bucket of milk splashing along the side of her dress. She has long black hair and her bashful brown eyes screamed for attention. She was capable of stifling a conversation without speaking a word. Since then she has done nothing short of becoming more elegant with time. God has worked a wonder of beauty in her creation. Abram, with every ounce of his being, believes that one day she will give birth to God blessed children that carry not only her physical appearance but her heart. Not a day goes by without him taking the time to give thanks to God for giving him such a gift as Sarai.

The next few days were filled with exhaustion. There were many things that needed to be settled and wrapped up. Every day the train of wagons grew longer as the packing continued. After three full days of work, tomorrow morning Abram, Sarai, all their belongings and the hired hands that worked for them would begin their trip west.

Chapter 2

Leaving the ranch

Genesis 12: 1-5

At the front of a long line of anxious families, Abram sits tall upon the back of the Bay. Behind him the wagon train prepares to make its way down the trail clanking with pans and tools. The children are climbing in and out of the wagons while the mothers are scrambling to make sure everything is packed. The men, for the most part, are gathering livestock. Abram stands in his stirrups and motions with his hand for first of the wagons to move out. With a couple of whistles and few cowboy hollers, the whips of reins across the hindquarters of horses and mules cause the wagons to head away from the homes they have had for many years. Abram reins the Bay to the side and watches with excitement as family after family ride by in their wagons with plenty to say. Some of them seem as excited as he is, some seem scared and some seem very unsure of what they are about to do. As the last few wagons pass him by he spins the Bay around and lopes back to his Pa.

The ol' man tries hard to be strong but Abram can see right through it.

"Pa, thanks for everything. I promise, soon as we get settled I'll send a message."

His Pa nods his head and removes his hat as he places his hand on Abram's leg. Looking up to him he says,

"You know I'll pray for ya ever day I'm alive. Right son?"

"I'm count'n on it Pa." Abram answers.

He reaches down for one last firm hand shake. Pa takes a deep breath fighting off the lump in his throat. Abrams adjusts his saddle and rides up along side the wagon train. Many of the families that are staying behind stand in front of their homes waving and watching as the rest ride out of sight. The dust has barely settled at the ranch as the last wagon slowly fades into the horizon. With Jake making one last yell into the sky, the only sign that Abram and his followers had ever been there were the wagon tracks, straying dogs and fact that Pa is still looking down the trail. Other than that, the ranch goes on.

It's been several days of hard travel. Whether you wear britches or skirts, sitting on rough cut timber of a wagon bench for fifteen hours a day will flat wear out your clothes, not to mention your attitude. You would think by traveling as hard as they have that they would be a great distance from the home. Truth is you just don't move cattle, chickens, goats, children and irritated women all that fast. Sooner or later you just have to stop, get everything back in order and try again in a couple of days.

Most of the time, Abram keeps himself a good distance from the actual train of wagons. He does so as a means of watching all aspects of travel. He can keep an eye on the wagons, the herd and any thing that may be coming to threaten them.

As he watches from above the ridge Lot comes riding along side;

"Abe, you reckon we oughta think about settle'n for a couple of days?"

Abram slides down from the Bay and wrestles one of his boots off his foot.

"How do ya get a rock in the toe of your boot when ya been on the back of horse all day long?"

He shakes his boot upside down and is caught off guard when the rock is joined by a baby scorpion.

"Oh!" Lot yells, "That coulda been bad if he'd been old enough to bite."

Abram shakes his head and smashes the scorpion between his fingers.

"How does that happen?" he asks.

He takes a seat on the ground beside the Bay and receiving a strange look from Lot he explains;

"It's the only way I can get my boots on."

Lot glances sharply to Abram's left and forcefully points.

"Is that another scorpion!?"

Abram quickly rolls away with the grace of a crippled buffalo, the boot half way on, flapping like a fish out of water and preventing him from any form of standing. Lot almost falls off his horse in laughter.

"I'm josh'n ya." Lot says through the laughter.

Abram can't help but laugh as he knows he looked ridiculous. As soon as he quits hopping around, he once again sits down and with a few hip to hip wiggles and an awkward grunt he pulls his boot on. He stands up and tries to knock a little of the dirt off his back.

Looking back at the wagon train;

"Looks like they've had enough for a few days. There's a good flat area over there by the creek bed. Head'em up in that direction and we'll rest for a while."

"Thank the Lord!" Lot exclaims.

He spurs his horse around and gallops toward the weary travelers. Lot no more gets spun and gone when one of the other men come riding up.

"Abe, you better come see this. Johnny's boy ain't look'n good."

Abram climbs onto the Bay and hustles back to the wagons. As he gets closer he can see that Sarai has gotten out of their wagon and is crawling into the back of Johnny's wagon. Many of the other women have begun to walk back towards them. Abram unsaddles from his horse, dallies his reins to the wagon wheel and moves the cover from the back of the wagon bed to look inside.

"What's go'n on?" he asks.

"Not sure yet." Sarai answers. "It's not just the fever. Something else is wrong. It ain't the sweats or shakes. Don't seem to have a fever. But he hasn't eaten in two days. We need to get some water down him pretty quick."

"Johnny" Abram says as he unties his horse from the wagon, "Pull your wagon down by the creek bed. Pete, get a fire started as quick as possible, we may need to boil some water."

Johnny thrashes the reins across the backs of his horses and rushes the wagon to the creek. The women grab the front of their skirts and scamper along behind. Abram rides off a short distance to make sure that everyone knows where they are going, mainly the hired hands that are pushing the cattle. As he heads out toward the herd he can see that Lot has already gone out to spread the word they were stopping for a while. Many of the children have prematurely jumped from the beds of the wagons and are in a race for the creek. Never noticing that the one affectionately called "Slick" was lying still and partially unconscious in the back of his wagon.

The wagon bed is packed with cloth sacks of seed, clothes and jars of canned vegetables and tools. There are worn out blankets, pots and pans, extra saddles and gear. Among all of that and years of dirt, lay a handsome three year old child.

His hair is as blonde as the sun and waved like rolling hills. His chubby cheeks are parched from hours of fun. His baby fat makes him adorable to the ladies and easy to run from for the other children. But today this normally jubilant boy lay motionless, physically and spiritually sinking into another place.

As soon as the wagon detours out of line the rest of the families realize something is up. In minutes many have gathered around Johnny's wagon near the water. The uncertainty of what is causing this sudden lifelessness is baffling and no one can seem to create a good explanation. For now the boy must get liquid and stay warm. Sabrina, the boy's mother, lifts him from the bed of wagon and is holding him in her lap. His body is limp and clammy, his eyes remain closed. His lips are beginning to crack from dryness and his tongue is as dry as cotton. She is nervously rubbing water over his mouth but has yet to be able to get any water down his throat. Rocking back and forth with her streaming tears washing his dirty face she is in a constant and excruciating prayer for the life of her child. Johnny, the father, can do nothing but pace outside the wagon. Nothing is worse for the man of the house than to realize there is nothing he can do when his son is in dire straights. The thought of the worst case scenario causes him to dry heave beside the wagon.

"Slick" is a first and only child to this young couple and they are trying desperately to trust in God. Every family in this camp has had the opportunity to baby sit this boy. Not because Johnny and Sabrina needed them to, but because this boy never met a stranger. He is the most adored little boy in camp. There are a few others his age, but he was the shortest, chubbiest, cutest fireball little cowboy in the camp. His smile, constant giggling and pleasant personality allowed him to spend nights with others because they asked him to, not because his parents asked them to keep him. *Even for children their actions tell everyone around them what kind of person they are. The parents on this trail all know losing any child is almost unbearable and the older couples know that Johnny and Sabrina's faith will be heavily challenged if the boy does not pull through.

Abram crawls into the wagon and lays his hand on the boys head. He closes his eyes and begins to pray. The others that have gathered around the wagon also join hands in unison yet individual prayers. Abram places his rough callused hand around the back of the boy's chilled neck and realizes that his pulse has gotten weaker. He gives a concerned look toward Sarai and she can tell that he is in fear of the worst. The complicating part still remains that no one can figure out what is going on. Why has a perfectly healthy little boy suddenly and unexplainably reached a point of gasping for his last breath of life?

The rest of the children have spent the past hour playing in the creek and now the alarms in their stomachs have told them that supper should be getting close. As a small pack of coyotes they come wandering aimlessly over the hill. One by one they find their parents gathered around the wagon where Slick has been lying. The older children can sense the tension and ask the question of "What's wrong?" simply by adjusting their eyebrows. Some of the parents take them aside for a short explanation, others point into the wagon. Some just shake their head. Either way these children realize something is up with Slick. The youngest children, however, have not gotten past their rumbling stomachs.

Tugging on skirts, "Mom, I'm hungry", the children repeat as they each find their mother.

The mothers are all struggling between assisting their children and leaving Sabrina. Their hearts are torn as to what they should do. The tension in the air is a thick as a morning fog.

And then it happened.

Everyone hears Sabrina gasp in horror from inside the wagon.

"Oh my God! No! NO!" She screams, "Johnny! My baby! Please! Please!

She is rocking feverishly back and forth and holding the unresponsive baby tight to her chest as if some spirit was tugging him away. Every breath she takes seems harder for her to gasp to the point that she can barely scream her husband's name.

Johnny burst his way through the crowd and leaps into the bed of wagon busting the back board in half with his knee. His worse nightmare has come true. Sabrina continues screaming and crying. The boy is being held lifeless in her arms. His eyes have rolled back, his breath is gone and his tender heart has stopped.

"Oh my Lord!" Johnny cries out as his eyes are inundated with tears and his body begins to quiver.

He turns the baby's face toward him and yells with heart wrenching agony. He feels as if his chest is about to explode. His breath seems to have left him stranded and he struggles to stand among everything in the belly of the wagon. He throws his arms around both the boy and Sabrina. They rock frantically from side to side in disbelief and shock crying out to God for help. They can't talk, they can't breath, they can't think, "Ahhh!" is about all they have. Their life, in essence, is being stolen. Their cries are contagious and spread to the other mothers and children standing around the wagon. Some of the women have crawled into the front of the wagon and are placing their hands on the young couple and praying for God's comfort and wisdom. Even in a time of such horrible loss the elders know that it is *God who will give them the understanding they need. Soon you can begin to see the shock and disbelief quickly turning toward anger in the cries of these young parents.

"Why!?" Johnny yells in furious anger to the very top of his lungs.

He push's away from Sabrina and suddenly rose to his feet. He kicks a few pans and lunges out of the wagon. He is completely distraught and falls to the ground when he tries to climb on to the saddle of his horse. In the weakness of loss he pulls himself back to his feet and jumps on to the back his horse like a wild man. He thrashes his horse with the reins and stampedes across the field kicking and whipping as if to literally chase the angel that has taken his son. Abram tries to catch him but was unable. Instead, with the simple nod of his head, Abram sends one of the other riders after him. This opens the door for the other ladies to swarm Sabrina and the body of her son with a common compassion of mothers.

"What happen?" the children began to cry. "What's wrong with Slick?"

Their faces light up in fear from hearing the screaming and the rushing of everyone in and out of the wagon. Johnny blasting out of the wagon, yelling in anger and rushing across the field on his horse has most of the children scrambling for their parents.

"Mommy I don't want Slick to be dead." Their little voices cracked in bewilderment.

The sudden chaos causes them all to cry in fear, perplexity and the sadness that only a true heart of a child can understand. The mothers of the children are especially shaken as they watch Sabrina react in despair while they hold their own children in their arms.

Several minutes of imaginable mourning passes as the men move away from the emotion and women move closer. It seems the men handle this situation better when they are also handling chores. Each will be fighting back tears and having nothing to say until the pain in their throat has subsided.

The wagon is surrounded by every woman in the camp. One of them is a very pretty young lady of a different descent. Her hair is long and black, her skin darker than any of the others. Her eyes are deep brown. As Sabrina raises her boy to her face and holds him cheek to cheek, this particular young lady looking in from outside the wagon notices a blood spot on Sabrina's dress. She steps to the side and can see that there is a small stream of blood that has drained from the boy's ear. Her eyes widen as she places her hand over her mouth. She spins away and rests her back against the side of the wagon wheel. Her eyes are moving wildly from side to side and she begins to slip down the side of the wheel hyperventilating. A couple of the women see that she is struggling and try to help her. The shock of what she has seen overwhelms her and she faints. She goes limp in the arms of two other ladies and they struggle to lower her to the ground. Once she is laid down, her breathing regulates and she begins to awaken. For a moment she can't figure out why she is on the ground and why her eyes are glazed until she begins to focus on the ladies that are standing above her.

"Are you okay young lady?" one asks.

She lies there silently trying to wrap her mind around what has happen. Then she remembers she has just witness the death of the little boy. She extends her hand and they help her to her feet. They hold her for a second as she stabilizes herself wiping dirt from her cheek with a damp handkerchief. She weakly makes her way through the small group of women around to the back side of the wagon. Though there were several women between this young lady and Sabrina, it seemed as if God intended for them to see each other eye to eye.

Sabrina has not been able to take her eyes off of her child as she continues to cry in wonder of what had happen. But for what ever reason, she looks up through her distress and gazes right into the deep brown eyes of this young woman. A few seconds pass as they stare motionless and then the young woman whispers something that no one else heard, Sabrina, however, could see her lips.

"He fell." The young woman whispers.

The expression on Sabrina's face changes instantly when she sees the woman's lips whisper that word. She knows the woman is telling her something vital. She stops rocking; slightly squint's her eyes and looks more attentively as if to ask her to repeat what she said. Again the woman whispers,

"He fell."

It is as if some clarity is racing through Sabrina's mind. Her mouth falls slightly open, she looks down at the face of her child and then back toward the women. You can literally see her mind at work. She looks at the child, raises her head toward heaven and looks once again to the woman. This time Sabrina whispers back,

"He fell."

The woman's head slightly moves forward in agreement.

A few days earlier this dark complexioned woman had been walking along the trail behind the wagon of Johnny and Sabrina while the boy had been lying on a sack cloth in the wagon. He rose up to his knees and saw her following behind them. He crawled toward the back of the wagon bed and peered at her over the back board as a quick game of peak-a-boo ensued. His bashful behavior was actually a game of flirting. The woman walked a little closer to the wagon as he was hiding and surprised him when he rose up again. Sabrina heard him giggle and turned to see him playing with the woman.

"Do you mind if he walks with me for a bit?" The woman asked Sabrina.

"He would probably love that." Sabrina answered.

The woman lifted Slick out of the wagon and allowed him to walk along side her. Sometimes he walked, sometimes he ran, sometimes he stopped and sat down. But once, he fell. He didn't cry or yell and, as a matter of fact, he didn't even move. She was only few steps from him so she quickly picked him up.

"You okay?" she asked.

She held him in her arms as she looked him over to see if he had any injuries. No matter what she asked him, he had no answer. She notices that he is abnormally blinking his eyes although when she looked closer at his face she could see that there was no dirt in eyes. She asked him if he wanted to walk again but he laid his head on her shoulder with nothing to say. She made her way back to the wagon and lifted him over the back board and placed him in the wagon. Sabrina looked back as Slick was lifted in.

"He fell down and kind of bumped his head." The woman told Sabrina.

Sabrina looked him over briefly and didn't see any scratches or bruising. She kissed him on the forehead and he fumbled his way back to the sack cloth bags. Both women smiled as they watched him grab his favorite toy, neither of them realizing this would be the last time he would lay down and would not get back up. It was such a small event in comparison to what all happens on the trail that it just never came to mind. But now it has dawned on the young lady that his head had landed on a pointed rock around his temple. There was no bump or scratch but it had apparently caused internal bleeding.

Now Sabrina notices the blood on her dress and in her son's ear.

"He fell." She states with a sigh.

She rubs her fingers through his hair and massages his temple. She closes her eyes and cries a while longer.

"You fell" she moans as she rocks her son. "My baby fell down."

She has still lost her son but at least now she knows why. In her sorrow she weeps to the Lord;

"My God, You gave us this child and I have blamed You for his death. Please God, forgive me. We have loved him as You."

She chokes and brakes into another moment of uncontrollable sobbing.

"We called him Slick. Please tell him how much we love him." She prays.

The rest of the women wrap her in their arms. Many of them have now seen the blood and heard her say, "He fell." They do not know the story but they can tell that Sabrina realized what has happen. The word spreads as time passes into the evening hours.

It is a common practice in times of death for friends to come and take care of preparing the body for burial.

"Sabrina" Sarai softly says, "We can hold him for you when you're ready."

Naturally Sabrina doesn't want to give him up, but she trusts in Sarai. Reluctantly she hands his body over to one of the ladies as several of the others scurry off and get the attention of their husbands to come help. Many of the women would like to console Sabrina but instead she delicately steps through them and climbs out of the wagon. She goes directly to the young lady who is backing away in fear. Sabrina takes the woman's hand and holds it with both of hers. They stand face to face both looking through tired, tear-filled eyes. The woman fears what Sabrina is about to say.

"He fell." Sabrina spoke softly, "It happens, it wouldn't have mattered if you had been there or not. He just fell."

The young lady starts crying as Sabrina puts her arms around the woman's neck. They hold each other for a minute as the weeping increases.

"Thank you for helping me to remember." Sabrina whispers in her ear.

Sabrina kisses her on the cheek then turns toward the rest of the women to be held in their sympathy. But first she turns back toward the woman one last time;

"I don't know you, do I?" Sabrina asks.

Wiping tears from her own eyes the woman shakes her head "no".

Once again Sabrina takes her hand;

"I'm Sabrina, my husband is Johnny" . . . . she pauses . . . . "We called our son Slick. And you?"

Hesitantly the woman answers, "My name is Hagar".

Sabrina nods her head and then wanders into the middle of the crowd of women. She is completely encircled in the outstretched arms of the other wives and mothers. There is, however, a small group of women separated from the rest. They can't help but be curious about this young quiet mysterious younger lady.

"Excuse me", one of them speaks, "What family are you with?"

Hagar looks at them with worry in her heart.

"I'm not with a family."

They seem to be caught off guard and move a little closer.

"Who are you with?"

Hagar tries to slip away but they maneuver in front of her. From behind Hagar a voice answers,

"She's with me."

Hagar's heart races as a woman's hand massages her shoulder from behind. It's Sarai.

"With you?" one of the others replies.

"That's right." Sarai answers with a tone that suggests questioning her could result in conflict.

"Well, then it's nice to meet ya." The women all stated sarcastically as they walk toward the wagon and struggle not to stare at Hagar.

As soon as they are far enough away Hagar turns toward Sarai.

"Thank you."

"Your welcome", Sarai says as she puts her arm around Hagar's waist, "Now, who are you and how did you get here?"

Hagar takes a deep breath as they begin to walk.

"My name is Hagar. My father was hired at the ranch a day before we left. I didn't want to move to the ranch when he took the job. I decided that coming with you may be the only chance I ever have to get away. So I hid in the bed of the feed wagon for the first two days. I finally climbed out and started walking. That's when I saw the little boy."

"Where have you been sleeping?" asks Sarai.

"Just wherever. I make do."

"And food?" Sarai asks.

"You'd be surprised what you find when dinner is over." Hagar says as she struggles to smile.

Sarai stops and looks at the woman head to toe. She shakes her head in amazement. She cannot believe that this beautiful woman has run away from home to join their camp.

"Well, you're here now, might as well make the best of it. From now on you will be with me and Abram. You can earn your keep by helping me with chores."

Hagar is ecstatic. "You don't have to do that." she says although praying Sarai will not change her mind.

Sarai grabs her by the hand and starts to lead her toward the camp;

"It's already done. Now come on, we have work to do."

It's been several hours since Johnny hastened out on his horse. The sun is starting to settle as the rider that had chased after him returns to camp. Abram and Sabrina walk out to meet him. She can only fear the worst as the man's horse tucks its hindquarters and slides to a stop. She prays that Johnny has not done any thing desperate. She prays that God has been with him. The rider's horse is lathered and is panting hard through its nostrils. It's been a long fast chase. The cowboy climbs off his horse and awkwardly moves toward Sabrina. He embraces her with strength he is unaware he has and squeezes her to his barreled chest. He has nothing to say but the posture of his body speaks volumes.

"Did ya find him?" Abram asks.

The cowboy turns and faces the wooded ridge across the field. Out of breath he replies,

"See that flicker'n of fire under those trees? That's him. He wouldn't come back so I built 'em a fire."

He hands the reins to Sabrina. She needs no help mounting up. With a firm jerk of the reins she rides his horse in full stride toward her husband. She is as dedicated in her marriage as she is in her motherhood. The relationship between Sabrina and Johnny has been blessed by God. Johnny has said on many occasions that *he receives favor from the Lord because of Sabrina.

Johnny is sitting on a rotted ant infested log glaring into the flickering flames of a small fire. He is mentally, emotionally and spiritually wasted. He has no more tears and no more words. When Sabrina reaches him she holds up the horse and has it walk slowly through the tree line. She steps down and dallies the horse to a tree. She stands under the neck of horse hesitating to approach any closer. There are very few people that can understand the sadness of this moment. Johnny is sitting there with his head in his hands and his elbows on his knees. His clothes are torn and filthy. She doesn't know that he had bailed off the horse in full stride as he cried out to God in anger. She doesn't realize that his horse has run away.

"He fell." She says softly as she remains by her horse.

Johnny barely raises his head out of his hands and turns his face a little toward her.

Sabrina put her arms around the face of the horse and rested her forehead on the horse's neck. Sabrina's voice is hindered from the soreness of her throat. She can barely speak;

"He fell on a rock a few days ago. I reckon it caused his brain to bleed. The lady with the dark complexion remembered. Do ya remember when she walked with 'em?"

Still remaining by the horse when Johnny stands, Sabrina's takes a step back with a small measure of fear of his emotion.

Johnny takes a deep breath, "I already miss him." He whispers.

Unable to control himself he breaks into a heart wrenching cry.

"I know." She answers.

Again he bends over and rests his elbows on his knees. A few seconds of silence pass and without facing her he holds his hand out toward her.

"Sabrina . . . "

She walks to him once again being struck with sadness. She sits beside him and lays the cheek of her face against his wet, bloodied and torn shirt. She can hear his heart racing as they think about their loss. She runs her fingers through his blonde wavy hair, the same hair as his son. Her husband's heart beat is the only life of her son that she has left. Together they weep. They sit on the ground and lean against the log. The flickering of the fire reflects off their spiritually wounded eyes. With little to say for the rest of the night, they hold each other in their sorrow. They dream of their son while resting in the arms of God and mourning their loss.

As expected, the others at camp have taken the necessary steps to prepare the body of the boy for burial. By morning a small grave has been dug on the top of a hill under an oak tree. The grave itself is covered with the best hand made blankets found in the camp. The dirt to the side of the grave that will bury the young boy is covered with a leather tarp. The entire camp, including the herdsmen, gatherer around the grave and wait until Johnny and Sabrina arrive. A little after dawn, the young worn out couple ride up to the burial site. They look beaten and hungry. They have complete understanding and appreciation for what has been handled. They slowly make their way through the friends and family hugging as many as possible until they have come to the side of the grave. The boy's body is wrapped in a hand made blanket like a papoose and is being held by Sarai at the foot of the grave. He appears to sleep in peace. He has yet to lose his color. At first, neither of his parents looks in that direction, instead they continue to stare at the ground.

Abram moves out in front of the families. You can see the anguish on his face.

"I know, that, this'll be a day that well . . . . none of us will ever forget and hope we never re-live. It don't seem right that such a young boy should be taken from us, or better yet, from his parents, at his young age, and theirs. I wish I could tell ya why it happens, but I can't. It's only natural for some to think we should question God. But I would tell ya, God didn't take the life of this boy. So then ya think; could it have just been sin? And again I would say "no". Sometimes things occur that cause events to happen that interfere with our lives plans. The boy fell down, and that's all it was. Johnny, Sabrina, we can either dwell on the fact that he's gone, or we can celebrate the time you had. You'll be better suited to do the latter. None of us can make the pain go away. Only God can help ya move through it."

He faces the camp;

"Now, let me tell all of ya, I can understand that someth'n like this, this early in our journey can cause many of ya, maybe without speak'n it, to wonder if ya made the right decision by come'n. We have traveled hard and yet not far. And in just a short time we are forced to burry one of our youngest and most lovable members of our families. It's hard, I understand your concern and I will not hold it against ya if ya turn back. But for those of ya who stay I will make ya this promise, this will not be easy, I never said it would, but God will surely reward us for doing what He asked. He has already rewarded Slick. Not in a way we expected or desired. But He has nevertheless"

He turns and places his hand on Johnny's shoulder.

"Johnny, your boys in good hands, God's hands. That little boy was already a cowboy. I already saw 'em ride and play'n with his rope. He was funny but he didn't take anything nonsense from those kids. He was a fighter. But in life, it don't matter how soon *we saddle up the horses, it's God who gives us victory. Slick's victory has been given by God. He has won the fight."

Johnny looks up toward Abram as his tears make a trail through the dust on his cheeks. He nods his head in agreement.

Lot makes his way over to the limp body of the boy and lifts him from Sarai's arms. He carries him over to Johnny and Sabrina with heart broken tears rolling down his face. Once again the rush of emotion began to flow throughout the entire group. Johnny takes the boy in his arms as Sabrina wraps her arms around Johnny's waist. Johnny leans his head back toward the skies and does all he can to keep from screaming. They make their way to the grave and kneel to their knees. It's an eerie silence that makes its way through the shadows of those standing. They pause for a moment with their heads bowed and then place their child in the grave. A little dirt from the side of the grave slides onto the body of the boy, Sabrina grabs it and throws it to the side. They take the rest of the blankets and cover him to rest for the last time.

At this time all the families walk away leaving only Johnny, Sabrina, Abram and Lot to bury the child. As Lot begins to burry the child it is too much for the parents to bear and they turn away. They don't leave, they just don't watch. Sabrina covers her ears to prevent having to hear the sound of dirt landing on the blankets that cover her child. When they realize he has completed the burial they turn and face the grave. At the head of the grave Lot places a simple stone with the child's name engraved.

Johnny "Slick" Johnson, Jr.

Sabrina kisses her fingers and rubs the top of the stone.

"Abe" Johnny says, "We'd like to leave out today and travel about a day out. We cain't stay here. We'll wait for ya up the trail."

He places his hat on his head and looks back at the camp.

"We're not turning back to the ranch, just so you'll know. This is God's journey and we intend to see it through."

Abram extends his hand. Johnny reaches out and shakes it. Enough had been said.

Johnny and Sabrina return to the camp. Naturally, they are hugged and held by every family. Many of the women are bringing damp rags to help clean the injuries Johnny received from jumping off his horse. Every one helps as they straighten up their belongings before they head out on their own. They will travel for about a days ride or so and that will give them time to be alone until the rest of the camp catches up.

As for the rest of the families, the journey was just getting started. The loss of Slick remains on everyone's mind as they go about repairing wagon wheels, mending blankets and washing clothes in creek water. The men also slaughter a couple of calves in order to feed the camp for the next couple of days. Eventually, as hoped, everything has been reorganized and repaired and they are ready for another run at the trails. The herdsmen start moving the cattle early one morning as the wagons began to roll out. Some of the older children are pushing the goats. As it turns out the trail will ease right by the grave. As the wagons pass, the women observe the site brokenhearted. Each man removes his hat in respect and, ...

the journey continues.

CHAPTER 3

The Early Rain

Genesis 12: 6-9

For quite some time the wagons struggle to stay held together as they move along the trail. For the most part nothing too drastic has happened. There were your normal events of broken wagon wheels, sick cows, sick kids, and naturally the occasional frustrations of just a hard life. More than any thing, the fact that you have no idea where you are going or when you will stop, brought on most of the problems. For as much as they would love to forge on, Abram knows that *planning carefully makes for plenty and moving too fast gets you nowhere. Once again Abram could sense that it has become time to stop. As the wagon train tops another of the rolling hills Abram comes upon an extremely large Oak tree that is sitting unusually alone in the middle of a pasture. After pausing for a while to look the place over and decides this is a good place for rest.

"Lot!" he yells, "wrap 'em up!"

A look of relief and excitement comes across Lot. He gallops his horse around all the wagons;

"We're stopping here! Circle everything up!"

You can hear the cheers of every family come roaring out of the wagon seats. The kids begin to jump out of wagons and run ecstatically, no apparent direction, just running. Even the riders guiding the herds can hear the excitement from a distance and realize that they are stopping. No one knows for sure whether this is the final destination or not, but stopping is at least a benefit for now.

You would think it would only take a few minutes to get a bunch of broken down wagons in a circle and get stopped, unfortunately that is not the case. Circling up and getting camp set is quite a job. It will be a couple of days before anyone can actually relax as if they were staying for awhile. To begin, the men scotched the wheels of the wagons and commence unhitching the horses. There aren't enough trees around to run lines for tying the horses so they have to build a make shift corral out of ropes and fence post that they carried from destination to destination. A few of the men ride out to find the best place to gather water.

The women begin to unload the wagons, each setting up an out door kitchen beside their wagons. At times the families eat dinner individually but often they come together as a camp family for a pot luck feast. One of the most important chores would come on the second day as the women and children ventured to the water hole to wash clothes and just as important, themselves. Naturally they also hope the men will find time to return the favor.

By now most of the livestock have figured out their only means of surviving is to stay within the feeding distance of this camp. There is no need to worry about the herd of goats running off into the wilderness. For the most part, the herdsmen continue in shifts with the cattle to help prevent them from stampeding should a thunder storm blow up but also to protect them from bandits. The entire camp has been pretty fortunate to this point not to have any conflict with the bandits, but that could change at any time. The threat in this area is not tribes of Indians. Instead, there are gangs of men and women of different nationalities that parade in these areas without settling.

After a hard days work the night falls before all the chores are close to being complete. It will have to be the second night here before they receive a true peaceful time of rest.

Early the next morning Abram is once again the first to fire up a can of coffee. It's already very warm outside and surprisingly humid. He watches as some of his men get up early to slip off and make room in their stomachs for breakfast. The women are soon climbing out of the wagons and starting to cook that breakfast. After the women are up, he can hear the cries of the children and they are not as excited about jumping out of the wagon as they were when camp first pulled up. The common noises take him back to the days when he could spend a few minutes relaxing on the back porch of his house on the ranch.

As the sun brings vitality to the morning and the camp begins to take its shape Abram rides the Bay out to the big Oak tree he saw from the hill. He is not often surprised by the wonders of God's creations, but this tree is incredible. He strolls around the tree looking for signs of its age and admiring its remarkable height. It casts out a morning shade that transforms its shape along the ground with the ever so slow movement of the sun and covers Abram like a blanket as he unsaddles the Bay and pulls the bridle off its head. By now the Bay has no intention of running off but instead enjoys the coolness of the shade of this magnificent tree. The Bay gawkily lies to its side in the dust of the shade and tries several times to roll over from one side to the other until he finally makes the flop after momentarily hanging up mid-center. Apparently the dust helps to keep away the insects that bother him in the heat of the day. Abram watches the Bays antics, chuckling to himself, and then takes a seat at the base of the tree. He takes off his hat and watches as the Bay returns to its feet and shakes off the excess dirt. Taking in a deep breath of morning air Abram leans back against the tree and closes his eyes for a moment of silence and contemplation of the past two months on the trail.

In the distance a small echo of thunder catches the attention of the Bay.

Not a day passes that Abram doesn't spend time in prayer, but nothing has been as clear as when God spoke audibly to him before they left the ranch. That is, not until now. Just as Abram begins to pray a light rumble from the distant storm chases the breeze that glides across the land. Then, God speaks;

"To your offspring I will give this land."

Abram hears the voice and immediately opens his eyes. There is no one around and just as last time the simple breeze has sent chills down his spine. At first he questions what he heard but the Spirit of God confirms in his soul that God has spoken to him once again. As the bark of the tree indents its image into the back of his shirt Abram takes a few minutes to look around at the property that God has just promised him. And then it dawns on him, God has once again spoken of children that Abram does not have. This time, however, he will not be mentioning it to Sarai. He closes his eyes for about twenty more minutes and continues to pray. Meanwhile the thunderstorm marches its way over the field and swallows the shade of the tree. Abram continues to pray until he feels the sprinkles of rain against his face. It causes him to smile. It reminds him of something his father once told him about promises. *If a man makes promises he does not keep, it's like a cloud that doesn't bring rain.

Before he leaves he decides to mark the tree to signify the place where not only had God spoken to him, but where God first told him of the place where his children would live. He gathered a few rocks and laid them around the tree. He decides to call this place Mowreh which means "early rain". He gathers up his bridle and saddle and moves toward the Bay. Just as he prepares to put the bridle over the Bays ears the thunder claps and the Bay whirls like a tornado and runs across plains. Abram stands there in stupor. He watches as the Bay runs completely out of sight, hopefully back toward the camp. Now the rain begins to pour from the skies like God was pouring it straight out of His boot. Abram looks toward Heaven batting his eyes to fight off the cooling rain.

"Nice God. Real nice."

He laughs to himself while wrapping the bridle around the saddle horn and throwing his saddle over his shoulder. He tucks the saddle blanket under his arm and starts walking back toward the camp. There is nothing more fun than carrying a saddle and bridle on your back while stomping through mud. After a while he can see the remnants of his wagon camp in the distance. What would have been blazing campfires are now just water soaked ashes with small streams of smoke. Where children would have been playing, there is absence of life. He can tell there is not a soul doing any chores of any kind. It would be nice if someone would see him and come get him, but there is no one stirring around. The rain has put everyone in their wagons. He's amazed at how close the camp seems to appear to the naked eye and yet how long it is taking him to get there. He is soaked in the blessings of rain. His saturated pants have begun to rub his legs raw. His saddle gets heavier with each minute of soaked up water. Finally, he is forced to stop and catch his breath. As he drops his saddle to the side, he hears the blow of a horse behind him.

When he turns around he sees that Lot has ridden up. Lot is all wrapped up with oil clothe tarp to keep dry. His old hat allows the rain to flow off his head and out of his face. He is fairly dry although not completely. He also has a rope around the neck of the soaked Bay and is leading him beside his horse.

Through the rain Abram asks louder than normal, "Where'd ya find 'em?"

"He came to the herd" Lot answers "How'd he get away?"

"Never mind that" Abram answers.

He throws his wet blanket on the Bay.

"How long you been behind me?"

Lot gives him that mischievous smile; "Awhile".

Abram girths the saddle on the Bay and tightens the bridle around its head.

"You best be glad you're kin."

Lot laughs out loud; "I'll be out by the herd if ya need me."

He begins to trot his horse back toward the herd and yells out,

"You can also bring me some eggs for catch'n your horse and not tell'n everybody."

Abram climbs up on the Bay and mumbles to himself,

"Like everyone ain't gonna know."

He kicks up the Bay and gallops back to the wagons.

Abram gets the Bay put into the temporary corral and unsaddles when the storm worsens. He runs through the mud of the camp and crawls into his wagon soaking wet, much to Sarai's dismay.

"Ain't seen a storm like this in years!" He exclaims.

Sarai continues looking out the back of the wagon as Abram changes into some dry but just as dirty clothes. He stumbles over some potato sacks and falls into the pots and pans while pulling up his pants. He watches out the front of the wagon as the rains continue to increase. He can see that several of the other men are also keeping an eye on the weather. They all know that this type of storm can cause total chaos to the herd. In just a few minutes the rain is coming down so hard that he can't see the wagon in front or behind him. The winds are beginning to rock the wagons. Among the pounding of rain and roaring of the thunder he can hear the whipping of wagon tarps and rattling of tools and pans that are tied to the sides of the wagon beds. Abram hears a scream as the wind blows one of the tarps off of a family's wagon. The young couple scrambles to grab the tarp and tie it back over the rails with very little success and getting soaked in the process. The cooking facilities that were set outside each of the wagons are now being blown across the camp like tumbleweeds. The horses are starting to spook and the cowboys can't stand it any longer. They realize this storm has basically brought on a small war. Regardless of what you're wearing it's time to go to work. Every one of them bail out of their wagons and get after it. Some of them have start helping others adjust their tarps, some are gathering the horses, others have go as far as to saddle up and head toward the herd to help keep the cattle in line. All the while every creature in camp is scrambling for shelter.

The rain slowly begins to lighten up. However, it was not because it was over. In minutes, for the first time in years, they are getting riddled by hail. As expected cattle do not like being pounded by hail and they take off. The cowboys from the camp get there just in the nick of time. Once again it begins raining and hailing too hard to even see what any one else is doing in this dangerous stampede. All they can do is cowboy up and hope for the best. And until the hail stops they are doing nothing more than trying to keep from being thrown. They hurriedly search for a tree line to hide the horses under. When the hail ceases they are "whoop'n and ride'n" in a life and death situation. By now the cattle have a substantial head start so the men must ride with reckless abandon. If the cattle are lost or hurt you endanger your main supply of food for the entire camp and in all honesty, the herd is not that large to begin with. Every man there is just as accomplished in riding and handling cattle as the other. It's every man for himself but riding as a team. It's a major problem having to out run the cattle knowing neither you nor your horse can see ten feet in front of you. But the race is on. The horses are galloping through weeds and mud, leaping at last moments over fallen tree limbs and stumbling along rocks. The riders are doing their very best just to keep a deep seat in the saddle and a solid foot in stirrup. Just when it would seem as if no one would have a chance at turning the herd God sends out a beam of sun rays through a hole in the storm cloud that unexpectedly slows the cattle just long enough for some of the riders to get to the front of the herd. In a few reckless moments of full on riding they have turn the herd back and stop what could have been a catastrophe. The clouds begin to break up just a little and as fast as the summer storm moved in it moves out.

All of the riders have bruises and cuts from riding in the hail. The horses are also going to be scarred. Only one cowboy has lost his ride and he is standing under a tree with mud from head to toe. His horse is roaming about in the middle of the cattle herd. None of the other riders seem to be in too big of a hurry to catch it and take it back to him. It's as if they enjoy rubbing it in by having him stand there and shiver for a while.

Back at camp the beam of a fresh sun is shinning down on a ravished camp. Some of the tarps were blown completely off the wagons and are wrapped around the wheels of others. Some were torn by the hail. There are wet people everywhere trying to pick up their belongings. Children are cuddling up together crying and fighting, naturally. The goats, well, no change really. There are, however, a few dead chickens.

Abram notices that one of the tarps on the ground is moving around. He quickly runs to the tarp in fear that a child may have been caught up in the wind. When he moves the tarp, Pete, his dog, scrambles out and runs away with his tail tucked between his legs as if someone just threw hot coffee on him, again. As it turns out, all is well with the exception of the mess. This has been a great way to start the third day.

Abram had been excited about telling everyone that God has spoke to him again. He decides he'll hold off on that bit of information until everything is dried a little. By night fall everything is back into place with wet laundry hanging on ropes and trees limbs every where you look. It will be easier for the families to come together for dinner instead of cooking individually. Around the table the small storm is nothing more than a conversation piece and everyone has a funny story about their family's reaction to the winds. The main topic, however, is how long will they be there. The families are praying that Abram has decided to make this a permanent stop. Since everyone seems to be in a better mood and enjoying their dinner he decides to tell them about Gods message. Maybe not the part about Sarai having children but at least the part of this being the place they will live. Nonchalantly, Abram mentions,

"God spoke to me today." He then continues to eat.

At first it went without comment. Until finally Lot replies,

"Did you just say God spoke to you today?"

Abram nods his head "yes" and shoves another spoon full of beans into his mouth.

"Audibly?" Lot asks.

"Yep." Abram blurts as juice drips out of his mouth and onto his shirt.

"Seriously, Abe" Sarai remarks, "You shouldn't tease about something like that."

"Not tease'n." He answers with a mouth full of bread.

By now he has caught every ones attention.

Sarai asks, "God spoke to you audibly . . . just as I am speaking to you?"

With his mouth full of food Abram nods his head.

"The God!. . . . . The God that just dumped a bucket of water on us for no reason! . . . .That God?" Lot asks.

"That's Him." Abram answers.

"And what did He say?' Sarai asks as she moves from the fire near their wagon.

Abram is about to burst at the seams because he wants to tell her the whole thing, but he dares not. So he says,

"God has said that this is the land we have been looking for."

Several of those eating slightly choke on their food.

"This is it?" they are all asking one another.

Abram pushes his plate away and pours himself a mug of coffee.

"I said this is the land God is going to give us. I didn't say this is where we are staying. I don't know how long we'll be here. But one day this is definitely where we will remain."

"If this is the place God has promised you, then why would we leave?" Lot asks.

Abram takes another swig of the coffee and then throws the rest out toward his left side, and yes, right on his dog, Pete.

"Our instructions were to follow God, this may be where we will end, but it may not be where we stop for now. I think we will be here for a little bit but I don't know how long. So, we'll enjoy it for now and be ready to go when it's time."

From behind one of the wagons you can see two little boots covered with pants draped over them. Those around the table hear a young voice yell out,

"Mom, I'm done."

Mary Lynn recognizes her sons voice and spins to look behind her, "Oh good heavens!"

Laughter erupts as they all stand to their feet and begin to put things away. The attitude in camp is automatically lifted, both from the cool of the air and Abram's news, and everyone is in a joyful mood as the final chores are finished up and the children are readied for bed. By night fall camp is pretty much settled in. After everyone else has closed the covers on their wagons, Abram crawls into his and nestles up against Sarai. They basically sleep in under garments without blankets. Often Abram will just kick off his boots, take off his shirt and sleep in his pants. Tonight the night time temperature barely breaks below the mid seventies.

"You didn't find your way to the river did ya Abe?" Sarai asks.

He wraps his arms around her and pulls her a little tighter to his stained shirt that reeks of sweat, dirt and manure.

"That's real man your smell'n."

She wiggles away and places a duck feathered pillow between them.

"This is real clean woman that your get'n your sweat all over." She replies.

He chuckles to himself and reaches across the pillow to pat her back. After a hard day it would only be a few seconds before he would be sound asleep. Just before that happens Sarai turns to face him. He didn't even need to open his eyes. He could sense her staring at him and that usually doesn't mean anything good. Usually.

"Did God say anything about children?" she quietly asked.

Abram debated on whether or not he should act like he was already asleep, but again she asks.

Without opening his eyes;

"I don't wanna get you upset Sarai."

She leans up on one elbow and moves her hair behind her head.

"What did He say?"

Abram breaths out, opens his eyes and rolls them to the side in a way that shows his worry of Sarai's emotions;

"He actually said that this is the land He will give our kids."

"Our kids . . . " She replies cynically and then turns away crossing her arms and exhaling in exasperation.

Abram never moves. If nothing else is said, all is good. There is silence. The next thing he hears is a soft, female snore.

Another day down.

As it turns out Abram's own stench wakes him up about an hour before day break. As hot as it already is he is sweating again so he determines that this may be a good time to ease down to the river for a bath. He quietly climbs out of the wagon and mounts up bareback on the Bay. They slowly walk away from camp. Abram is not big on having anyone bathe at the same time he does. As he reaches the river bank he slides off of the Bay. He undresses himself down to his long johns and then surprisingly jumps back up on the bareback of the Bay. He grabs the nap of the mane and guides the horse out into the middle of the river. Apparently they both need a bath. He's a little surprised that he can guide the horse and even a little more surprised that he hasn't been thrown. He walks the Bay around in the deep water for a few seconds and then guides him up toward the bank. As Abram slides off he is taken back when the Bay decides to lay down in the water. Abram removes his shirt and begins to scrub his body with home made soap. When your standing in the river, lathered in soap making a weird face because your eyes are burning, it's hard to look like a brave leader of a ranch. As he splashes water up into his face he is startled;

"What's going on Boss?"

Abram ducks down into the water and can only see a blurred image of Lot.

"You touch those clothes and I'll kill ya."

It's then that he realizes Lot is joining him in the water, barefoot, shirtless and long johns that should have been thrown away many moons ago.

"Let me borrow your soap and I'll leave'm alone." Lot laughs.

Abram tosses him the bar of soap and finishes rinsing off his chest. The Bay is behind him pawing into the water and drinking in as much as he can hold. They spend the next several minutes doing nothing but soaking and swimming until Abram's stomach begins to remind him that he has not had his coffee. Before he gets out of the water he hears a large splash behind him, he turns quickly and sees Pete dog paddling in the water.

"A man gets no privacy out here." He says as he splashes water at the dog.

Lot makes his way out of the water and stands dripping on the dry clothes. He grabs Abram's shirt and uses it to dry off his hair before giving it back;

"I don't think that dogs gonna tell anyone what he saw."

"He better not or I'll dowse 'em with coffee."

They both laugh as Abram walks gingerly across the rocks to put on his clothes. It's quite a sight watching them put dry clothes over their wet skin before they ride back into the camp and find the normal morning activities beginning to take place.

Sarai is just finishing up some bacon and eggs as Abram slides up behind her for a refreshing morning hug.

"Thank You, God" she mumbles with a smile, "Are you ready for your coffee and some breakfast?"

Abram has his mug in his hand and looks towards Pete. Pete freezes in his tracks and ducks his head expecting the worse.

"Quit teasing that dog." Sarai says as she brings Abram his meal.

Every morning Abram tries to remind Sarai of how proud he is that she is his wife. *A good wife is her husbands pride but a bad wife is like cancer. He grabs an extra biscuit off the pan and throws it down to the dog. He sits on an old nail box beside the wagon wheel with his tin plate of food in his lap. He leans back against the wheel to enjoy his breakfast. Abram eats his meal as if it may be his last, making sure he wipes every bit of the greasy sunny side up fried eggs off the plate with the last biscuit left. When he has finished he lays the plate on the ground beside him so that Pete can lick the plate clean. He crosses his legs and examines the worn out soles of his boot as he sips his coffee. In a few moments Sarai walks by and wipes the excess egg off of his chin. She starts to walk right on by but he grabs her and pulls her in his lap.

"You're a beautiful woman Sarai." He says as he tickles her side.

She puts her arm around his neck, "Tell me more."

Abram gives her a kiss on the cheek as he stands to his feet lifting her in his arms. They catch the attention of a few others as he carries her towards the front of the wagon. Eyebrows rise as their rootless minds begin to scurry with their own imaginations. Abram places Sarai on her feet beside the dirty pots and pans.

"And I think you're sexy when you clean the dishes."

He gives her a husbandly love pat and turns away. She slaps him on the shoulder as he grabs his hat off the seat of the wagon.

"I'll tell ya what else I think later this evening." He says with a grin.

The snooping neighbors are a little disappointed but it doesn't take long for them to get back to the business at hand.

About two weeks have passed since they pulled up to camp and they have had quite a relaxing time. Many have already begun to discuss where they would like to build their house, make their lots and settle in. Abram has not made that type of statement and is not ready to do so until he is sure that God has finished his trip.

Abram and a couple others are mending the temporary corrals when two of the riders from the herd come storming into the camp. The dust flies in every direction as they halt their horses at the wagon. The riders are overcome with anxiety and are slightly out of breath.

"It's Canaanite's! We saw 'em watch'n us over the ridge! You best get some of the others and come out there Abe!"

The Canaanites are the local bandits that have always roamed that land. For the most part they are not always the kind of people that will attack for no reason. However, times have gotten hard, even with the storm that blew through several weeks ago the weather is drying up everything around them so their hunger may cause them to attack the camp or the herd.

Abram calls for a couple of the others to saddle up. He also has a few of the men prepare the women in case of an attack on the camp while they are out at the herd. One mention of Canaanites and even the smallest of children know what to do. Hide! Every woman in the camp has had an opportunity to learn to shoot. You don't get to live in this part of the country and just cook and make babies. They can shoot, hunt, ride, cook and fight. And when needed, pray a wart on your nose the size of a wooden nickel. If the Canaanite's plan to attack their children, they better mean it. Between the cries for God's protection and the ability to bust the core out of an apple at fifty yards with a twenty two caliber, this party could get western in a hurry.

After the women, children and few men that are staying at the camp get hidden in their wagons Abram rides off into the distance. The camp grounds are completely silent and empty. Through the holes and rips of the wagon covers the adults are watching with baited breath. The children are tucked under the feed and potato sacks for extra protection. But if needed, in a moments notice, and without notice, riffle barrels will be thrust out the sides of the wagons and bullets will fly like a swarm of irritated wasps. As expected, Abram just rides below the horizon when a small group of bandits emerge from the back side of camp. Quiet and nervous bodies inside each wagon move into shooting positions. At first all you can see are the shadows as the Canaanites moving along the edge of the tree line. They remind you of angels of death hovering over those about to enter hell.

They are a motley crew. They ride horses that are barely alive and they don't care. They intend to ride them to death and possibly eat them the next day. Their clothes are torn and worn, covered in the blood of men and animals. Even in the heat of summer some of them are dressed in jackets and cow hide. When running the plains you are forced to go through many rough areas. It's better to be hot and sweaty than riddled with thorns, poisons and who knows what. With them all wearing the same style of clothing it makes it hard to tell the women from the men. Even their greasy hair seems to be the same length. The characteristics of their faces finally take shape as the sun washes away the shadows of their hats. Their eyes seem to be as hallow as the darkness of their lives. Fighting is a way of life for the Canaanites and they know that the women and children are hiding in the wagons. They are prepared to kill if needed but are just as willing to slither in, steal what they need, and leave without confrontation.

That will not be permitted.

They ride into plain site as a group but soon spread out to prepare to cause confusion when needed. So far they have moved slowly and meticulously. They ride in and out of trees like serpents. The focus of the families is on the middle of the gang but from the side comes the attack. In a moments notice one of Canaanites comes crashing through the middle of camp screaming and yelling to the top of his lungs in hopes that he will scare the women and children into staying inside the wagons.

It was a wasted effort.

As the bandit reaches the half way mark of the circled wagons one resounding shot explodes his chest and splatters blood across the neck of his horse. He is dropped from his horse and dead before he hits the ground. That shot, however, was not fired from one of the wagons. Abram

is no fool. He knew that they would allow a few of the bandits to be seen
at the herd in hopes that all the men would run out there and leave the
camp open for attack. Instead, Abram and his men rode out of sight then
circled back. Women and children are much more important than the
herd of cattle. Before anyone could fire a shot from the wagons Abram had
dropped the Canaanite while the other riders with him were charging in
against the bandits.

Bullets rip through the woods and exploded the bark of the trees in
their path. The gunfire echoes through the valley like the cry of angelic
warriors. Several of the bandits try to fight back the charge of Abram but
in seconds three of the Canaanites lay dead, the rest are caught so off guard
they have no choice but flee for their lives. Their ability to rush through
brush and limbs of the broken trees is amazing. Bullets were hitting men,
trees, horses, dirt and anything else in sight. Among the flurry of shots
fired it has become apparent that the women are putting their training to
use. When Abram and the other riders have stopped the chase, shots are
still being fired at the Canaanites from the flaps of the wagons. It takes
several minutes to get angrily excited women to stop firing.

The Canaanites run right past the herd. Abram's men have been put on
alert by the shots being fired at camp. Once again a gun fight ensues. The
men from Abram's camp have no idea as to the extent of damage that has
been done to their families. They don't' know if anyone is alive or dead.
Their rage against the bandits is heightened by the fears of the unknown
and they take no prisoners when their anxiety and adrenaline soars to this
level. For now the herd is left unguarded as they race to kill those who have
come against their women and children. Before the bandits can manage
to run completely out of sight another one of them falls victim to his own
antics. As a bullet from the rifle of Johnny rips through the flesh of the
Canaanite neck, another shot cripples his horse and causes it to flip head
over heels. The Canaanite is smashed beneath the broken neck of the horse
and both lay dead among a desolate brush pile.

Back at the camp everyone scrambles from the wagons and horses
to search for other bandits that may be hiding. After several minutes of
searching the nearby ridge line it is obvious that the Canaanites have
vacated the area. All the adults return to camp and start cleaning up the
mess. Most of the women are checking to make sure that none of the

children were injured. It will take a while to calm them down from the fears of what they just saw and heard.

While charging toward the bandits Abram and his hired hands caused some destruction to the camp but no one is seriously injured. There was one flesh wound to the arm of a young lady named Cindy and one of the men had sprained his ankle while jumping out of the wagon. Other than that, all is well. Before the children are allowed to leave the wagons everything is cleaned up including the bodies. It's a horrible thing to have to kill another human especially when you know that God could have changed their lives. Even though they have forced their own demise Abram still requires that the men bury the bodies out of respect to the Lord.

It actually takes late into the evening before everything is put back into order and supper was more of just grab what you can get. Not many people will sleep tonight.

Several days and indeed weeks pass by and there have been no further signs of the bandits. That being said, it has been an interesting time during this stay at Mowreh.

With all the craziness Sarai has enjoyed having Hagar with her to help with chores and to keep her company while Abram was out and about. Abram has built a bed frame for Hagar to sleep on outside the wagon. Sometimes she decides to share beds with kids in the feed wagons just for fun.

Many of the couples have become very attached to this place and it will be hard to pull up roots. Families have even grown during the time here as three of the women are now pregnant. As suspected by Abram the time has come to move on. He knows that they will one day return but he is being led to move out by God's Spirit. So as God calls, ...

the journey continues.

CHAPTER 4

Little Egypt

Genesis 12: 10-20

For days the families of the camp prepare to move the wagon train forward again. Three of the families ask to stay here and wait for Abram to return. Naturally he is giving them his blessings and they couldn't be happier. For the rest of the families, however, the trail will be no easier than before. Nevertheless they feel confident that God will provide and protect.

Once again the time to travel happens in the hottest season of the year. A heated gust of wind lifts the particles of dust through the air and runs them across the faces that have been covered with handkerchiefs. There is not much talking going on today as the suffering continues for the families that have chosen to follow Abram. A month and a half passes as they tread down lonesome trails. Their emotions have ranged from the highest of mountain peaks to lowest of valleys. Birthdays have passed, anniversaries have been celebrated, but no more than three nights in a row have ever been spent in the same place. The weather has become torment. There has not been a drop of rain since they were back at Mowreh and the temperatures have been scorching. Several of the cattle have gotten sick and the herd has been diminished to about a third of what they originally had when this trip began. Even Abram has began to wonder how God will provide if things do not change. Eventually they can travel no further.

Abram brings the camp to rest just outside a town called Little Egypt. They have found a small water creek that will be big enough to keep the cattle from going thirsty and will provide enough water to drink and wash. Food however is scarce. After such a long hot time of travel it is impossible to expect everyone to get camp set up as fast as they did several months back. Even the children refrain from jumping into the heat of the day. When the wagons saunter in to their circled up formation, and this time in a much smaller circle, everyone is content to crawl in the back of the wagons and hide in the shade for the rest of the afternoon. The men herding the cattle are slow to move after watching several head fall to the wayside from the heat. They are also very aware of making sure their own canteen is full every chance they get. They ride on the back of their horse while being cooked like sizzling fried chicken from the afternoon heat. If they run out of water they may not have a chance to get to the creek before they are dehydrated. Their main objective is to keep the cattle, horses and themselves still and in a shade as much as possible. Their slumped bodies, leathered necks and face tell stories of the pain of this drought.

For several weeks Abram, Sarai, Hagar, Lot and four other families survive on what they have available. Finally, Abram makes a decision that they should go into Little Egypt for food. He decides that He and Sarai will ride into the town to check things out and bring back food for the others. His idea was that if he had Sarai with him it would be a lot less likely that someone would cause him grief. Not to mention, it would be better for them to suffer hostility than to take everyone with them.

Early one morning Abram and Sarai mount up and head in for a days ride to town. It has been almost a year since either one of them have seen civilization outside the camp. Needless to say they are a little anxious about going. Other than the dust of the trail, some dead trees and the occasional rodent there is not a lot to see as they ease along the trail that is barely walked out by travelers. But in the far distance they have begin to see the silhouette of Little Egypt. It's called Little Egypt because of the top of the hotel that was built before the town really emerged. Abram and Sarai have no idea about the people that live there or how they will treat strangers. Apprehension will be their best defense. Abram intends to reach the town before sunset and find a nice place to rest for the night.

From the middle of the glazing sun the movement of another man riding their way emerges. It will take over an hour before they cross paths and during that time all kinds of thoughts are passing through their minds. Is he a good man or bad? Is he a murderer or thief? Is he a Christian? Is he sick? He finally begins to get close enough to see.

"Is he ride'n a mule?" Sarai asks.

"Looks like." Abram answers as he blocks the sun with his hat.

"He doesn't look like he's very big." She whispers

"Ya don't have to be big to carry a gun. Stay a half behind and block yourself from him by using me and the Bay. If someth'n goes down kill him and don't go into town. If ya go in by yourself they'll abuse ya."

Abram un-sheaths his rifle and loads a round in the chamber.

Sarai's mind is now racing with all sorts of ideas of what may happen in just a few moments but as Abram has instructed, she slows her horse to follow about a half length back and slides her pistol under her belt behind her back.

The stranger from Little Egypt approaches. He is riding a small young mule and leading another behind him loaded with blankets, pots and pans, riffles and personal objects. He is a relatively short stature man. His hair has not been cut or perhaps cleaned in a coon's age. His hat displays the sweat bands of age like the rings inside an oak tree. His beard is ratted and stained from chewing tobacco and spilt coffee. His eyes are old and tired and yet still express a bit of a wild life. His old shirt may have been the same one he was given at his sixteenth birthday. Strapped to his thigh is a pistol older than he is. Bullets wrap his waist on a partially rotted leather belt. If it weren't for the young mule he might look a little intimidating, as is, he just looks a little different. In his mind, he is just as curious about Abram and Sarai as they are about him.

"Even'n." Abram remarks.

The old man rides up a little closer and looks Abram over either to see if he should feel threatened or perhaps he just can't see.

"Even'n" He answers.

The man rides just a little past Abram to catch a glance of Sarai.

"That your bride?"

Abram glances back at Sarai and smiles.

"That she is. We're just head'n into town for some supplies. You?"

Again the man leans around Abram and gets a good look at Sarai. She pulls the reins of her horse to move behind Abram and block the strangers view.

"You're a dead man ya ride in there with her."

His spit a mouth full of tobacco juice to the ground beside his mule and smiles a mischievous smile. At first Abram has no idea what he is talking about but understands* it is smarter to withhold his comments until the man explains.

"Why's that?" Abram asks.

"You ain't been to Lil Egypt before have ya? Ya don't know bout Sheriff Pharaoh.

The stranger's mule lunges forward and almost dumps him to the ground. Abram quickly grabs the headstall and holds the mule still.

Under his chuckle Abram replies,

"Don't reckon I do."

The old man slides off the mule and begins re-tightening the girth of his saddle.

"Pharaoh is the sheriff. Better yet, he runs the town. Between him and his so called deputies, people do what he says when he says it and how he says to do it or they come up miss'n. And many have come up miss'n."

"How does Pharaoh affect us?" Abram asks.

The old man tries to swing his leg back over the small mule but hangs it on his saddlebags. The mule starts dancing a circle around Abram's horse and forces Sarai to move out of the way. The whole time the old man is yelling "Whoa!" and spitting tobacco everywhere. He finally drags his leg over and grabs the reins from Abram. He settles into the saddle and smiles a tobacco stained grin at Sarai.

"Well, one thing Pharaoh won't do is steal another man's wife. He figures that would be the straw that breaks the camels back and might cause the whole town to come down on 'em."

He begins to ride past Abram still talking although having his back to them as he rides off;

"However!" he exclaims, "If some beautiful wife's husband was to die or get killed then she is free for the taken."

He stops his mule and turns to face them one last time. After pausing for a few seconds;

"She sure is a beautiful wife!" He laughs.

Once again he spits out a jaw full of tobacco juice, laughs out loud and turns to mosey away. Abram and Sarai watch him for a few minutes to make sure he was honestly riding off and not planning on coming up behind them.

"Well that's good to know." Abram mumbles.

They are only an hour or so from the entrance of Little Egypt and have no idea what they are going to do. They ride in silence for quite some time. Sarai can tell that Abram is pondering on how to handle what the stranger had told them, if, he were telling the truth to begin with. As they top over the last hill the entrance to the town is in plain sight. Two of the deputies that are posted at the gate see Abram and Sarai. They throw down their hand rolled cigarettes, mount their horses and ride out to meet them. The closer they get the faster Abram's heart begins to race. Just before the deputies get to them he turns to Sarai;

"Tell 'em you're my sister."

At first Sarai thinks he is kidding and laughs. But when Abram looks at her she can see the fear in his face and again he says,

"Tell 'em you're my sister or they'll kill me."

The fear in the countenance of Abram has now caused fear in Sarai as the deputies arrive. They look like anything but deputies, rebel Canaanites, perhaps, but not deputies.

"You two got business in Lil Egypt?"

Abram slides his hand down beside his pistol.

"We're camped out about a days ride. We're run'n a little low on supplies so me and my sister decided to ride in and get some stuff for our camp."

The other deputy makes his way around behind Sarai and is looking her over like new candy.

"Sister? You ain't his wife?"

Sarai looks down to the ground without answering. The deputy rides up beside her and raises her chin with the barrel of his rifle. It is all Abram could do to keep from shooting lead through the hooligan's evil heart. For the first time in his life he feels that he is not prepared to protect her. They look desperately to each other but neither move.

"This is a pretty lil sis ya got here cowboy. Someth'n tells me Pharaoh's gonna want to meet her." He says with a sinful laugh, "How long ya'll plan'n on be'n in town?"

Abram continues to stare straight ahead.

"Just long enough to get what we need."

The deputy runs his hand along Sarai's shoulder and down her waist. She can feel the callous of his hands and it makes her stomach turn.

"I tell ya what, you go get what ya need and we'll introduce your sister to the Sheriff."

Abram grips his pistol and debates what to do. His hands are sweating and his finger is quivering above the trigger. Only wisdom is keeping him steady. He knows there are times when it is *better to be a patient man than a warrior.

"I think she'd be better off with me." He says with trembling voice.

The first deputy rides up tightly beside Abram and sternly looks him face to face.

"Not if you plan on get'n outta here alive." He grumbles

The sweat of his shirt and the smell of his breath reek of violence and satanic air.

"Find yourself a place to sleep and we'll get back with ya tomorrow." He commands with a raspy voice.

With a tear rolling down the cheek of Sarai she calls out to her husband,

"Abram, go do what ya need to do. I'll be okay."

With that the deputy hits her horse on the rear with his rope and the three of them gallop into the middle of town. Abram pauses and then follows. He's watching from a distance as they help her off her horse and drag her into the saloon. She looks back to Abram as they hurry her inside and the sounds of an old piano blare into the road. As they escort her through the swinging doors she hears the laughter and swearing that surrounds each table. Shadows are cast across the floor from the scandalous romances of each corner of the room. Drunks and thieves clamor around the bar telling lies and threatening the lives of anyone who questions them. Like spirits of the night they drift from place to place with repulsive behavior. Abram's heart is like a rock in the bottom of the river. In all his life he has never feared another man especially to the point of allowing them to take his wife. As he has been taught,* fear has always been a snare but had he trusted in God he would have been safe.

He slowly rides the Bay through the middle of town. People from both sides of the road stare as he rides by like he was swollen from a plague. The sin of this town could be felt like thick fog. Instead of actual people all he could see was sadness, anger, depression and fear. Those who have chosen to live here have apparently made a decision that they can not retract. He can't bear the thought of paying for a good place to sleep while Sarai was held in the saloon. Instead he ties the Bay to the back of store just behind the main road and makes a bed on the ground. A bed he will lie on, but not that he will sleep on.

The town itself is quite run down. There is much more concern for drinking and fighting than there is for maintenance. The wood of most buildings is rotting and infested with bugs. The people drink from the same water troughs as the horses. Many of them still lie sleeping in the same place they passed out in after too much alcohol. The dust covers the bottom half of every window facing the main road. The constant heat increases the smells of dead varmints and manure.

It is a hell on earth.

In the saloon Sarai is quickly handed over to the madam and they rush her up stairs. Several of the women who work in the saloon are told to spruce her up and get her ready for Pharaoh. At first Sarai resists, but she is swiftly slapped around by one of the older women and she realizes that her resistance will only bring on more trouble. The whores remove Sarai's modest and dirty clothing and brutally wash and dress her in a much more scandalous dress. They pull her hair from the bun and allow it to hang long onto her back. Perfume is sprayed all over her body and they leave her in the room upstairs alone and crying for the rest of the night.

She stands from the bed and watches out the window hoping she will get some glance of Abram. Instead all she can see are drunken cowboys and ladies of the night as they stagger back and forth from sidewalk to sidewalk. Throughout the night there is constant gun fire and yelling, laughing and screaming, and crying of children who have been left in the road by the parents who have forgotten they were there. In the middle of the road stands a baby who is clothed only in a cloth diaper. He is dirty from head to toe. His cries echo along the road and yet no one bothers to help him. Several drunken riders have barely missed him as they gallop their horses by. Sarai watches with tears in her eyes as the boy makes his way into an alley by the saloon. The rest of her night is spent pacing, worrying and praying.

Across the road Abram lays on the blanket in the heat of the night as insects crawl along his legs. All he can do is cry out to God.

"My God, what have I done? How can I trust You for my descendants and not realize that You will not allow me to be killed? How will You take us from this mess? Forgive me God. I am weak. *If I am weak in trouble I am weak indeed. I am not worthy of Your mercy. I have forced Sarai to sin against You. Please God, see past my lack of faith. Show us Your power. We cry out to You, we need You."

There is no way he can sleep as he worries about Sarai and listens to the same noises of the night that she is hearing. His only thought is how to get out of the turmoil he has gotten them into.

Sarai also spends the night in prayer. Although many have always looked to Abram for guidance in the way of God, Sarai too has a relationship with God that is second to none. Her fault now comes from agreeing with Abram to go along with this lie.

That next morning Sarai is sitting on the edge of the bed and she can hear the clinking of spurs as someone makes their way up the stairs. The shadows under the crack of the bottom of the door stop and stand at the entrance of the room. The knob slowly turns and then the door is flung open. Standing in the doorway is a large arrogant beer gutted man. His presence screams of violence and filth. He does not stand proud behind the badge on his chest but hides behind its power. He glares down at Sarai without speaking a word and absorbs her beauty as if he had just won the final hand at a poker table. She refuses to look at him. She can hear him breathing and smells the scent of his cigar. It seems as if he stands there forever, then, for some reason, he backs out of the room and closes the door. She listens as he makes his way back down the stairs.

"Where's her brother?" He yells out.

One of the deputies speak up,

"I saw him make a bed back behind the store."

Pharaoh walks out onto the porch of the saloon and kicks a bum off the steps. He then motions for a few of his deputies to come to him.

"Find the new girl's brother. Round up a couple of good horses, a few head of cattle and some food. Give 'em a couple of people that work for us. Tell 'em to take what I have given 'em and leave out. His sister's gonna be my wife."

Several of the deputies burst into laughter and fire random shots into the air as they hear his proclamation. However, as soon as those dreadful words slithered from his lips he cough's up a fowl taste into his mouth. With a slight gag he spits onto the road and realizes it was blood. He rubs the bloody saliva into the dirt with his boot and starts to walk away without giving it a second thought. As he walks away he hears his name being spoken from inside the saloon as one of the ladies calls for him;

"Sheriff Pharaoh, you need to come check on your sister and children. Something is wrong!"

Pharaoh goes into the rustic house beside the saloon. In the shaded and yet humid bedroom are two of his sisters children. Both lay shivering in the blankets of his hickory framed bed. Their faces are flushed red and their hair is soaked in sweat. Their eyes are glazed over as they both stare with emptiness into the air. They have the fever. His sister sits in the curled wrought iron rocking chair of the living room with a rash about her whole body. Her lips are white as powder. She tries to speak but her throat is as dry as the dust he stands on. She covers herself in a blanket and shakes from the chills. He himself begins to feel the temperature within his body rising with every minute. He is confused.

"When did this happen?" he asks.

"It started last night. Just about the time we went up to dress that woman." She replies.

Something catches the eye of Pharaoh and he looks toward the darkness in the corner of the room. He is staggered by the image of a stern demanding spirit of an angel that glares into his soul. Pharaoh wipes his eyes to make sure of what he is seeing. The Spirit stands strong and vigilant. Pharaoh's heart races at a pace that seems as if he is having a heart attack. The Holy Spirit speaks to his mind and instantly he knows the sickness of his family and himself is because he has Sarai. A wind swirls around the room and blows the curtains to the side of the windows. The angel quickly breezes by Pharaoh and out the door knocking him against the wall as he goes by. Pharaoh turns to chase him and stumbles out into middle of the street. He finds himself on his hands and knees in the dust of the main road looking into the sky to see where the angel has gone. Those that are outside are shocked as they watch him crawl around like a maniac. They haven't seen the angel and it takes Pharaoh but a second to realize everyone is staring at him. His fever is raging, his shirt is now full of sweat and his voice is about gone from the blood that is caking on his vocal cords. He stands to his feet, stumbles to one of the deputies and grabs him by the arm to stabilize himself;

"Bring me the cowboy!" he whispers.

Three of the deputies run to find Abram and rush him to Pharaoh. They find him behind the store on his knees praying to God. The deputies grab him and forcefully hurry him to Sheriff Pharaoh. Abram has no idea what has happen and is in fear that something is terribly wrong with Sarai. When they get him to the middle of the road in front of the Sheriff it is obvious that Pharaoh is sick. At first Abram doesn't want to get too close but the Sheriff staggers up to him and grabs him by the shirt.

"Why have you done this to me?" he asks as blood spatters from his mouth.

Abram tries to pull away and the Sheriff grabs tighter and pulls him to his face.

"What are you talking about?" Abram says in fear.

Gasping for air the Sheriff staggers as he drags Abram into his house and yells,

"That woman ain't your sister is she? Is she your wife? Look what your God has done to my family!"

All the bystanders that are gathering in the street have no idea what he is talking about. Many think that he is going crazy with the fever. But Abram knows exactly what has happen. Although he is scared he is calmed in the mercy of God and quietly speaks.

"I feared that you would kill me for her. She is my wife."

Pharaoh pushes him against the wall and then walks outside falling onto the porch post and moving back toward the saloon. Searching for water he sits down on the stairs of the porch and spits up blood.

"Bring me water!" he yells to a whore, "and get that woman out here!"

He looks up to Abram;

"Take the gifts I have told them to give ya and go! . . . . Go now!"

He looks to his deputies;

"Get 'em out of here and make sure no one hurts 'em! Give him double what I promised and anyone that wants to go with him can go! Get 'em out of here before his God kills me and my whole family!"

A few of the men run upstairs and rush Sarai outside to Abram. He never notices how she is dressed as they embrace in the middle of the street. Then, Abram makes his way toward the Sheriff and lays his hands on the weakened shoulder of Pharaoh.

"God will bless you for what you are doing. The sickness of you and your family will pass."

Many families hear what Pharaoh has said. They rush to gather as much of their personal belongings as possible and meet Abram and Sarai at the entrance of the town. They are full of anxiety and fear. Would they really get to leave or would they be shot in the back? They are herding what few head of cattle and goats they have. Some bring chickens others push hogs. It was actually quite amazing how many people have chosen to follow Abram. All of them are escorted out of the town of Little Egypt by several of deputies. After a short ride the deputies stop and head back toward Little Egypt.

Abram and the others ride all night and into the morning herding cattle, horses, hogs and wild children. They are also bringing extra pack mules with enough food and supplies to get Abram's entire camp through this drought. God has not only saved them from the death Abram feared but has taken this awful circumstance and found a way to be glorified by many. The whole time they are riding away Abram is in quiet pray thanking God and asking for forgiveness. After a while Abram stops.

He faces all those who have followed him;

"Listen to me! If you have simply come with us to get out of that town, then you are free to go. You don't need to continue on with us. If you choose to follow me, you must know that the only way you can be a part of this camp is to completely believe in the God that has provided for me and Sarai. If you do not believe, do not follow us any longer. Turn and go your own way. Otherwise, you must ask God, the God of heaven, to forgive you of your sins. Now is the time for your choice."

A few seconds pass as Abram waits to see what will happen. One of the men from the third wagon back jump out of the seat and walk out into the open beside the row of wagons. He removes his hat and bows to his knee. Following suit his wife makes her way out of the wagon to join him. It was all the others needed to see. Each member of those who have followed moves out from their wagons and kneels to their knees in a group.

From the back of the wagon train they are all surprised to see one of the deputies's riding up behind them.

"Who is this God you talk about?" He yells out.

Abram is also surprised to see him. He thought that they had all gone back to Little Egypt. It seems a little awkward to tell someone about God and grip your pistol to kill them at the same time.

"He is the God of all creation." Abram answers. "Look around you, everything you see including every man, woman and child, every tree, the land and water, the air, everything is created by God. He is the only living God and the only God that can grant you forgiveness of your sins and the hope for an eternal life after your life here is done. He is the only One that can free you from what you have been bound with in Little Egypt."

One of the men bowing down spoke,

"Sir, we do not know what to pray."

Abram dismounted from the Bay and stood in the middle of the group of families.

"Say what I say."

Before Abram begins to pray the deputy throws his leg over the neck of his horse and slides off the side. He walks toward the rest of the group and the people move away still in fear of what they remember. He kneels down in the open area of the middle of the group. He looks around at those who have moved back until one of the young and unknowing children walk up and kneel down beside him. He places his hand on the shoulder of the little boy. Abram then leads them in a prayer as they ask God to forgive them of their sins and accept Him as their God. As he finishes his prayer they all raise their eyes toward the Heavens. The look upon their faces is as those who have seen a new sun for the first time in their life. There are tears, excitement, relief and joy, they are new people. What has once had them bound and headed for hell has now been cast away and they are made new in the Spirit of God. Smiles replace the burden of sadness and they cannot wait to move further away from Little Egypt. They stand and simultaneously begin hugging one another and shaking each others hands. It was as if they have accomplished something they had never dreamed of doing. There is reluctance at first to embrace the deputy but they finally give in.

Abram makes his way to Sarai. The two of them have not spoken since they left town. He is ashamed and disgusted with his actions. He can only imagine what she thinks of him now. He walks up behind her but does not touch her;

"I don't know what to say."

She moves a little away from him and begins to pull her hair back up off her neck.

"There is nothing to say."

Abram reaches down and lightly pulls on the sleeve of her dress to stop her from walking away.

"I failed you. I failed you and God. I should have known that God would not allow anything to happen to either one of us. I allowed the ol man to make me act like a fool. I'm sorry."

Sarai is not quick to forgive or forget how close she came to relations with a man whose life is of the devil. She understands that God has protected them. She understands that God intends for her and Abram to live long lives together. She knows that she loves Abram, but she also knows that she needs time to work through all that had just happen. Sarai turns and looks at Abram. She nods her head forward and walks to her horse.

Abram knows that she is hurt. He knows that her faith in him has been damaged. However, like Sarai, he also knows the plans of God. He prays that God will begin to mend the distance this trip has placed between the two of them. As they continue on their ride back to the camp Abram ponders on how easy it was for him to fall away from the trust he has always had in God. Simple words from a stranger shifted his entire thought process of his life. In the smallest of ways he allowed Satan to creep into his life and cause chaos.

"It'll not happen again." He mumbles to himself.

In the darkness of the night he is pleased to see the distant camp fires of his friends and family. They have quite a story to tell. A story many will find hard to believe.

CHAPTER 5

Lot moves away

Genesis 13

Once Abram and Sarai return from their adventure they realize their group had instantly doubled in size. It takes some doing to get those who had followed Abram from the ranch to welcome those who had followed him from Little Egypt. Needless to say the life styles have been considerably different. Those coming from the ranch have basically grown up living a life directed by God. Those coming from Little Egypt know nothing of the sort. They are young Christians, spiritually speaking, with much to learn. Their desire to do well in the eyes of God and Abram would depend, somewhat, on the willingness of the others to teach them with patience. There will absolutely be times when they mess up, but the idea was to put out the effort.

They have stayed outside Little Egypt until the drought is just about over. Eventually they load up all they had gathered over the last several years and heading back to where the rest of Abram's original camp had stayed, Mowreh. During this time the herd has flourished and through trading, God has also blessed them financially. This small group of Godly nomads has grown in substantial number. Their stock and supplies are vast in comparison to the day they stopped outside Little Egypt. When they return to the rest of those who had stayed behind they were excited to find that they had been immeasurably blessed as well. Abram had left them with several head of cattle, goats, hogs and chickens. Because of their dedication to Abram they had treated the livestock as if the animals belong to them and the herd had flourished.

The new ranch was increasingly consecrated. Several years passed after the trip to Little Egypt and as Abram had expected, God had once again blessed him and his family in a way that only God can do.

Because of Lot's relationship with Abram he had been given a large amount of the riches. As time passes the ranch hands have also been divided between Abram and Lot. As the herds continued to grow, the hired hands began to argue among each other about whose cattle needed to be where. Abram could see that the time was coming when he and Lot would be forced to separate their camps.

A gentle wind brings in the morning and before the sun crowns the ridge Abram is sitting underneath the large oak tree where God had first spoken to him at Mowreh. He has been there praying for about an hour as the sounds of bawling cattle and calves echoed through the valley. His heart has grown heavy with the idea of separating from Lot. He remembers how hard it was when he and his father stood outside the barn and first discuss him leaving the ranch. Now, he will be playing the part of the father. Fortunately he didn't feel they needed to separate in such a distance as he and his father.

As if God has directed it straight from heaven, Lot finds himself slowly riding his horse up to the tree. Before Abram opens his eyes from prayer Lot eases up and sits down beside him. Tears are filling Abram's eyes as he looks up.

"Ya alright?" Lot asks.

Abram takes a deep breath and tries to put on his stern look, but it doesn't work.

"Not really."

Abram stands to his feet and looks out across the fields in amazement at the blessings he can see. There are no longer wagons circled up in some random simulated formation of protection, but instead there is a community of log houses, barns of hay and stables, cattle lots, play grounds and a center area where the camp meetings are held. Even larger than the ranch he had left years ago. As he reflects back he is reminded of how many lives have changed over the years. Lot himself has taken a wife and has been blessed with a couple of daughters. The riches of God's glory are at every corner of their lives. They both understand that their *riches have come because of their faith, not because of the eagerness for wealth.

Abram wonders to himself how a man gets so blessed from God that he is forced to separate himself from people he loves? In his true and unusual character, Lot walks up beside Abram bearing a stench of flatulence that drifts past their nostrils like the serpent of Satan. Neither say a word. Abram covers his nose with his hand and Lot struggles to keep from laughing out loud.

"Can you believe how this place has grown?" Lot asks amidst his quiet laughter.

Abram puts his arm around Lot's neck as if to share the moment but squeezes him into a head lock.

"God is good, ain't He!" Abram exclaims as he rustles Lot around

Lot laughs through his choking;

"Ain't He though."

Abram releases Lot and reaches down into the dust of the land, picks up a broken twig and begins to sharpen it with the worn but incredibly sharp knife his dad had given him for his fifteenth birthday.

"Lot, I hear our men are fight'n among each other a lil bit bout where our cattle should be."

Lot spits into the shadow of his boots while adjusting his shirt collar.

"That's what your upset about ain't it Abe?" Lot asks, "Your upset cause ya know it's time for me to go just like it was time for you to leave the ranch."

Caught off guard by Lot's remarks Abram leans against the tree;

"Is that what you're feeling?"

Lot kind of laughs to himself, "Yeah, I been see'n it come'n for awhile."

For a moment Abram stands there staring into nothing. That is, until he hears Lot's stomach roar.

Again Lot smiles;

"Does that smell like bacon to you?"

Abram shakes his head at the smell and begins to fan the air with his hat.

"Maybe you should just move off by yourself, I don't think your family can handle the evil your back side is possessed with."

Lot choked on air as he began to laugh.

"My wife fed me food that made my backside be possessed with an evil stench!" he chokingly says.

Both men are laughing out loud and avoiding the topic of separating. But eventually they regain their composure and focus on their matters at hand.

I reckon if it's really time for me to go, God'l be okay with it, won't He Abe?

Abram smiles as he looks toward the haze of distant clouds.

"God will always take care of us."

Both of them walk back to the tree and take a seat.

"So what do we do?" ask Lot.

"That's gonna be up to you, Lot. You look around and decide which direction you'd like to go and I'll work our herds in the opposite direction. There's plenty of land and water both ways. The city of Sodom is to the east and open fields and Canaan to the west. The call is yours. *You've worked hard in the summers and weren't lazy during any harvest. You've been as faithful to me as my own son. You deserve to get to choose."

Suddenly the emotion begins to get to Lot and his voice cracks as he looks away quickly blinking his eyes but not able to withhold the drip of a tear.

"I owe my life to you Abe. If it weren't for you I don't know where I'd be. My wife and daughters are all blessed because of you. Leave'n will be the hardest thing I'll ever do. I ain't even sure I can do it, at least not like you. All you got to do is send word and I'll be back before the moon can change."

Abram squeezes Lot's shoulder, "I know that's true, Lot. You've always been an honest and trustworthy man."

Both sit quietly for a moment.

"So what do you think? Ya wanna go east or west?

Lot leisurely stands to his feet, rubs his belly and smiles at Abram insinuating that he may need to relieve some of the pressure of breakfast.

"Don't!" Abram insists.

Lot continues to rub his belly in a circular motion, groaning and laughing at the same time, mainly as a means of trying to relieve the emotions that are threatening the masculinity of them both. After taking a few minutes to look around Lot takes a deep breath;

"If it's all the same to you, I'll go east toward Sodom."

Abram gives a grin of approval and stands to his feet. He dusts the dirt from his home made chaps and puts his arm around Lot. He looks into the rose colored morning sky and holds Lot firm as he returns the favor of flatulence.

"Oh my!" Lot yells as he pushes away from Abram. "Where did that come from?"

Laughing Abram answers, "*Hard work and a good living keeps me from being enslaved to bad substance!"

"Then it's settled" Abram laughs "I'll be tell'n my people to follow me west."

A smile comes across the face of Lot. He is saddened by the idea of leaving the man who has cared for him basically all his life, but he can't help but be excited about leaving to be on his own with his family and hired hands.

"It's gonna take a while for me to get everything ready to move." He replies as he watches Abram mount up onto the Bay.

"Take all the time ya need, Sarai ain't gonna be too anxious to see ya leave. By the way, it would probably be best if ya tell everyone tonight what's go'n on."

He sits there for a moment looking up into the top of the oak tree. He then looks down to Lot. In his mind he can picture a full series of pictures of Lot's life. From the time he was a small boy barely able to climb into a saddle, to the time he had his first fight on the ranch, he remembers when Lot broke his first horse and his first arm, his thirteenth birthday when he spent a week in bed as sick as a dog, his first girlfriend, the first time Lot killed a man while protecting the family, to his marriage and the birth of his girls. Once again Abram's eyes fill with tears and he turns the Bay to ride away.

Lot slides down the bark of the trunk of the oak tree and settles in on the surrounding dirt. He watches as Abram rides back to the new ranch and then bows his head to pray;

"My God, the God of Abram, I just wanna say thank Ya. I ain't a great prayer like Abe. So, forgive me when I don't know what to say. I just wanna ask Ya to take care of all us as we go our separate ways. I don't know what's gonna happen. But I thank Ya for given us what all we got."

He remembers that his hat is still on his head so he quickly grabs it off and holds it to his chest. "Thank Ya."

Lot stands to his feet, adjusts a crick in his neck and the catch in his jeans. He walks toward his horse and pats it on the neck and dares not to look the jug headed gelding in the eye for fear he would run off into the pasture.

"Get ready ol boy, it's fix'n to be a long ride."

A good jump into the air and he throws his leg up over the saddle. He slides his feet into the stirrups and spurs the horse up to a gallop. He rides back toward the herd that is slowly migrating toward the river. You can imagine what the horse does in the first two lunges, and "no", it didn't smell like bacon.

Lot stays away from the main part of the ranch for the rest of the day and into evening. The longer he can put off having to tell his wife and daughters about the move, the better, as far as he is concerned.

That night the ranch has come together for one of their much endeared pot luck suppers. Each family has created its own special plate of vegetables or deserts. The meat is the fatted calf that the ranch hands have brought in from the pasture and are cooking over the open fire. The kids are playing and fighting, the babies are laughing and crying, the dogs are barking and chasing chickens and yet it all seems somewhat peaceful in its own way. Eventually all the families have settled in around the long wooden tables enjoying the feast and fellowship.

Lot is nowhere as good at hiding his feelings of excitement as Abram might have been. In all honesty, most every one can sense that something is fixing to happen. Right in the middle of the supper Lot tells everyone what he and Abram had decided. No beating around the bush or slow explanation, just drop the hammer and let it fly.

"Well, I'm move'n out!" Lot blurts out.

His wife lowers her eyebrows;

"Move'n outta what?" she asks.

"Well, I didn't mean to say "me", I meant to say "us"!

Again she gives him a puzzled look.

"Us is moving outta of what?"

"Okay I didn't mean to say "us" I meant "we". We are move'n out. Me, you, the girls, my boys and their families. We're taking our stuff and moving down by Sodom and Gomorrah."

She stands to her feet and places her hands on her hips.

"Now why on earth would we do that?" She asks.

A little nervous Lot stands beside her;

"Abe told me to."

Sarai gives Abram an uncomfortable look.

"You what, Abe?"

Abram looks to Lot with eyebrows raised and without a word insinuates to him that he had best tell the truth.

"Okay, okay!" Lot laughs. "Abe didn't tell me to. Look God's done both of us real good. Now we got too much to keep everthing together. So I decided I'd move all my stuff down east and Abe's gonna work his herd up west. We ain't even gonna be that far apart."

"I don't wanna move." Both his girls exclaim.

"You'll like it down there. Just relax."

"Relax?" His wife asks.

"Hey, I'm the man of the house and that's what I decided. So . . . . . There it is." Lot meekly commands.

Abram looks to Lot with a half cocked smile as Lot stands there shuffling his feet and adjusting the waste band of his britches.

"I'm the man of the house." Lot whispers to himself.

His wife and daughters stomp off to their house as Abram smiles and eventually begins to laugh;

"Yah handled that like a true champion, Lot. It should be quite pleasant around your place the next day or so."

Lot takes a deep breath.

"Well, nevertheless It's out there."

As expected there are some that are just as excited as Lot and some that are not excited at all. For many of them, although it has been many years since the time they left the ranch of Abram's father, it only seems like a few days since they went through the work it takes to move out. Now, it's time to do it again. This time however, they at least know where they are going.

Lot has decided to move into the land outside the cities of Sodom and Gomorrah. Both of these cities have a reputation for being full of sin but Lot has convinced himself neither he nor his family will be persuaded by the temptations that come from living in that area. Both Sodom and

Gomorrah have become almost mythical legends for the lack of morals and rampant violence of the inner parts of the town. Both towns are surrounded by destitute housing of those who work for a chance to stay alive. They are generally beaten and abused and work to the point of exhaustion. Saloons and houses of ill repute seem to be on every corner. Slavery of children in every aspect is a way of life. The women are as hard and ruthless as the men and homosexual behaviors are a part of life from the youth through oldest of filthy adults. And yet, the towns seem to thrive in the riches of the land.

A simple thought of God has not entered into the minds of any of them for many years. It would seem impossible for a man of God to exist in a place where the "prince of the air" has taken total control.

A few months later Lot, his family and all those who are going with him are finally ready to move. It has been very tense around his house and emotions have been running high, but finally, they all seem to be ready for their adventure. Every day a few of the families have started moving away from the ranch and in the direction of Sodom. The hired hands that are going with Lot have separated his cattle from Abram's and even the farm animals have been picked over. The families have once again gathered everything they can carry and with fearful anticipation, a little excitement and a touch of apprehension they head out.

Sarai is standing by Lot's wagon hugging his daughters as if they were her own. His wife is sitting up front wiping tears with nothing to say.

Lot walks over to Abe.

"We're just up the trail a couple days ride. Ya know that, right?"

Abram shakes his head; "I know Lot."

"If ya need me for anything, I'll come run'n." Lot insists.

"I know." Abram says.

"Okay then, I guess we best get go'n." He pauses; "Sarai, you come see us, okay?"

Sarai hugs Lot as tight as she can;

"I love you like a son. You take care of these girls."

"I know." He whispers. "I will."

Lot climbs into the seat of his wagon and whips the reins across the back of his mules. With a quick jerk the wagon moves out and Lot is headed out on his own. Abram stands in the tracks of their wagon and watches as they drive off. Sarai walks up beside him and wraps her arms around his waste. She lays her head on his chest as tears flow down her soft cheek. Abram is not settled. Something inside him is stirred. He shakes it off as a thought that he is probably upset about Lot moving away since Lot is the closes thing to a son that he and Sarai have ever had. But that is not the case. The spirit inside him is giving him warning. Trouble is coming.

As feared, it will seem that Lot's desire for the pleasures of life will overtake his ability to focus on a righteous behavior. *If you make your friends with people of God then you are protected, but if you make friends with evil, then you get what you get. His time away from Abram will not serve him well.

CHAPTER 6

Abram rescues Lot

Genesis 14

For many years both Lot and Abram continue to grow in their individual riches and, as one would expect, Lot has become closer and closer to the people of Sodom and Gomorrah and trouble looms in the distance. Eventually Lot had taken all his possessions and moved into Sodom. His life style is anything but the life Abram has taught him throughout his childhood. He and his family have fallen captive to the social ways of evil.

In this area of vast riches there are many small towns that desire to have the final say in who gets what part of the wealth of the land. In each town, there are also malicious men who are willing to do whatever it takes to increase their riches. "Whatever it takes" will now mean rampaging the towns and communities of those around them.

In the middle of a balmy night a small group of men are gathering outside one of the towns to the east of Sodom to drink and discuss their plans of animosity. For quite a while they have been plotting to invade both Sodom and Gomorrah and take over its wealth in all means possible. These men are not led by leaders of other cities they are rebels on their own. They steal, kill and deceive. They may be mean but nobody said they were all that smart, so, they neglect to assure that their meetings are held in secret and that word does not get out. Which it does. Unfortunately, word of their planned incursion has spread to the wicked men of Sodom and Gomorrah and you might as well have spit in their eye. They will not stand still for such an attack. Fear does not enter the minds of any man living in the cities of evil and the chance to fight and kill are welcomed with open arms. Strange as it may sound, an oncoming war with a rival gang seems to be a good reason to get drunk the night before. And they do.

There is place between the towns called the Valley of Siddim where the summer's heat bears down on the land and an excess of tar oozes through the cracks of the ground giving the valley its name. The men of Sodom and Gomorrah have decide to surprise those coming against them and kill them in the valley where there is no place for them to run. As it turns out their plan of attack is about to meet a desperate outcome.

Before sunrise they are gathering outside the gates. Many of them are still drunk from the night before. Most of them are riding horses that are as wild as the rider. The men of Sodom and Gomorrah are armed with every firearm and knife they can scrounge up. They are soiled in their own sun baked fluids and reek of disgusting sloth. In a wayward trot they head to the Valley of Siddim. What would normally seem to be a beautiful sunrise, will now radiate the beginning of a murderous morning.

As they get to the valley they slow to a walk and begin weaving through the valley dodging the ditches of tar. They have no idea they are riding in to an ambush and their enemy has already taken place above them in the crevices of the mountains. * Their understanding of battle is limited and the fools they call leaders have brought them straight into the serpents den.

Though it is early morning the heat is already beginning to impress its wrath on the backs of these drunken warriors. A quiet and somber mentality of an oncoming fight rides along inside their heads. The sounds of twisting saddle leather, horse hooves stomping along the dry surface and the occasional rolling of horse lips echoes through the valley. The sodomites are intent on getting to the middle of the valley before taking cover to surprise their foe.

The riders of Sodom and Gomorrah enter deep into the valley before a single shot from their rival is fired. Before evil fights evil a deathly silence fills the day.

There's stillness, and then . . . .

When the first shot is discharged, it is immediately followed by continuous gunfire raining lead down on them from every direction imaginable. Before a man can draw his pistol many of them have bullets rip through their flesh and explode their lungs. The bullets are soaring past their heads and rupturing the bones of those beside them. The blood of their wounded horses flows into the tar filled cracks of the ground as they fall to their death. Many of the men never know what hit them, the others, however, lay in the torturous pain of having parts of the bodies torn apart from gun shots. The smell of gun powder fills the scorching air that is clouded with gun smoke. Some men are yelling commands, others are shouting for help, some roar in violent rage, but most are screaming in pain.

The enemies attack is emerging from both ends of the valley to join the downpour of violence coming from those hiding on the ridges of the sides. The men from Sodom and Gomorrah realize that they are seriously out numbered. Those who are not dead, or being killed as they lay injured, are trying desperately to escape. While spurring their horses in fury many become victims of their own plot by falling to their death in the deep steaming tar pits that have given the valley its reputation. Eventually, the dissenters of Sodom and Gomorrah are over taken. The enemy carries their vicious charge through the valley killing every living man and creature in their path. Without as much as a second thought they continue out of the valley and into the towns. It is several days of bloody massacre and fire. They destroy anything and everything in their course and take all they want including men, women and children that they intend to enslave. Lot, his wife and daughters and all his possessions are among those taken. *He has forsaken all that Abram has taught him about God and righteousness and it has landed him in the company of the spiritually dead.

When the battle ends one of Lot's hired hands manages to stay alive. Beaten and battered he finds a horse and escapes from Sodom. For the next three days he struggles to stay alive and on the horse as he rides toward Abram. He is barely conscious when Johnny, from Abram's ranch, sees him riding through the thickets. Johnny swiftly jumps up on his horse and rushes toward the injured man. Even from a distance Johnny can tell that an angel of death is riding in this man's soul as he gallops his horse out to meet the half dead stranger. Quickly Johnny dismounts from his horse and pulls the rider off of the injured and dehydrated mare. The man's face is beaten and swollen. One eye is completely shut the other struggles to focus through the dried blood caught in his lashes. He is coughing from the internal bleeding. He has numerous stab wounds and has been shot in the leg. His clothes are stained in dry blood which has actually caused a coagulation of the blood around the injuries and have kept the man from dying. Johnny lays him on the ground and grabs a cantina that he has been carrying on his saddle horn. He tries to pour water down the man's throat but realizes the injuries are preventing him from swallowing. Most of the water runs out of his mouth and down his bloody face. The stranger coughs and spits. He gasps even harder for a breath of air. A few minutes pass as Johnny works feverously to keep him alive. With a blood stained hand the lone rider grips the wrist of Johnny and mouths the name, "Lot."

Johnny moves his face closer to the mouth of the dying rider;

"Did you say Lot?!"

The man raises his arm to Johnny's shoulder;

"They took him." He whispered., "His wife and girls"

"Who took him!?" Johnny yelled as he shook the man, "Took him where?!"

With every shake of his head the man's eyes barely rolled back into a consciousness. Again the he spits up blood and his breathing stops. Johnny feels a warm wetness on the ground where he is kneeling and realizes the wounds of this stranger have re-opened and blood is pouring across his thighs and onto the ground.

"Who took Lot!?" he begs.

The rider was gone.

Without hesitation Johnny slides the man off his lap and lays him on the ground. His jeans are drenched with the blood of stranger and the mud of the earth. He places a blanket that was tied to the saddle of the exhausted horse over the man's face. The chestnut mare stumbles and falls to her side. Johnny has no choice but to put her down. He then jumps onto the back of his own horse and rushes back to the ranch fearing that Lot and his family may have been brutally killed.

Abram is in the main barn putting new shoes on the Bay and can hear the commotion when Johnny comes racing through the ranch.

"Abe! Abe!"

Abram can tell by the sound of Johnny's voice that there is trouble. Finishing the clipping of the last nail he drops his horse's foot and wipes his hands on his jeans as he walks to the barn door.

"Johnny! I'm over here. What's the problem?"

Gasping for air from a dangerous ride and the anxiety of what has happen;

"Lots been taken! They took his wife and girls and I don't know what all!"

A look of concern and confusion comes over the face of Abram as Johnny leaps from his horse and stands uncomfortably close while panting with anticipation.

Abram grabs the reigns of Johnny's horse,

"Who took Lot? What are talking about?"

Johnny explains about the man that has just passed away out in the field. He tells of his injuries and the blood. He could tell that there has been a serious fight and Lot is in desperate trouble. Immediately Abram tells Johnny to call up the men from all parts of the ranch and then he rushes into his house. Many other men were around as Johnny was telling Abram what he has seen and when they hear that Lot is in trouble they rush off to prepare themselves for war. Abram begins trying to give Sarai a brief description of what he knows while frantically gathering every firearm he can find. The more he moves about the more Sarai and Hagar begin to worry. Abram doesn't know enough information to tell them everything they want to know and now all three are frustrated.

"Abe, stop for a minute and tell me what's go'n on!"

Abe keeps gathering his guns;

"I don't know what all's go'n on! I just know Lot's in trouble!"

"What about the girls?!" Hagar asks.

"From what I know they're with him. I just don't know if they're hurt or not."

Abe wraps an extra leather strap of bullets over his shoulder.

"Oh my Lord." Sarai says as she places her hand over her mouth.

Abram places his hand on her shoulder;

"If they're alive I'll find 'em and get out!"

She nods her head.

Johnny rides hard out to the herd to gather up the rest of the men. Within twenty minutes every man of the ranch is mounted up on horse back and waiting in front of Abram's house. They are armed with rifles, pistols, knives, and every shell they have ever made in their life. Among the worn out leathers of chaps, gloves and boots they are wrapped in ropes and straps. The spurs rattle in anticipation and the call for revenge begins to be heard from the voices of angered friends of Lot. The anxiety of war running through their bodies is even evident in the attitudes of their horses. A man's nerves when sitting horseback are captivated in the sensations of their horse. The horses dance in circles, blow and even rare up with a desire to stampede into the field for a reason they know nothing about.

Abram has given as much explanation of the situation to Sarai and Hagar as he can. All three of them walk out onto the porch to address the rest of the ranch. The distinct and frightening look of anger on Abram's entire body is something many of them have never seen. Behind him Sarai and Hagar stand holding to each other in fear and worry and anger. Fear for Lot and his family, worry for what the men are about to face and anger toward those that Abram will soon attack. They are not, however, in fear for Abram whom God protects.

"Listen!" Abram commands, "I don't know what's happen. All we know is that Lot and his family been taken and accord'n to what Johnny has seen people been killed. Men! We'll ride to Sodom and find out what's happen. There's a good chance we could have to fight."

Suddenly shots are being fired into the sky and the men yell in eagerness to protect one of their own.

"Ladies! The ranch is yours! God be with you until we return. And we will return!"

Abram turns and kisses Sarai. Johnny has saddled the Bay for him and hands him the reins. Without another word he slings himself upon the saddle and spurs up the Bay leading the men toward Sodom. In normal circumstance this would be at least a two day leisurely ride but these are not normal circumstances. The horses are ridden as hard as they can go with the understanding that they are also the men's only means of transportation. Late in the night Abram stops the ride. They can get to Sodom by noon the next day if they rest now and head out again tomorrow morning.

"Johnny, spread the word, no fires tonight."

Johnny rides back through the rest of the men telling them to unsaddle here for the night with no fire which also means unless you brought something from your house to eat you were probably missing supper. The men unsaddle and tie their horses to anything they can find. Most of them throw their saddle on the ground beside their horse and use it as a pillow. None of them worried with bringing bedding. Not much sleep will happen tonight anyway. The rest in the cooler temperatures of the night is more intended for the horses than the men.

As Johnny lies on the ground and props his head and shoulders against his saddle he recalls the gruesome body of the man that had told him about Lot. It dawns on him that no one has gone out to bury him. The pictures of the pain screaming through the tears in rider's eyes are forever embedded into Johnny's memory. He can only imagine what may be happening to Lot's family. He sits up and looks across the men that are trying to lie still for the night. To his left the moon light shines down on the silhouette of Abram and the Bay. Abram is not preparing to sleep. He is preparing for war. He is not doing so by checking his rifle or shells, he is putting on armor in a way that he knows will bring forth success. He is praying.

An occasional blow of a horse, the sounds of crickets and the howls of coyotes are the music of the night. The beating of each man's heart pounds in their breast and delays any good rest. Before the sun rises the next morning Abram personally walks to each man to stir them around and express his gratitude for their loyalty. As the red sun barely peeks its eyes over the rugged horizon the army of men from Abram's ranch are already beginning to move toward the battle.

Micah has ridden ahead several hours to scout out the enemy. Abram and the rest of the men have been riding for about an hour and half when they see Micah riding back toward them. He doesn't seem to be in a hurry and it takes about thirty minutes until they reach each other.

Micah rides up along side Abram.

"I found 'em."

The look on Abram's face changes from a look of concern to a look of anger.

"What are they do'n?" he asks.

Micah finishes a drink from his canteen.

"There's about a hundred of 'em. They got Lot and his family along with several others all gathered up in a corner. They got a lot of cattle, wagons, pretty much anything they could steal and take with 'em. They're drink'n pretty hard. Lot's of guns."

Abram takes a deep breath.

"Can we circle 'em up?"

Micah nods his head forward.

"They're bout half a day ahead and in no hurry to go anywhere. We could probably get there and get set then take 'em down right before sunset."

Abram adjusts himself in his worn out saddle.

"Lead the way."

With that Micah winks at one of his buddies and turns to lead Abram's men to the battle. They will ride easy and slowly knowing that they are not chasing men on a run. The quieter they ride the less noise and dust will be stirred up that may give them away. As Micah had stated, it took them about a half a day to ride up to the ridge above the enemy's camp.

While the others wait back Abram eases up through a tree line to look over the camp. He can smell the burning of cow hide. They are cooking and better yet, wasting many of the cattle they have stolen. He notices the guns lying on the ground around all the clothing and saddles. The camp is in total disarray. He searches the camp over from a distance for Lot and his family. When he finally catches a glimpse of them he can see that they have been beaten and abused. They are dirty, their clothes are torn, and he can tell that they had not eaten or had much to drink in days. Many of the enemy either lay asleep or passed out. The view to the eyes of Abram is not only one of wicked men, but also of men soaked in the sin of their lives. His Spirit is almost overwhelmed at the evilness that seems to be weaving its way through the camp. This will not just be a battle of man on man, but principalities of darkness against the Family of God.

He slowly backs the Bay away from the ridge and then turns to ride to his men. He motions for them to follow him a little ways away from where they were so he can talk with them.

"Listen up. I have feared for my life in the recent past when the man inside me over powered my trust in God. I am telling you now, this is not just a battle of us against them. It is a battle of those who oppose our God against those of us who are of God's family. Do not fear! We will circle them and at dusk we will attack them and conquer them or run them to another land. Ride hard, shoot straight and go with the heart of bravery that God has placed within you."

Abram assigns a few to be the leaders of smaller bands of men. For the next several hours they quietly ride all around the ridge that completely encircles the camp of evil. From where Abram sits he can see the movement of his men until they have each reached their position. Then, they wait patiently.

While they wait, Abram prays to God. He prays for strength, direction and the safety of his men. He also gives thanks for the opportunity to defend the name of God against those who have come to spread despair. He prays that the first person to lead the charge into this camp will be the Holy Spirit. Finally, he prays for the protection of Lot, Lot's family and all the others that are being held prisoner.

As he finishes his prayer and opens his eyes he can see the last of the sun preparing to rest behind the mountain. Then as if it were the middle of winter he feels a chill run through his body. This is not the chill of the air but the presence of the Holy Spirit.

He adjusts his seat in the saddle and waits as the Spirit of God calms him.

He raises his rifle to take aim and his Spirit settles.

With that Abram takes a bead on the chest of one of the bandits and fires the first shot that drops the guard standing beside Lot. Instantly a stampede of horses and riders from every direction charge down upon an unsuspecting repulsive tribe.

"Take cover!" Lot yells to his family. "Get down! Get down!"

Lot's family and friends scramble together and do the best they can to hide from the fury. Lot is laying over his wife and daughters as one of Abram's men crash through a tent on his horse. Lot recognizes him;

"It's Abe! It's Abe and his men!" He yells.

Rifle shots and yells echo through the valley. The sounds of bullets ricocheting off the rocks and the wind screaming the whisper of shells through the weeds tell the prisoners to take cover. Many of the enemy are killed before they ever wake from their drunken slumber. Several race for a loaded weapon but the bullets of Abram's men rip through their flesh and drop them to a blood-splattered death. The battle rages for more than twenty minutes until several of the enemy flee for their lives. Abram's men chase them for quite a distance with every intention of killing them if they can. Eventually the noise of gun fire ceases and is replaced by the screaming of women and children.

When it is all said and done Abram sits high above the campground on his Bay spinning in circles and looking for anyone that remains alive and is representing the darkness of iniquity. To those who are huddled together the flames of several campfires and the glow of the moon draw their attention to the face of the Man of God. When he finally stops his horse he is facing directly toward Lot.

Through the smoke of the night Lot stands looking toward him as a beaten man. He has changed. He is not the rough rider that he once was when he rode with Abram. His clothes, though torn and filthy, are city clothes. His demeanor does not express the confidence of the man that Abram once knew. Abram dismounts from the Bay and walks toward Lot.

Lot's eyes are bruised and filled with tears.

"I prayed you would come."

Abram wraps his arms around Lot's neck.

"I will always come, and bring our God with me."

In the back ground Abram's men are untying some of the prisoners that had been bound with wet leather. It takes an hour or so to make sure that none of the enemy were lying in the camp pretending to be dead and still posing a threat. When it is determined to be safe all the men begin moving the women and children to a place above the ridge to sleep for the rest of the night away from the death of the original camp. It would have been nice just to load everyone up and head for home but there was way too much property and stolen goods that needs to be retrieved to try and leave at night.

The next morning it takes several hours for everyone to separate the property the thieves had stolen from all the families of Sodom. Once they have gathered the clothing, money, jewelry, gold and livestock they are ready to begin the trip back toward Sodom.

Throughout the day, into the night and following morning Abram had spent most of his time tending to the needs of those they have rescued. Occasionally he would catch a glimpse of Lot huddling up with his wife and daughters. Judging by the Lot's demeanor, evilness has built up his pride and then crumbled his ego. Only the Spirit of God can lift him back to the place he once stood with Abram.

The next day the band of wounded Sodomites, the ranch hands and Abram begin the final leg of their slow meandering trip back home. It will be a very slow procedure because of the injuries and mass of property being brought back. In due course they have found sight of Sodom. On their way they are greeted by the Mayor of Salem. Several of the prisoners that had been taken were from this small town. The Mayor also happens to be a Pastor of their small community church. The old man rides slowly up to Abram on his swayed back mule. He removes his hat and wipes his forehead with a dust covered handkerchief.

"You're a man of God, Abram. In your own way, you've punished the guilty. *Many would have avoided 'em and let 'em run. They woulda destroyed us. May God bless you for all you've done."

Abram can see the Spirit of the Lord in the eyes of the Pastor. He can tell that he has honest love and concern for the people of Salem. For that reason Abram gives him ten percent of all the stolen property he has recovered. The Pastor was completely humbled by Abram's generosity. Those from his town quickly swarm around him and hug each other in a jubilant celebration of life and safety and hope.

Abram and the rest of the assembly continued on to Sodom. As they approach the entry of Sodom they are welcomed by the Mayor of Sodom. Unlike the gentleman from Salem this man was anything but a Godly man. He is arrogant, prideful, filled with lust and debauchery. He rides his black stud up to Abram with an air of sinful conceit that disgusted the Spirit within Abram.

"Nice job Mr. Abram." He replies sarcastically, "I got to tell ya, I wasn't really expect'n ya to make it back alive."

He laughs abruptly as his rotted teeth hide behind the food infested hair of his filthy mustache and beard.

"I tell ya what, you leave the people here and you can take all the other stuff with ya . . . My gift"

Abram is not impressed. He removes his hat and wipes his forehead with his sleeve. He leans his head from side to side stretching his neck, takes a deep breath and looks the Mayor dead in the eye.

"I promised my God that I'd never take a single thing from you sir. Not one single thread. You'll never have the opportunity to say you had anything to do with what I own."

A look of surprise comes across the sun aged face of the Mayor of Sodom. He is offended and yet not crazy enough to offer up sarcasm. Instead he casts a sneering smirk and turns his horse away from Abram.

"Whatever big man, your loss."

Several others have followed the Mayor out to meet Abram. They gather up the rest of the stolen property and citizens of Sodom and begin separating from Abram and his men. Meanwhile Abram and his camp have set up for the night. As the fires burn in the barren air most of the men sit and drink coffee watching as those they had rescued sauntered away without so much as a simple "thank you" for the risk these men have taken.

Abram stands at the front of the camp holding a tin cup of coffee and watching as the heat waves flowing across the ground cause the silhouettes of the Sodomites to glide in a phantom-like motion toward the horizon. He can smell the aroma behind him of a man that has not been cleansed in several moons.

"Abe." Lot says lightly

Abram turns and faces Lot for the first time since the battle. For days they have traveled together through the rough terrain but other than the initial contact at the rebel camp Abram has not taken the time to sit and talk with Lot.

"You look a little worn." Abram says without actually looking at Lot.

"I feel a little worn". Lot answers.

Abram spits the last of his coffee onto the ground.

"I noticed that Mayor took all your stuff back to Sodom with 'em. You plan'n on go'n back there Lot?"

Lot walks up beside Abram and stares at the crowd Sodomites limping their way through the dust of the night.

"It's where I live. My families there, my friends, my hands. Ya don't just walk away."

Abram turns toward him and sizes him up from head to toe with a look of discernment.

"Ya do if ya cain't take God in there with ya."

"It ain't like ya think, Abe. They're not all bad."

He pauses.

"I cain't thank ya enough for come'n after me, but ya know I gotta go."

"Just like that?" Abram asks

Lot has nothing to say.

Abram was hoping that Lot would consider coming back to the ranch for while but it was not to be. As he turns to continue his conversation he is surprised to see Lot's wife and daughters standing with Lot and encouraging him to head out with the rest of the others. They have lost their understanding of respect. Without another word Abram steps to the side and nods his head.

"I'll come see ya soon." Lot replies.

As they walk by, the wife and girls hug Abram, lower their face and head out for Sodom.

Abram's heart is burdened. He knows without any doubt this will not be the last time he comes for Lot. He also knows that Lot will soon have more struggles with his faith in God. But "a man's got to make a man's decisions". For now, they are safe and none of Abram's men had been killed or injured. Tomorrow, the excitement of the past few days will just be talk as they ride back to their own families. Sometimes people just don't seem to understand where true love of a brother comes from and the weight it carries.

As Lot continues on into the night it strikes Abram hard in his heart as if he were losing the son he has never had. He continues to watch his nephew disappear into the haze of the horizon but his mind finds its way back to the promise God had given him, the promise of children. The years have continued to press forward as Abram and Sarai climb further past what most would consider to be an age that would allow for child bearing. He takes a deep breath, looks to heaven and sheds a quiet tear.

As the night matures deeper into the darkness Abram falls into a sleep and gives God a chance to talk. Once again through the Spirit of God Abram is assured that he will have children and that his children will have children to a measure too large to count.

It is often argued as to whether or not a man can be righteous or if it is the Spirit within in him that is righteous. On this night God tells Abram that it is his faith that has made him righteous.

CHAPTER 7

Abram and Hagar

Genesis 16

Many seasons have come and gone and though there have been days of hard work, despair and loss that normally come with running a ranch, God has continued to bless Abram and the families that work for him. And yet both he and Sarai are still concerned with the fact that they do not have a child to inherit all the blessings that God has given them. But, life continues.

Abram pushes himself away from the cedar kitchen table after eating another incredible meal that Sarai has prepared. He tries to expand his belly to insinuate that he was getting fat but even at his age his body is still ripped with working muscle.

"There's still some apple pie for later." Sarai says as she gathers up the metal plates.

Abram gets up and slides his chair under the table then follows her over to the sink. He wraps his partially washed arms around her shoulders and hugs her to his chest.

"Whoo, I may have to hold off for now. Besides, you're sweet enough for me."

Sarai pats his wrists,

"Why don't ya grab me a bucket of water from outside so I can wash these plates, Mr. Romance."

Abram laughs and goes to the back porch where he had earlier placed a bucket of water for just this purpose. You would think he would try to get it to the kitchen without spilling the majority of it across the floor. That never crosses his mind. He pours what is left into the sink while Sarai shakes her head in humorous dismay. Sarai finishes cleaning the kitchen as Abram sharpens his knife in the front room. In a moment she walks out of kitchen and leans against the log wall of the fireplace. Looking bashfully over the rag that she is using to dry her hands, she replies,

"Something has crossed my mind."

Abram spits on the blade of his knife, begins sliding the blade across a wet rock and then presses back in his chair with a look of inquisitiveness.

"Oh yeah, what's that?"

Sarai sashays over to him in a seductive interwoven path and sits on his lap running her fingers through his hair and kissing him on the forehead;

"I think I have come to grips with how God intends for us to have children."

The excitement he has in her flirtatious actions to this point is overtaken by the surprise of her statement. He doesn't care for surprises. Over his life he has found that most often *surprises turn in to rude awakenings and only good willed actions make for happy days. Abram gently presses her to a distance that allows them to look eye to eye;

"What are you talking about?"

She stands to her feet and faces away from him hiding the fact that her heart is beating in her chest like the pounding of wild Indians on leather drums.

"It's obvious to me that I ain't gonna give ya no children, however, I do think we can have children."

"And how is that?" Abram asks.

Sarai crosses her arms, turns and looks him straight in the eye with a stern look of resolve;

"Hagar."

Abrams eyebrows sink in uncertainty as he places his wet rock on the table next to his chair;

"What about her?"

Sarai quickly kneels down in front of him and places her hands on his knees;

"Hear me out Abe."

His body relaxes back into his chair as a way of telling her he was listening.

Taking a deep breath she continues,

"Perhaps God has brought Hagar into our lives as a means of give'n us children to build a family around. I know they won't be my blood but I think I can still love 'em as if they were my own."

For a moment they both stare breathlessly into each others eyes as Abram considers whether or not she suggesting what he thinks. Sarai is filled with a considerable amount of emotional pain and begins to cry.

"What I'm say'n is, I want you to have a baby with Hagar."

Abram stands abruptly to his feet; "You're crazy!"

"Wait!" Sarai exclaims.

Abram grabs her by the shoulders and stops her at an arms distance.

"You're say'n ya want me to cheat on you and get Hagar pregnant? I've never heard such a thing! Even if I did, what do ya think our hands are gonna say?"

She interrupts, "I'll tell 'em it was me, that I asked ya to do it for me!"

He turns to grab his hat, "It ain't right Sarai!" he says with a bit of anger.

Sarai steps in front of him and blocks his path.

"Ain't right for who?! You!? Me!? Ya keep tell'n me God said we'll have children and I keep get'n older by the day! I don't know no other way, Abe!"

He moves her aside to leave but stops just inside the door. He can hear the tone of desperation in her voice as she makes her plea. His hesitation gives her one last chance.

She takes one step towards him; "Just tell me you'll think about it, that's all I'm ask'n."

He honestly has no other choice. Making a decision now would be ludicrous. *If he has any wisdom he will act as a prudent man and give thought to his actions. Abram takes a deep breath and then walks out into the darkness. Sarai is as exhausted as if she had just worked a full day of branding. She knows that she has either given Abram a serious way to begin a family or driven a horrible stake between them. She falls onto the bed and cries into the pillow smothered in his scent. That night he never makes it back to the house and she cries herself to sleep.

A ray of sun light squeezes its way between a splinter in the wall and warms her tear swollen eyes. She smells the aroma of coffee and hears the creaking of a rocking chair on the front porch. He's home. As she sets up in bed her mind debates on whether to go out or stay in. History tells her to get it over with. Either he has thought it through and will agree or he will put her in her place and she will be months trying to repair the damage. Her shadow crawls across the wooden slats of the porch for Abram to see as she approaches the door.

He is filled with turmoil. Truthfully, he was deeply hurt by the proposition. How can a woman he loves allow herself to share her husband with another woman? In a way his relationship was cheapened. But as the night passes, so too does his thought process. Can a woman so desire a child that she is willing to share the love of her life to experience the opportunity of raising a baby? He also remembers several years back when he feared for his life in the town of Little Egypt and Sarai agreed to say she was his sister. If she was willing to sacrifice for him should he not be willing to sacrifice for her. And yes, although for many men this would not be considered a sacrifice, for Abram, a man of God, it is just that.

"This could really hurt us if it's not what you really want." He says softly into his cup of coffee.

A little surprised she stands quietly for a few seconds;

"It's what I want. It's what I need."

Abram sits his cup on the porch beside his chair and stands to his feet never looking toward her. He slightly nods his head forward, slaps his hat on the side of his leg and watches the dust float into the air;

"Then make it happen."

Again he never looks her way as he walks out toward the branding rink and goes to work. Sarai has gotten her way. She will soon have a child in her house. How it will work out is anybody's guess. Nevertheless, something is about to give way. All the while, Hagar has no idea of what is about to transpire. Sarai has no idea if Hagar will agree.

Many years ago Hagar had hidden in the back of a wagon as Abram's family left his father's ranch. It was the death of a child that brought

Sarai and Hagar together and now the birth of a child could weave them together in a whole new way.

Over the years Hagar has grown from a quiet cute little girl to a vibrant young woman. She is petit in size yet very strong in build. Though her clothing is always modest and worn mainly in ways of comfort and necessity for the work she is given, every man in camp has noticed her beauty. Her long black hair is like the mane of a beautiful stallion. Her eyes are deep in chocolate with a soft look that causes every young single man to drool. All of her attractiveness is matched by the love that she has shown to everyone she comes into contact with. Even the females of the camp have found it hard to be jealous of her because they are drawn to her by the warmth she displays to them on a daily basis. Even with the compassion and love she possesses this request from Sarai will not come easy.

Today is a gorgeous day. The suns triumphant appearance is announced in the echoes of the brilliantly colored roosters that bring life to the morning. As Hagar enters her one room cabin from an early morning shower Sarai places her dish rag on her kitchen cabinet, unties her hand-woven apron and goes to see Hagar.

This will be one of the most awkward conversations that Hagar and Sarai have ever encountered. How do you ask a girl you have basically adopted and parented from childhood, to have sex with your husband? How do you, as the young lady, answer?

Sarai steps up on the porch of Hagar's small home and adjust a few pots that are cluttered around the entry. Hagar walks around the corner and sees Sarai straightening up her room. As Hagar enters Sarai stands up straight and rubs her hands on her skirt.

"Still clean'n up after me, huh?" Hagar asks with a smile as she buttons her skirt around her waist.

Sarai smiles, "It never ends I guess."

Sarai walks over toward a wall where Hagar has a picture of a deer that she had painted using the color from flowers.

"You're so talented Hagar. Beautiful and talented."

For some reason that compliment did not settle with Hagar. Sarai has often paid Hagar a compliment over the years and with true heart. Something about the way this one was said didn't settle with her.

With a look of curiosity Hagar approaches Sarai. Looking over her shoulder at the painting;

"Sarai, you've seen that pictures a hundred times. What's really on your mind?'

Sarai walks away without facing her;

"I just like the colors."

"Oh, Okay." Hagar knows she is not being truthful. "Would you like a cup of water?"

Sarai's chin rises into a proud and stern position;

"I have something I want to ask you and there is no easy way to go about it."

Hagar brushes her hair away from her face;

"Then just ask. You know I'm here for ya."

Sarai approaches Hagar and takes her by the hand.

"This is awkward for me." She pauses, "You have been the closest thing to a daughter that we've had. Now, I'm about to ask you to do someth'n that no real mother would ever ask."

A small case of uncomfortable fear crosses the mind of Hagar;

"Your kinda scare'n me Sarai."

Sarai moves them over to a wooden couch that is covered in tanned cow hide.

"Ya know how bad I've wanted a baby. I'm way past the age of being able to bear a child and yet Abram insists that God has told 'em we will raise children. As far as I can see it, there is only one way that will come to pass."

Hagar unclasps her hands from Sarai;

"I don't understand."

Sarai stands to her feet and walks across the room toward the painting. Not facing Hagar she continues;

"Everyone wants their children to be blessed with gifts and talents and physical beauty. Abe is a very strong and handsome man, as you know."

"Yes he is." Hagar interrupts

"You too are very blessed."

Again she pauses and takes a deep breath;

"I believe that God may have brought you to us as a way of giving us a child."

"I beg your pardon? Hagar asks in disbelief

Sarai turns to face her and stands firm and in an almost militant stance;

"I'm asking you to have a child by Abe."

Hagar gasps. "Are you kid'n me? He would kill both of us if he knew you were asking me this."

"He knows." Sarai answers.

Hagar's chin drops.

"He knows?" He knows you're here? Oh my Lord, I'm so embarrassed!"

Again Sarai grabs her by the hands only to have Hagar pull them away.

"I'm a virgin! I have been waiting for the man I will marry! What will everyone think of me? My heavens Sarai, he's your husband! How can I do that?"

With every word her breaths become deeper and deeper. She is rapidly wiping the tears of her eyes with her apron. She moves into her kitchen to pour a cup of water. She tries to drink but chokes.

A desperate Sarai continues her charge;

"Think of all we have done for you! We brought you out of that nasty land and gave you every thing you have needed."

"I know!" Hagar screams. "But this is how ya want me to pay ya back? Is this why you have acted like ya love me?! Have you known all along one day you'd ask this of me?!"

Sarai grabs her again and this time refuses to let go;

"No!"

She grabs Hagar by the chin and turns her face toward her;

"I've never thought of this til now. You have to believe me. But this is the only way I can see us have'n a child! You're the only one I would trust with Abe."

Again Hagar fights away;

"I don't want you to trust me with your husband! I want to have my own husband!"

"And you will!" Sarai answers.

Hagar is now in full tears.

"What man will want me? Who will want a woman that gives herself up to another woman's husband? I'll be despised!

"I won't let that happen." Sarai says as she wipes the tears from her own eyes.

"These people will understand the sacrifice you're willing to take in order to show your love to me and Abe. They'll respect what you're do'n. Look, all I'm ask'n is that ya think about it. Then you can let me know. Just think about it."

Hagar turns away from Sarai and covers her face with her hands.

Sarai stands for a few seconds in silence.

Without touching her she whispers; "Just think about it."

She lowers her head and leaves Hagar to ponder her request.

Abram is standing beside a fire built for the branding iron. Through the smoke and heat waves of the fire he catches a glimpse of Sarai walking back to his house. There is no doubt in his mind about what has probably transpired. In a way he would love to go see Hagar to see how she's feeling. His concern is not about their relationship as far as a physical relationship, but he clearly understands the odd emotions that must be going through her mind. His connection with her has been anything but physical. If she has agreed with Sarai's request, regardless of how hard they try, their rapport may never be the same. After pondering it for a while he decides not to go but continue working. No doubt, Sarai will fill him in soon enough.

Meanwhile Hagar is pacing nervously back and forth through her house. It may have seemed easy for Sarai to just walk off, but for Hagar the physical and emotional stress of this appeal has her flabbergasted. She has never considered such a strange twist in her young life. She has no idea if the child would still be hers or if she will be forced to give it to Sarai. Will she be treated as a member of Abram's family in reference to inheritance or will she simply be seen as a tool to provide the child? Will it happen again? She also wonders if the rest of the ranch will consider her a whore. Will they really appreciate her sacrifice as Sarai said or will they look down on her for the rest of her life? And if she says "No.", then what? Will she be forced to leave? Will she be shunned by the one woman who saved her years ago? All she wants is to someday be married and continue to follow Abram as the rest of the ranch. From what it appears, there really is no choice. It's as if the decision was made long before the question was asked. So far her emotions have prevented her from considering prayer.

It's a shame actually,*her heart is good and she cherishes the Father. He would surely hear her.

In the middle of the night there are no more tears to be shed, there are no more questions to ask, it is what it is and she decides she will have to handle what circumstances come. This is where her life reaches a split in the trail and her best chance of survival is to stay with the ranch.

"So be it." She whispers to herself. She pulls the blankets over her head and fades to sleep early in the morning hours.

In the house of Abram the night came and went and not a word was spoken about Hagar. Abram was a little surprised but did not press the issue. Best case scenario is Sarai chose not to ask or Hagar said no and he will never hear of it again. Unfortunately the morning will hold a completely different scenario.

Hagar knows that Abram and Sarai are always the first to get up in the morning. Though she has gotten but a few hours of sleep she is sitting on their porch when Abram steps out for his morning cup of coffee. He is stunned when he sees her and his heart drops. She is sitting on the end of the porch hugging the rustic pole that holds up the roof of the porch. She hears him walk out but does not turn to look at him. It is the most uncomfortable morning of their lives. His spurs rake across the wooden slats of the porch as he moves toward his chair and takes a seat. Still not a word is spoken. In a moment Sarai comes outside for a breath of morning air and is caught off guard seeing Hagar. She stops in her tracks just inside the door.

Hagar's voice has been weakened by the night of crying so she softly asks,

"When will it happen?"

Abram has no answer. All he can do is look across the field and slightly shake his head.

"Soon." Sarai replies.

With that Abram stands, adjusts his hat and walks toward Hagar. He places his hand on her shoulder;

"I'm sorry."

He gives a quick look back toward Sarai and can see no sign of her backing away so he leaves. Both Sarai and Hagar watch him as he walks around the corner. Each of them now see him in a way they never have.

Hagar stands to her feet;

"I hope you know what this will do."

Sarai looks toward the horizon and then walks into the house without a reply.

Several silent nights pass and there has never been a greater distance between Abram and Sarai as there is during these past few nights in bed. They have always bedded down at night in peace with each other and comfortable in their lives. Until now that is. For Abram it is as if he is in bed with a stranger. Every night he gets into bed he can feel the disappointment of his wife. He can't understand how a man's wife can look forward to the night he does not come home, especially when she knows he is sleeping with another woman. *What happiness there once was has been robbed by worry and there are no words to fix it. There is little rest to be had when tension overwhelms your ability to sleep.

It's been four nights since Abram or Sarai have spoken a word to Hagar. Once again they are both lying in bed together, at least for a while. Abram has not moved in several hours and yet continues to stare at the walls. Torn as he has ever been in his life he quietly slips out of bed and leaves the room. Sarai is not asleep. She keeps her eyes focused on the ground beside the bed and never moves. Her mind fills with anxiety but she fears that if she moves he will stop. For a while she can't seem to think of anything. She can't keep a single thought processed. As the minutes pass a cloak of sadness drapes itself over her heart. She can't help but realize what she has caused. The man she has dedicated her life to and who has dedicated his life to her is in the house next door with a young woman they basically raised. Feeling as if she is frozen in time, she knows she can stop it and yet chooses not to.

Now she has gotten out of bed and is walking about the house trying desperately to prevent the images in her mind. As the time passes she faces the cold hard truth that it is too late. Eventually Abram walks out the front door of Hagar's house. His head is hanging down like a beaten man. This is not a man that Sarai has ever seen. He turns away from his house and walks out to the corral. Sarai watches from the front door as he saddles up the Bay and rides away.

As the dust from the Bay settles into the belly of the moons shadows the silhouette of a man leans against the inside of the barn. A glimmer of light faintly shines to the ground from the reflection of his spurs. Young Taylor Wilham spends many nights alone thinking and dreaming of the day he and Hagar will be wed. His quiet demeanor has prevented anyone other than Hagar from knowing that they have feelings for one another. Tonight he has seen Abram leave her house, he has heard her cries and he has seen Sarai watch as Abram rides away. His anger for what he thinks may have just happened is only out burned by his knowing it is Abram. His world may have just been stampeded by Sarai's desires for a child. Sarai turns to go back inside but stops as she hears the quiet cry coming from Hagar. Deciding not to go comfort her she returns to bed for the rest of the night. One decision, two sinful acts, three broken hearts. Now, the consequences of their choices.

Understandably it took quite a while for Abram and Hagar to be comfortable around each other after spending the most uncomfortable night of their lives together. But eventually things begin to change. It's a strange twist of fate that occurs over the next several months. Slowly but surely their relationship mends and actually grows stronger. For the longest no one in the ranch ever knew that Hagar was pregnant, but now she is starting to show. Sarai will have to step forward on her behalf soon or the rumors will fly. Problem is, Sarai has not become fond of the relationship that Hagar has created with Abram.

"I think people are start's to notice that Hagar's gain'n weight." Abram says to Sarai.

With a bit of attitude Sarai turns toward Abram;

"What's that got to do with me?"

Abram is caught a little off guard;

"Are you kid'n?"

Sarai begins brushing her hair as she turns her back to him;

"No I'm not kid'n. I can't help it if she puts on weight. It happens. What did you expect. You got her pregnant."

Abram stands there in amazement. For the first time he has seen a glimpse of resentment from Sarai. This is not a good thing.

"Sarai you owe it to her to protect her. You promised her you'd stand for her, for both of us. Now is the time."

"Why don't you stand for her? Since you and her are so close now."

Abram takes a deep breath. It's like she has become a different woman.

"This baby is as much on you as it is any of us. You'll go out there and tell those who need to know, and you'll do it today!"

Sarai spins quickly around as if to argue with him, but seeing the expression on his face quickly changes her mind. He's not kidding.

"Fine, but no one will believe it."

Abram's tone gets a little deeper;

"I suggest you see to it that they do."

Sarai turns her back to him again and continues brushing her hair. The door slams shut behind her and he is gone.

Since the night of conception the relationship between Hagar and Taylor has been strained. He has not bothered to tell her that he was standing outside the night Abram came to see her. Nor has she chosen to discussed what has happen. All they know is that there is something wrong in their relationship. Without saying anything, he has noticed that she is showing the physical sign of pregnancy. Neither of them can find a way to get a conversation started in the right direction until the day that Sarai finally comes forth.

Sarai is sitting with several of the other women while they mend the clothing of the hired hands;

"Well, I have something to share with all of you." Sarai says as she continues to sew, "It appears that Hagar is with child."

A congregational gasp comes from the small group. All of them asking questions at the same time and all of them wanting to know who the father is.

"Wait, wait!" Sarai whispers as she shushes them with her hands.

"It's complicated."

Several of them snicker, "I magine so.", one states.

Sarai sits and sews as if she has nothing to say knowing that they are about to burst with curiosity.

"It's Abrams." Sarai says under her breath.

There is deathly quiet until one of them drops her needle.

"That little whore." Another says.

Suddenly they are all on their feet and surrounding Sarai with hugs and kisses.

"I knew the day we first saw her on the wagon trail we shoulda kicked her away." The third replies.

For a few minutes Sarai sits and absorbs the sympathy but finally moves away.

"I should tell ya'll the whole story."

All of them encourage her that it is not necessary to put herself through the details, they perfectly understand and assure her that Hagar will be punished and sent away. It takes several minutes for Sarai to finally get them to quiet down and listen.

"As you know, Abram and I have never been fortunate to have a baby. So, Hagar said she would have a baby for us. That way we would have a child to raise that we could call our own. So, Abram agreed."

Again the women all sit back in their chairs. Such a thing has never been heard of. They are looking quickly to one another and back to Sarai like hens hiding from a knife.

"Is she gonna give you that baby?" One asks.

"That was the plan. But I have a feel'n things are change'n and she's got thoughts of her own now." Sarai answers.

All the ladies sit around the table nodding their head back and forth. This was going to be gossip at the highest level.

"So now what?" They all ask.

"She might'a had good thoughts at first but now I want her gone." Sarai exclaims.

"Then you best be tell'n Abram before it gets too late." The youngest says as she picks up her needle.

All of them agree with grunts and body wiggles of attitude.

"I know." Sarai replies, "But for now, you keep this to yourselves."

Before the night moon smiles on the back of the cattle the news of Hagar's pregnancy has spread around the ranch. The idea of her heroism and sacrifice is not what has been told. Some however, can see her side, but mainly men. The women are siding hard with Sarai.

The news finally makes its way to Taylor. It's not surprising to him based on what he witnessed. As he walks across the lane he's met by Hagar. At first they stand face to face in an awkward minute of silence.

"I just couldn't tell ya." Hagar says.

"I know." He answers.

She steps a little closer. "I guess ya hate me now, huh?"

"What made you decide to it?" he asks.

"It was Sarai's idea. She felt like I owed it to her." Hagar answers.

A stern look comes across Taylor's face.

"I thought they said it was your idea."

Slightly surprised she interrupts, "No, Sarai almost demanded it of me."

You could see the anger rising in his young eyes;

"Where was Abe in all this?"

Hagar looks to the ground. "He just wanted to make Sarai happy."

Slapping his hat against a tie post, "Yeah I bet he did! I bet he never thought bout get'n to have sex with a young virgin! Did he!? It's as much his fault as it is hers!"

She places her hand on his chest and can feel his heart beating through his shirt.

"It's as much my fault as it is theirs. We all made the mistake. But we still have a baby to take care of."

Still disgusted he smashes his hat back on his head crooked and moves her hand.

"And what about us?! What about our lives?!"

She shakes her head. "I don't know. We just gotta wait."

That's not an answer he was willing to accept. He brusquely moves her to the side and stomps off. Though she tries to see him again later that afternoon he keeps to himself and is nowhere to be found.

The next morning he is in the corral working a horse when Abram comes to help him.

"Need me to help ya Taylor?"

"I think you bout helped me enough Abe." Taylor answers.

That attitude catches Abram by surprise.

"What's that suppose to mean?" he asks.

At first Taylor bites his tongue but it gets the best of him;

"There's more people in this ranch than just you and Mrs. Sarai, ya know! Many of us ain't had a wife much less a kid. Bunch of us wonder if we're even gonna get a chance to have a family!"

Abram knows exactly what he's talking about;

"Look Taylor, I ain't say'n what happen was right. Matter of fact I know it wasn't. But Sarai felt like it might be a God thing."

"You know better than that!" Taylor blurts.

That draws a look from Abe that would normally cause Taylor to tighten up. But today he's ready to take the whipping if it comes to that.

Abram takes a second to gather himself. Pointing his finger toward Taylor's chest;

"She's my wife and I reckon you should remember that. Nevertheless, you're right, it wasn't God's plan. But it's still done and I can't change it. All I can do now is play this out and see what happens."

"I reckon that's what we'll all have to do then." Taylor remarks in sarcasm.

With that he throws the rope over the neck of the horse and goes back to work. Without the help of Abram.

If the drama over the past several days wasn't enough, it would just get more interesting as Abram gets home for lunch.

"I tried to tell everyone what Hagar did for us." Sarai says as they sit at the table to eat, "I don't think their believe'n me. I think they can see that she has feelings for ya Abe."

Abram is too tired and mentally worn to discuss it. Instead he chooses to just keep eating.

Sarai continues, "I thought this would be a good thing, but she's changed. She don't like me anymore. I don't think both of us can live here. I think she's got to go."

Abram has a million thoughts going through his head but none of them will exit his mouth. He finishes his meal, throws his plate in the bucket on the counter and says,

"Do whatever ya want Sarai, I'm tired of fight'n it."

That's exactly what Sarai wants to hear.

From that day forward Sarai does everything she can think of to cause Hagar problems. She treats her as if she is an outcast. She turns friends against her, argues with her and even goes as far as to threaten her. Sarai is not the woman that had come to Hagar's protection many years ago on the trail. *Not trusting God for His promise of children and leaning on her own thoughts is causing her to act and make decisions that are far from normal in her characteristics. It's the exact opposite of what she has been taught. Eventually Hagar can't take anymore.

In the middle of the night Hagar slips out of her house with an arm full of clothes wrapped in her blanket and a few supplies. She sneaks across the lane and into the barn. Just like most of the women in the ranch, she is not a stranger to riding or guiding a wagon. She gets an old tote wagon from the side of the barn and hitches up one of the weaker horses in hopes that no one will hate her for taking him. In just a short while she's loaded and headed out the back side. Where she's going is a good question. When she'll get there is an even better one. Right now, even the fear of the unknown is better than Sarai's wrath. Only a few nosey dogs notice that she is fading into the distance. When morning comes, she's long gone.

The morning comes and goes as she continues traveling the wagon trail. In all of her anxiousness she only grabbed enough food and water for a few days travel. She grabbed nothing for the horse. The heat of midday has her pulling to a stop while the lathered horse tries to survive. She pours a bit of her water from a canteen into a pan she found in the back of the wagon and holds it to his mouth. In two sucks of air the water is gone. A small sip for herself and she crawls back into the wagon and reins him back to the trail. Slowly and methodically they travel through the evening hours and late into the night. Her lack of food and pregnancy causes her to be excessively tired and she falls asleep as the horse meanders aimlessly about until he finally just stops in his tracks. She remains slumped in the wagon seat for a while longer until the pain in her back wakes her up. As she straightens her back and moves her hair from her face the baby inside her kicks. Trying to awaken her senses she realizes she has no idea where she is. She is nowhere. She is scared.

She climbs down from the wagon and throws a blanket on the ground next to it. She loosens the harness from the horse and helps him sip another small drink of water. It's a hot evening.

She slowly lies down on the blanket and once again begins cry.

In the midst of her cries a voice is heard.

"Hagar, where are you going?"

She lies motionless with her arm across her eyes. She is pondering to herself whether she really heard a voice. She moves her arm and is startled to see a man sitting beside her. She quickly rolls to her side and screams as she tries to get to her feet.

"Don't be afraid." He states, *"I'm not here to hurt you."*

She grabs her skirt as she sits up to her knees. She takes a quick look around to see if anyone is with him. There is no one. There is also no horse, no buggy, nothing. He stands to his feet and is every bit as tall as Abe. He is a well built man with an unyielding and yet peaceful expression on his face. He is dark in complexion with facial hair. His clothes seem worn and yet not torn. His vest wraps around him like swaddling leather. He has no supplies and seems to have no concerns. Hagar is mystified.

Catching her breath, she asks, "How did you know my name?"

He smiles, *"I know you. Where are you going?"*

Again she looks around trying to figure out where this man has come from and how he got there. From what she can see there is not even evidence of foot prints.

"I'm going home." She whispers as she stands to her feet and continues to look around.

"Why?" He asks.

"It's a long story."

He moves toward the horse rubbing it on its neck. He places his hand over the horse's mouth and she can hear the horse sucking as if it were drinking for his life from a river.

"I've got time." He says.

For what ever reason he doesn't present a demeanor that is causing Hagar to fear for her life. His presence is settling.

"Did you give that horse the rest of my water?" she asked.

He shook his head no. *"Your canteen is full."*

She knows her canteen is not full. As a matter of fact it was almost empty. She lifts if from the wagon seat where it was hanging and finds that He was telling the truth, it's full. She quickly takes a drink and pours a little on her face. She's not sure where the water came from but she knows she's thirsty.

Hagar is holding her stomach when the stranger turns to look at her.

"I'm with child."

"I know." He mutters.

"I'm not married." She says while trying to hold back tears.

"I know." He gently says.

Hagar walks away from the buggy.

"So how did you get here Hagar?"

She can't quit looking around and looking at Him.

"It's a strange life of events."

She walks a circle around the Man; "When I was young I hid in a wagon and ran away from home. A lady by the name of Sarai took me in. Her husband is a great man named Abram."

She continues to move slowly around the buggy;

"They pretty much raised me. They couldn't have children of their own. When I became a woman Sarai talked me into have'n this child by Abe. Now, she's jealous and threatened me. I had to leave."

The Gentleman walks over to the bed of the wagon, reaches into Hagar's bag and pulls out a loaf of bread that she had not packed. He tore a piece off for each of them. Again she is taken back and baffled.

"She's not going to hurt you. You need to go back."

"Go back?! You don't know her!"

He smiles; *"I know her. Listen to me, this baby you're carrying is indeed a boy. You will name him Ishmael. He will be as wild as a donkey. He will be a fighter against others and sometimes even his brothers. But he will be okay and he will have many children of his own. I promise."*

The man's voice seems to transcend through the wind. It surrounds Hagar and causes her to look behind her. She turns to see where it is coming from and sees nothing. When she turns back to ask Him a question He is gone.

Hagar is bewildered. She runs around the buggy looking over and under.

"Mr.! Mr.!, She exclaims!

She can't find him.

"My Lord! My Lord!" She screams!

She has realized who He was. She falls to her knees and prays.

"I have seen the Man who sees me."

She spent a few more hours in prayer and quiet peace before loading onto the buggy and heading back to face Sarai. Not sure of what she would find she felt confident that God would protect her.

It's midmorning when she comes riding back into site of the camp. Several of the hired hands see her and come loping their horses out to meet her.

"You bout had us scared to death!"

She smiles; "I'm sorry. I just needed some time."

Taylor comes racing up behind them. You can see panic and worry in his eyes.

Again she smiles; "I'm okay, sorry I had ya scared."

"We aren't near as worried as ya had Abram. He's bout to have a heart attack."

They all laugh except Taylor.

They escort her back to the barn and help her out of the wagon. She gathers the clothes she had wrapped in a blanket and walks away.

The two ranch hands see a loaf of bread lying on a blanket and grab it each of them began eating a bite.

"Man, Hagar cooks good bread!" one exclaims.

"I didn't cook it." She says as she walks out of barn.

They have no idea what she means. But, since she wasn't taking it with her they tare it apart and stick it in their saddles bags for later.

She walks across the lane and into her house where she finds Sarai standing in the middle of the room. Sarai's eyes are filling with tears as she runs over to Hagar. She grabs her arms and pulls her close hugging her firmly.

"I shouldn't run you off. I should'a made sure people knew what really happen. I'm sorry."

"It's okay." Hagar answers, "Let's just move past it. Is Abe around?"

Sarai gives her a kiss on the cheek and tells her that Abram is out front. Immediately Hagar goes to see him. She runs off the porch and out toward the area where they are keeping the hogs.

"Abe!"

Abram turns the instant he hears her voice.

"Hagar! Girl you've had me worried to death!"

"I know, I'm sorry" she interrupts, "But I saw Him."

While he is hugging her Abram asks, "Saw who?"

She pulls away and looks him dead in his eyes;

"The Lord! The Man you're always tell'n us about that speaks to you. I saw Him . . . . He told me our baby is a boy. We gotta name him Ishmael. . . . .I saw Him Abe, I ain't kid'n and I ain't crazy."

Abram has no idea what to think. Did she really speak to the Lord? Who is Abram to question especially when he expects others to believe him when he tells them God has spoken to him.

"Okay, okay, I believe ya. If it's a boy, we'll name him Ishmael."

He can see the excitement generating through every parcel of her body. He's not sure what happen but its obvious Hagar has had a life changing experience. For now Abram is just glad she is back and healthy.

Sarai takes the time over the next several days to correct the controversy that has spread throughout the ranch. Though some find it hard to distinguish between what was true and false, for the most part everyone just accepted that bad choices were made but now it was time to move on.

The full moons come and go rather quickly and the time for Hagar to give birth has arrived.

"Sarai! Sarai!" Hagar screams

Sarai can tell by the tone of her voice that something was wrong. She drops the bucket she is carrying and runs into Hagar's house. Hagar is sitting on the floor leaned up against the wall. She has sweat coming from her forehead and her face is flushed with a look of fear and pain. A broken plate lies on the floor beside her. The floor is wet under her. She is sliding her feet back and forth on the floor and her hands are white knuckled clinched as she suffers in labor.

"Oh my, you're getting ready to have a baby!" Sarai says with excitement.

She helps Hagar up from the floor and moves her to the bed.

"Ahh!" Hagar screams.

Sarai rushes outside and sees a couple of women by the well.

"Hagar is having her baby! Don't let anyone in here!"

The word spreads like a wild fire. Within minutes the front of the house is surrounded by well wishers. Sarai will not allow anyone in the house. From outside the walls many women, a few men, some children, Taylor and Abram hear the screams of birthing pains that carries on for a couple of hours.

Then, there was one last yell of excruciating pain followed by the cry of a baby.

Then silence.

In a few minutes Sarai comes busting through the door to the front porch.

"It's a boy! . . . . It's a boy! . . . . She calls him Ishmael!"

CHAPTER 8

Abram becomes Abraham

Genesis 17

Thirteen years pass and Ishmael continues to grow into a young cowboy. The father/son relationship is very strong and for the most part all is well with Hagar and Sarai. Together all three of them are having a part in raising Ishmael.

Abe is standing beside the corrals when Ishmael walks up beside him.

"Whatcha look'n at Pa?" the boy asks.

"It's the filly." Abe answers.

Ishmael climbs to the top rail so he can see the young four year old horse jumping around and trying to adjust to her first experience of being hobbled.

"She's gonna take the place of the Bay for me."

"I bet ya miss your old horse don't ya Pa?" Ishmael asks.

"Yes I do. I hope this filly will be as good as the Bay."

Abram stands in silence and watches as the filly begins to settle down with the hobbles on her front legs. Abram has spent the last thirty days or so working on this new horse and today he decides to ride her out in to field. It shouldn't be an issue. No one trains a horse better than Abram.

*"You best get back to your chores and stay outta trouble." Abram says as he kicks the boy in the britches. "Got to earn your lunch."

He's watching as young Ishmael takes off running and laughing his way right in front of oncoming horses ridden by ranch hands.

"Whoa!" they yell as the dust flies.

It startles Ishmael causing him to fall stiff legged onto his rear. Wide eyed he smiles at his dad then jumps up and grabs his hat. He waves at the riders and moves on like nothing happened. The hired hands look over towards Abram. He shakes his head and they return to work.

Abram climbs into the corral and grabs a bridal and brush. The filly seems to have finally settled in with the hobbles. This is one fine young horse. He begins to brush and curry his horse and his mind ventures back to his days on his father's ranch. Abram and the Bay had many good rides, many hard rides, and many dangerous rides; it will take several years for this young filly to get the experience the Bay had. He saddles the young filly and rides out into the open range. He rides away from the ranch about a mornings ride and then stops among a group of trees by the twisting river. Abram's tradition of getting alone and praying has never ceased regardless of how crazy his life events may have been. He ties the filly up to a branch. Abram grabs his knife and sits down to think as he whittles on a small stick. He sits quietly and watches as a doe and spotted fawn cautiously sneak their way down to the opposite bank of the river for a drink. Through the briar swamped hedges he hears the blow of a cantankerous buck that causes the doe and fawn to sprint back up the ridge and into the woods.

The filly begins to get a little anxious tugging on the reins and blowing through her nostrils. Abram grabs his gun and quickly stands to his feet but can see nothing that should be spooking the horse. Then he notices that familiar breeze. He turns back toward the river and there, knelt down getting a drink out of the river, was a stranger. Abram is not sure if the man knows he is there. There is something familiar about him but Abram can't put his finger on it. Then is dawns on him, the man looks just like the stranger that Hagar had described when she said the Lord visited her. Abram knows exactly who it is. He immediately bows his face and kneels down.

"Stand up Abram." The Man says as He walks up the bank of the river to Abram.

Abram is a little apprehensive about standing up and facing Him. Just the air about Him is causing Abram to remain humble in the presence of the Spirit. The Man reaches down and takes Abram by the hand to help him up from his knee. He looks peacefully into Abrams eyes;

"I have decided to make a pact with you. You should walk before me and do your best to be blameless in your life. I will give you many descendants and Sarai will have a son for you."

Admittedly Abram has heard this before and is a little frustrated.

Abram prays, "Lord, can You not just bless Ishmael? He is my son and there is no way I can continue to lead Sarai on with the idea of her giving birth."

"I have heard your prayers for Ishmael and I will bless him. But my pact will be with the son given you by Sarai. I want you to name him Isaac."

Abram laughs. "How can I have another son at my age?"

The Man walks away from Abram and back to the rolling waters of the river. He stands in silence for a bit.

"You will have another and I will bless him. However, you must show your commitment to my pact. You and your sons and all your descendants after them must be circumcised. And as for you, you will no longer be called Abram but instead, Abraham, which means "father of many". And Sarai will no longer be called Sarai but Sarah which is "princess of a multitude". Within the year, Sarah will have your son."

Abraham is at a loss. *He knows his heart had best follow the instructions and his ears adhere to the words of knowledge. With a mischievous grin he takes in the appearance of the Lord as this nomadic cowboy;

"That's a good look for You Lord."

The Man smiles and turns away. The filly stomps the ground behind Abram and causes him to turn around. With that, the breeze is gone. The filly is standing loose in the field eating grass as if the day was made especially for her. Abram slowly makes his way out to her realizing that in such a short conversation he has been given a head full of information to decipher.

"I have a new name?" He says to himself. "I gotta tell Sarai I'm calling her Sarah from now on? And me and Ishmael are not gonna be happy for a few days!"

He laughs to himself but at the same time understands the importance of the great gift God has given him. It will be a pact that is hard to maintain but complete in blessing for every generation of Abrahams to come.

Abraham leaps upon the saddle of the filly and races back to the ranch. When they get back Abraham heads toward the house. He ties the filly up to the corner post of his porch, rushes into the house and begins gathering blankets and food.

"What are doing?" Sarah asks

"Me and Ishmael are go'n camp'n for a few days. Where is he?"

"He's next door. What's the hurry?" she asks.

"We got things to do. We'll be back in about three or four days."

"Three of four days?! Abe, he's not ready for that."

He stands up straight and looks at her;

"He'll be fine. I'll take care of 'em."

He walks through the kitchen loading up a saddle bag with food, grabs some blankets and kisses her on the cheek.

"See ya in a few days Sarah." And he's out the door.

It takes her just a second to realize he had called her Sarah. She puts it aside figuring he is excited about going camping and just mispronounced his wife's name.

He rushes into Hagar's. "Where is Ishmael?"

The boy comes sliding around the corner, crashes into an end table and slams into the wall. He jumps up and dust's himself off quickly putting everything back on the table hoping his mother doesn't get after him.

"Come on son, we're go'n camp'n. Hagar, we'll be back in three or four days. Don't worry about 'em. We're just go'n out for a while."

Abraham hurries out the door. Hagar is standing in the living room smiling at the two of them but not having much to say. Suddenly, Abraham stops in the door and looks back to Hagar. It Appears he's about to ask a question then turns back to leave. Again he pauses and looks back. He lowers his eyebrows;

"Was he wearing leathers, kinda tall man, tough looking with hair on his face?"

Hagar is caught off guard. She doesn't catch on at first. Then her eyes light up. She doesn't speak but nods her head yes.

Abraham smiles, "I talk to Him today down by the river. You were right."

He grabs up Ishmael and takes him to the filly. Abraham climbs into the saddle then lifts Ishmael up and sits him behind him on the saddle blanket. The filly snorts around for a second but Abraham has the handle. He spins the horse around and off they go.

This camping trip is not going to be as much fun as everyone would think. But somehow Abraham knows God is going to make it work. He's not sure how just yet, but that's what faith is all about. Abraham knows that his God given *wisdom, truth, learning and good sense are worth more than anything he has, actually, too valuable to see.

No one ever finds out what happened during the four days Abraham and Ishmael were gone. But Abraham has done just as the Lord has asked. Now it was time to return to the ranch.

After a long day of working cattle the ranch has decided to spend Friday night with a good group dinner. The women have been cooking for several hours as the men are finishing up the final chores. Abraham and Ishmael have been home for about two hours when it becomes time for dinner.

Everyone begins to gather around all the picnic tables that have been lined down the lane. It's controlled chaos all over again. Mom's trying to control little kids, teenagers fighting over position and wives griping at their husbands for taking too long to get in line. Eventually everyone drifts about until they find a place to sit down and eat. The kids are down at one end of the row having their own conversations and allowing the adults a little time to socialize. Abraham sits at the head of the row.

After getting a belly full of beef, mashed potatoes, gravy, corn and even some fresh deer meat, he lifts his tin cup for a toast to the ladies. All the other men raise their cups in agreement giving complements of whistles and yelps and one loud and embarrassing burp.

"I have news." Abraham says as he stands to his feet clanking his spoon on his cup.

"Oh my Lord. Please tell me we're not moving." A ranch hand remarks.

Abraham laughs, "Well, not yet. But I did have another time with the Lord."

That statement gets everyone's attention.

"He is very proud of all ya. He has made a promise to me, as a matter of fact, He has made a pact with me, that we will all be blessed for generations to come; Your children, your children's children and on and on."

He moves away from the head of the table and walks down the side placing his hand on the shoulder of everyone he passes;

"But there must be a commitment from each man and boy who wanna be blessed by this pact. It's a physical commitment not just spiritual."

He pauses.

"So what's the commitment?" Daniel asks.

Abraham smiles; "You have to be circumcised."

The men all bust into laughter and the women blush with embarrassment.

"Abe!" Sarah gasp, "That's not nice." Then she hides her face to laugh.

"I know you think I'm kid'n, but I ain't. I've already completed the process with me and Ishmael."

That shuts them up in a hurry.

"You what!?" Asks Hagar.

"He's fine. And so am I" He looks at Sarah.

"It ain't my idea and you ain't gotta do it if ya don't believe me. But I'm just tell'n ya it's what the Lord wants. So, take it at that. I ain't say'n ya got to do it in the next couple of minutes. But ya got to do it sometime. That's just the way it is."

There is no more laughing, instead, just a bunch of men looking back and forth at each other and a bunch of young boys who are frantically shaking their heads "no".

"There's more . . . . I'm tell'n ya, the Lord is very proud of all ya. Despite all the craziness of our life, He still finds favor in us. He is change'n my name. I am no longer Abram, but instead, Abraham."

"What?"

"Who?" they ask.

"And Sarai, you'll be called Sarah. We are Gods children and He has named us as He pleases."

"Is Abraham suppose to have some special meaning?" one of the ladies asks.

Abraham smiles slightly; "Father of a multitude."

The crowd laughs under their breath.

"Well, he is old enough to be Dad to us all!" A hand yells out jokingly.

They all laugh out loud with mouths full of food and drink.

"What about Sarah?" another asks.

"It means princess." Abraham answers.

Sarah cocks an eyebrow as to dare anyone to make remarks about that.

A moment's pause and one of the men lifts his cup, "Well suited!"

An abounding "Here! Here!" and they laugh again.

"Do we call ya Abraham or Abe?" a young boy asks.

"You can still call me Abe."

"Or Pa!" another jokes.

Abraham throws a piece of bread at him and laughs.

"For now, that's all I got. What you do with the information is up to you. It's a beautiful night and I'm glad you're all here. Now, where's that dessert?"

It takes a second for the women to begin moving around to bring out the pie. That was quite a load of information. Not near as shocking to them as it is to their husbands and sons. Many of the men sit their in a daze twisting their forks through the calf slobber on top of the pie until one of the old men finally speaks,

"Well, it can only hurt for a little while, ain't gonna kill me, so, let's eat!"

And once again the party was on. Sarah walks by Abraham and he smiled at her in a different way.

"Don't even start," she says, "I don't wanna hear noth'n about me have'n no baby."

In all honesty it takes several days for each man to separate himself in a secluded area for a few days to do as the Lord requested. But each man and his son would eventually show their dedication to both Abraham and the Lord. Taylor was the last to go.

By the way, it didn't take long for Sarah to get use to being called by her new name, being the" Princess" and all.

CHAPTER 9

Sarah Hears God

Genesis 18:1-15

It's about 2:30 in the afternoon and Abraham has decided to take an uncommon cat nap. He's sitting in his oak rocking chair on the front porch with his legs crossed and propped up on the rustic porch rail. His arms lay crossed on his sweat stained shirt with his worn out hat pulled forward and covering his face from the sun. His occasional snore causes the dog to get up and move to the other side of the porch. However, he finds it a little hard to go to sleep with the sounds of bawling calves, yelling hired hands, hammers, playing children and occasional laughter that's coming from the women washing clothes together. Just when he is about to fade into the deep afternoon sleep something causes him to open his eyes under his hat. It's a breeze. Though it appears to be an uncommon breeze, it's the breeze he's all too familiar with.

He slowly moves his feet from the porch rail, lifts his hat and sits up in the rocking chair. The unknown scent causes his dog to lift its head and give a deep throated growl warning that something is different. The breeze glides its way along the right side of Abraham's bristly face and causes him to look down the lane. He stands to his feet and through his slightly blurred eyes can see three cowboys riding into the ranch. They're not ranch hands. They're not from surrounding cities. They're strangers to most, but not to him. As his vision clears Abraham immediately *knows Who it is.

The cowboys on the outsides ride tall above their Palomino studs. Their horses dance with energy. The men are not dressed in work clothes like everyone is used to seeing on the ranch. Instead, their clothes, though similar in style, are fresh and clean. They are both wrapped with leather belts that are loaded with shells. Their pistols extend from the holsters on each side of their hips and they have rifles at easy access from their saddles. It's as if they were about to engage in war. Their flopped brim hats sit low on their brows and shadow their eyes. They are indeed an intimidating pair. But the Man in the middle was different. He rides a white quarter horse stud that is a hand taller than any horse the ranch hands have ever seen. The horse's muscles are defined to the smallest twitch and convex in strength and quickness. His bridle and saddle are an exquisite hand crafted leather design. Though the Man's clothing seems common in style they are not worn from work. He carries only one weapon, a sword. His demeanor commands the attention of the other two riders.

Abraham steps off his porch, walks out into the lane, removes his hat and bows his head as they ride up.

"Men, it's suddenly an even more wonderful day." He says with a smile, "Please tell me you're gonna stop for a while and let me feed You and Your horses."

The two riders on the outside glance to the Man in the middle and await His response;

"How are you Abraham?" He asks.

"Honored." Abraham answers, "Can You come in and eat?"

"I believe we have time for that." The Man answers.

Ishmael is standing a little off watching his Dad talk to these unknown men.

"Ishmael! Come take their horses to the barn. Make sure you feed and water 'em. Wash 'em down and give 'em a good comb out."

"Yes Sir, Pa." Ishmael answers.

The men crawl off their horses and hand the reins to Ishmael. It's all the boy can do to hold the studs from galloping away. The Man in the middle places His hand on Ishmael's shoulder and causes a sensation that forces Ishmael to wonder if he knew Him. Then all three of them follow Abraham into the house.

As they come in Sarah is sitting in her chair beside the window sewing.

"Sarah, quit what your do'n I need ya to cook these men something to eat." Abraham whispers with excitement and then pats her across her knee.

At first she just sits there with a confused look on her face. Abraham motions to her as a means of saying "now". *It's important for him to be a good servant to this Man and he knows it will bring him honor. She puts her sewing to the side and scurries into the kitchen as the men enter the door. The clumping of boot leather and ringing of spurs fill the air of Abraham's house as the three men come strolling in.

Abraham moves his chair away from the fireplace and says,

"Men, there's a bucket of wash water right there so ya can clean up if ya need it."

He looks outside and sees Salam, his ranch foreman.

"Excuse me." He says as he makes his way past one of the riders and walks back to the front door.

"Salam! I want cha to go find our best fatted calf and get it here quick as ya can. Have some men stir up a fire and have Ellen come help Sarah cook it. Make it quick, I got special guests here today. Go! Make it quick!"

Salam has no idea what the hurry is but he's not going to question Abraham, so off he goes. Next door Hagar is standing outside washing some clothing on a scrub board. Abraham catches a glimpse of her as he turns to go back inside.

"Hagar, come help Sarah for while."

Without looking up; "I need to finish scrub'n these shirts then I . . . ."

"Now!" he interrupts.

Hagar looks up and sees him prancing around on the porch like a little boy in need of an outhouse and encouraging her to come on. She makes a slight sigh of disgust as she lifts the water bucket and places it on her porch.

"What could be so important? She mutters to herself.

When she walks into Abraham's house she can see the images and shadows of the men in the front room with Abraham but she has no idea who they are. Sarah is already hard at work over the cabinets with flour flying while she prepares the bread. Hagar also notices that several men had gotten busy building a fire in the pit out back that is usually used when they kill a calf for the ranch to eat.

"What's all the fuss?" She asks Sarah.

Sarah wipes flour across her forehead; "I don't know. I just know he wants these men to eat really well."

"Who are they?" Hagar asks as she picks up a towel to wipe Sarah's forehead.

"Beats me." Sarah answers. "Here take these cups of water in there to 'em."

Sarah places four cups of water on a tin plate and hands it to Hagar. Hagar pretends she is about to spill them just to watch Sarah squirm. They both laugh quietly and Sarah pats her on the back of the arm. Hagar shakes her head back in order to move her hair out of her face and then walks toward the front room. She puts on her best smile and posture to be presentable to these strange men who have come to visit Abraham.

As she enters from around the corner the Man in the middle raises His head and looks her straight in the eyes with a smile of recognition. She is stunned. Her eyes widen, her jaw drops and she is frozen in her tracks as she unknowingly drops the plate. Only the crashing of the cups and splashing of the water on the floor causes her to look away and everyone else to immediately stand to their feet.

"Hagar!" Abraham exclaims.

Her eyes cut to Abraham and then quickly back to the Man dressed in leathers. She squats down and is trying to pick up the cups but can't get herself to quit looking at the Man. He moves over and helps her pick up the cups.

She is still speechless.

"How are you Hagar?" He quietly asks.

Her voice trembles as she answers, "I'm blessed."

Sarah has rushes over to help with the mess and is wiping up the water when she hears what He says. She is surprised to think that this Man knows Hagar.

"Let me re-fill these for ya." Sarah states.

She grabs Hagar by the arm and they saunter toward the kitchen. Hagar is glancing back and forth between the Man and Abraham. Abraham is simply standing there and smiling. Sarah is tugging frantically at Hagar to come on. Once they are in the kitchen Sarah pull's her to the side.

"How do you know that Man?" Sarah quietly asks Hagar.

"It's Him." She whispers.

"Him, who?" Sarah asks as she dips another cup of water.

Wiping tears of joy from her eyes Hagar whispers to Sarah, "It's the Lord."

Sarah takes a full step away from Hagar and looks at her as if she had just said something blasphemous. But there is something about the glow in Hagar's eyes and the confidence of her posture that is not normal.

"It's the same Man that came to me in the range. It's the same Man that spoke to Abraham about changing your name. Why do you think Abraham is acting so crazy?"

Hagar sneaks a peak around the corner and then leans back against the wall.

"He's the Lord."

Realizing she is standing there with her mouth open, Sarah quickly dusts herself off and this time carries the drinks into the front room herself. First she hands a fresh cup of water to each of the other two men. She tries to get a better look at them under the brim of their hats but has very little success. Then she takes a cup to Abraham and gives him "the look". Wishing to her self that if at anytime, and of all times, he could read her mind, he would perhaps introduce her to the Man. But he does not. Finally she turns to the Man sitting in the middle.

"And this one is for You." She states with a smile.

"Thank you Sarah." He replies.

She stands motionless for a second.

"Oh, ... I didn't realize Abe had told You my name."

The Man smiles and from behind her Abraham remarks,

"I believe He told me your name."

Sarah is startled and steps away. She has no idea what to do, where to go, what to say.

"Sarah", ... Abraham snickers, "why don't you continue get'n dinner ready for now?"

A tear slides its way from her eye and down her cheek. She wipes it away with her apron. *Sarah's ravishing beauty is no comparison for her true love of the Lord. Just as Abraham, that love has gained her praise in the ranch.

"Welcome." She softly speaks.

She then returns to join Hagar in the kitchen. They are like teenage girls knowing they have a chore to do but overwrought with a desire to return to the front room.

"Please have a seat and take a load off Your feet." Abraham suggest as he pulls up another chair.

Outside the hands are working frantically to get this calf butchered and over the fire. The calf is skinned, quartered, and now hangs from an oak tree limb over the fire pit that is tied between the "x" oak legs on each end. The smell of the cooking beef is already causing excitement around the ranch as the kids come running from every direction. The Man on the porch between the two armed cowboys stands and watches with a smile as the children run senselessly around the fire. As the adults begin to come around He eases His way back into Abraham's house. Not many know of the visitors, they just know there is going to be a good supper. A few other women join Sarah and Hagar in the kitchen but neither of them has yet to share with Who is actually in the house.

Outside, a large portion of the hired hands begin to shut it down for the afternoon. As they begin to put up their tools and unsaddle their horses, they can't help but notice the spectacular animals inside the corral with Ishmael. Slowly the men gather around the corrals for a closer look at these unique athletes the strangers rode in on. Most of the men are propped up along the fence rail as Ishmael is washing down the huge white stud. Everyone is amazed at the physical fitness of each horse. Even Abraham's prize horse is not a match for these specimens. Each man would love the opportunity to saddle one up and race across the range and as each story gets a little more daring about how he would ride, Sarah steps outside and rattles the triangle to let everyone know dinner is served.

Ishmael chunks the bucket of soapy water into the lane of the horse barn and outruns every man to the tables in the alley. It's an unusual gathering since it sprung up so quickly. For the most part, many are coming and going and only a few are actually sitting down to enjoy dinner with everyone else. All are still somewhat oblivious to the Man that has come to visit.

Inside Abraham's house Sarah and Hagar have prepared four special plates. The men have all gathered around the table after washing up and hanging their hats on the wall. Almost bashfully, Sarah and Hagar hand deliver the plates and place them on the table in front of the men. The two women stand patiently by for a few seconds like needy waitresses until Abraham thanks them and gives them a nod of his head.

Brushing her hair away from her face; "I think we'll just eat in the front room." Sarah says.

They each make themselves a plate and move in to the other room away from the eyesight of the men. They find a place to sit in the front room to carry on eating and talking about the day and life until the Man asks Abraham;

"Where did Sarah go?"

Abraham looked around from his chair, "I think she's in the front room."

The Man paused for a moment, took a sip of water, then states,

"When I return in nine months from now, Sarah will have had a child."

Abraham grimaced at first hoping Sarah didn't hear Him. Abraham doesn't want to get into that argument with her while he has company. As it turns out, Sarah has gotten up from her chair and was standing just on the other side of the wall and hears what He says. She laughs to herself when she hears Him and mumbles sarcastically;

"At my age, I'm gonna finally have a child."

The Man looks to Abraham;

"Why did Sarah laugh to herself? Does she not feel that I am capable of doing whatever I want?"

Abraham turns to see if Sarah was in the room and she is not. He has not heard her. Sarah didn't realize He could hear her either and became afraid when He questions Abraham.

Without stepping into view she answers from around the corner,

"I didn't laugh."

She was starring at Hagar and both were cold with the fear of lying.

But the Man disputed her, *"Yes you did, Sarah. You laughed."*

Wiping his mouth with a cloth He stands to His feet and drinks the last of His water.

"Abraham, would you like to go for a ride?"

Abraham slams his cup to the table and almost knocks his chair over getting up to grab his hat. The four men leave the kitchen and walk into the front room where Sarah and Hagar stand with their backs against the far wall. The armed cowboys walk toward the front door as the Lord moves in the direction of the women. He reaches out and takes the trembling hand of Sarah.

"Thank you for the meal."

This time she keeps her eyes directed more toward the floor with an occasional glancing up at Him. He turns and looks to Hagar;

"Bless you young lady."

She smiles and states, "You already have."

The men walk out of the house, stroll to the barn and gather their saddles from the top rail of the corral where Ishmael has left them. Within a few minutes they have saddled up and are headed away from the ranch without anyone even noticing.

They ride for quite some time without so much as a word. The Man in the middle leads the way as the other two cowboys ride about a half horse back on each side. Abraham follows from behind. They have traveled down several dusty cow trails and eventually leave off the trail and head up through the brush. Eventually they ride up to the top of a small mountain that overlooks the town of Sodom where Lot is now living. On the top of the mountain is a line of trees where they decide to stop and sit for a while. After they tie their reins to loose limbs and loosen the saddle girths from around their horses the other two cowboys ease down the path for a distance leaving Abraham a chance to visit with the Lord.

The two of them find a fallen tree and sit down together. They can look out over the valley and see the fires of Sodom. From where they are sitting it appears this is a peaceful community that the Lord would be happy to sit above. Unfortunately that is only the appearance from afar. Both of them sit for a while allowing the food to settle and taking in the sights of the night. As the Lord looks down toward Sodom it is as if He were literally looking into the very lives of each one living there.

"There are a lot of things going on down at Sodom and Gomorrah that I can't tolerate much longer."

Abraham picked up a small stick and pulled his knife from his sheath to whittle.

"Like . . . . What kinda things Ya talk'n about?"

The Lord straightens His back and answers, *"Sinful things."*

Abraham slices a couple of pieces of bark off the twig and begins sharpening the end.

"That's where Lot and his family live now."

"I know." The Lord answers, *"I need to go down and see how bad it really is."*

Abraham takes the sharpened twig and picks at his teeth while pondering on what he is hearing. He spits a sliver of wood to the ground.

"And what if it's as bad as You suspect?"

The face of the Lord is half shaded from the light of the moon as Abraham turns to Him and waits for His reply.

It's never offered.

Instead the Lord allows Abraham to discern His intentions of destroying the towns. Again they sit in silence for several minutes while both of them stare at the hazy glow of town. Finally, Abraham can't take the silence any longer;

"Would ya really destroy all those people just cause of the actions of some bush whackers? What if there are fifty people down there who still care about You? Are You really gonna kill 'em?

The Lord never moves His eyes;

"If there are fifty people, I'll spare the whole town."

Abraham puts his knife back in the sheath. He now wonders if he can continue to bargain for the survival of those who live in Sodom and Gomorrah.

"What if there is forty, better yet thirty? Do they need to die cause of other scoundrels?"

The Lord stands to His feet and walks a few steps away. Abraham is not sure if he has aggravated Him or not so he remains seated. The Lord grabs a limb above his head and leans into his arm. He knows Abraham's heart and can sense the passion and concern he has for Lot. He is moved by the apprehension of Abraham.

"If there are thirty, even twenty, I'll let them be."

Abraham walks up behind Him, nervous and understanding that he has already pressed the Lord twice he cannot resist but to ask once more.

"Lord, I don't know how many good people are down there. But I do know that Lot is. All I'm ask'n is for Ya to have mercy. If there are at least ten people who still got faith in You, will Ya let it be?

The Lord turns to watch as the other two cowboys have mounted their horses and headed down the trail to the city of Sodom. Abraham is amazed at how quietly they have begun to move through the bush and down the hill on their horses. He has always had a keen sense in the wilderness and yet he never heard them saddle up and move out. The Lord withholds His answer until He has watched them ride their way down a winding path and out of sight.

"Okay, Abraham, for you, if there are ten, I'll spare them."

For a brief time Abraham can breathe normally but his heart is still heavy with fear of how sinful the two towns have gotten. He lowers his head in relief just as a strong gust of wind blows up from the face of the mountain that causes Abraham to close his eyes for a second. When he re-opens them the Man and his horse are gone. Abraham looks about but quickly cast his attention to the flickering of fire lights he can see in Sodom. He knows that the other two cowboys will reach the town by morning. He fears for the life of Lot and for the souls of those who have brought on the wrath of God. His main concern is for Lot and Lot's family. *In truth he does not worry for the evil of others. He understands that they have nothing to look forward to and nothing to hope for. All he can do now is hope and trust.

CHAPTER 10

Sodom and Gomorrah

Genesis 18: 16-Genesis 19

The two cowboys stop outside Sodom just before lunch and find a watering hole for their horses. While the horses drink the two men stand vigilantly watching as the citizens of Sodom parade back and forth across the dusty streets of the mid town. No one from the town is even noticing that the strangers are watching from a distance. The two will not continue until the Lord moves on them to do so. They don't eat, they don't drink, they don't sit and they don't wander around. They stand alert to their surroundings and wait. Around mid-afternoon, almost simultaneously, they saddle up and begin ambling into Sodom.

The entrance to Sodom is a large rustic wooden gate with the name chiseled on the top plank. The name, Sodom, is representative of any place filled with immoral actions. At the foot of the entrance Lot is sitting and looking out toward the open range. He often finds himself sitting there and remembering the days when he rode with Abraham. When Lot sees the cowboys riding up to the gate the Spirit of God stirs within him and gives him wisdom as to who these riders are. It scares Lot beyond anything he has ever known. He jumps to his feet and runs out to meet them. When they get close to him he bows on one knee and removes his hat.

"Men, please come to my house and let me feed ya. I got water you can bathe with."

One of the riders moves a little closer to Lot;

"I think we'll just stay in town tonight."

Lot looks up and then stands to his feet. As he puts his hat back on his head he pleads with both of them.

"Seriously, come to my house for the night. I'll feed ya, let ya clean up and you can ride out first thing tomorrow morn'n."

The other rider moves up along side his partner, "Okay Lot. But just for tonight. You go ahead to your home, we'll be there in a bit"

Lot mounted up on his gelding paint. "I need to show you where I live and . . . . "

"We know where ya live." They interrupt.

"Alright then." Lot says.

He spins his horse and lopes through town and out of sight.

The cowboys ride inside the gates and enter the town of Sodom. Just inside the gate to the left is the ironsmith. His place is filled with trash and wasted iron. Horseshoes, hammers, nails and whiskey bottles have made it all but impossible to walk around. A very large, filthy shirtless man sits inside his rickety building sweating out the alcohol he consumed the night before and watches as the cowboys ride past. His face is stained by the smoke of his fire and covered with dirt. His spirit puts off a demon of anger.

Beside his place is the first house of ill repute. The alley between the two buildings is covered in trash. Hidden among the heaps of paper that have been blown there by years of wind is another man that has not woken from his intoxicated night of rest. Several ladies of all ages are loitering about the house. On the upper stairwell an overweight woman dressed in a worn out bar dress leans against a porch post smoking her hand rolled cigarette. Behind her a young twelve year old girl, whose hair is matted from days without a bath, is hanging torn undergarments on a rope tied between two other porch posts. In the darkness of the front room the cowboys can see a young women being attended to by two other ladies. She is cut and bruised by a patron who didn't feel like paying for service. *Here a prostitute was the price of bread, but that desire will cost him his life.

On the right side of the road is the jail. Although the place is filled beyond capacity with drunks, thieves, rapists, murderers or just general outlaws, there is not a deputy in sight. The jail itself is made of wood and clay. Rats can be seen scurrying around the rotted wooden floor looking for the scraps of wasted food. Several of the prisoners stand and peer out through the bars of the windows as they hang their arms outside giving gestures to anyone who dares to walk by. You can hear the yells of anger, fear, agony and even the ruthless vulgarity of senseless rambling. The stench that comes from within the building is disgusting sewage.

Just ahead is the town tavern. This is by far the largest building in the town. For the most part it is held together fairly well. One of the front windows is boarded up from gun shots that had pierced through them and killed a by-stander in the road a few weeks earlier. It appears that the saloon doors never stop swinging as men, women, boys and girls are constantly rushing in and out. There is apparently no age regulation either legally or morally in reference to who can come and go into the den of sin. The piano rings loudly into the streets and the dancers flash around the poker tables while drunken singing and loud laughter bounce off the walls. Many children huddle together outside the tavern at the end of the long porch and cling to each other in fear of what the night holds. It isn't long before two bodies come flailing through the doors and out into the street with fist flying. Behind them come two women doing their best to join the fight. When the dust settles around the brawl the four of them find themselves lying at the hooves of the two cowboy's horses. They all stand to their feet and begin knocking the dust off their clothes. At first they are still angry but in seconds one of them begins to laugh and one by one all four of them join in.

After reaching down to pick up his hat and then looking up to one of the cowboys, a fighter replies,

"Don't mind us, just a little family dispute."

The expression on the face of the cowboys sent from the Lord never changes. They are not impressed. The fighters each wrap their drunken arms around their women and they all stagger back into the saloon.

As the afternoon fades closer to evening the cowboy's attention is drawn to the grocery store ahead. They are curious as they watch the owner of the store wrap the door with chains to lock up then quickly run behind the building. As they ride up they can see the silhouette of a man and woman in uncompromising circumstances. One of the cowboys notices a woman across the street that seems to be looking for the owner. It's his wife and she is concerned about where he is.

"Honey!" She cries out, "Honey!"

They can see the silhouettes adjusting their clothing giving one last kiss and the man comes quickly walking from the alley. He walks right in front of the cowboys wiping lipstick from his face.

"I'm here." He exclaims, "I was throwing out some trash."

The woman runs out to him and wraps her arms around him. As the cowboys ride by, the store owner continues to embrace his wife and turns her back to them so that he can watch them without her noticing. He knows he has been seen, he does not know the circumstances that will result.

Beyond the grocery store were several other condemned buildings where homeless people have created a place to sleep. Just around the corner were several partially destroyed homes where gangs of bandits ride in and hide. The main street of the town stretches about a quarter of mile and is lined with small business that are constantly ravaged, robbed or burned. Those who have managed to stay in business only do so because of the back door arrangements they have made with the Mayor and Sheriff. Some pay money, some pay with sex, others run errands of danger. But one way or another they all pay.

As the cowboys continue to ride through town several of the patrons begin to notice the clean clothed intruders. A few of the children have run back through town along the wooden porches and spread the word. Before they have ridden half way through town, the streets are lined with people of all shapes and size, nationalities, economic status and authority. The Mayor and a band of Deputies step out of the barber shop and watch as the cowboys ease by. At the very end of the block the two are mocked by the people in the section of the town who sell favors for people looking for homosexual pleasures.

The lower income houses are just past the slaughter lot at the end of town and are randomly placed. Their rotted wood and decrepit roofs make them more like shacks than homes. There is very little maintenance being done on any of the houses or fences and of course the yards are solid dirt. When it rains it literally pours inside the house through the holes in the roofs and the yards become a play ground of mud. Most of the day is spent sitting on porches playing cards and drinking home made whiskey. For several of the families the meals come from the trash barrels behind the Saloon. Working for a living seems like a waste of time. *This attitude alone has caused much of the poor lifestyle.

As you stretch out a little further from town the homes get to be better quality. Most of these people are ranchers who are financially capable of taking care of their own property and also have enough ranch hands to protect themselves against thieves. The homes are nicer and the families are quite large often having as many as ten children. This is the money of Sodom. They are still as the commoners of Sodom and Gomorrah in the fact that they participate in the same lifestyles as the degenerates that live wherever they can find a bed. The only difference is that the ranchers seem to do it at a higher expense. Through the wagon made road that weaves its way around several of the ranches, the cowboys traverse up to Lot's house.

Lot is standing on the porch listening to all the random gunfire in Sodom and praying it didn't have anything to do with the cowboys sent from God. Eventually he sees them riding up his path. He throws down his drink and runs to meet them. When he gets to them his heart is racing. He's not sure why they are here and though he is excited to see them he is also worried for their well being, which makes no sense if he really believes they are angels of the Lord. The problem is that he can't separate what he knows to be true about the strength of God's people and what he knows of the ruthlessness of the citizens of Sodom. He stops short of reaching them in order to catch his breath as they ride up.

"We got dinner cook'n and a place for ya to clean up."

The cowboys never answer verbally but nod their head in acceptance of his offer. Lot turns and runs back to the house to let everyone know the two cowboys are here. Lot's daughters come to the men and take their horses to the barn. The girls are a little surprised that the cowboys are somewhat handsome. The girls try with best efforts to flirt but are completely ignored. Lot anxiously leads the men into the house. For some reason the cowboys stop just before entering the door and turn to look behind them. There's nothing unusual that Lot notices and yet they continue to watch as if they are sensing something other than what mortal man can see.

"Everything ok?" Lot ask

They stand there for about thirty more seconds, look at each other and then turn to go inside. Lot's house is filled with silver vases, gold memorabilia and expensive leathers. The cowboys never pay them a seconds worth of attention. They walk straight to the kitchen table where

Lot's wife is placing fresh vegetables and fruit. They have only sat there a very diminutive time when Lot's girls come running into the house.

"Girls! Girls!" Lot exclaims, "Slow it down."

"Pa, they're coming!" The eldest says frantically.

"Whose coming?" Lot asks as he walk to front window.

When he looks outside he is amazed at what he sees. It appears that every man and boy, young and old, is parading their way to Lot's house. Some begin to fire gunshots into the air, many of them have torches, most of them are carrying bottles of alcohol and all are laughing and cursing as they completely surround Lot's house. Lot is no fool, he knows exactly what they want.

The cowboys hear the commotion outside and move into the front room.

"Wait!" Lot says, "Let me handle it."

He slowly opens the screeching door and steps out onto the porch where he is confronted by a sex craving heard of perverted men. His shirt is pulsing from the pounding of his heart in his chest. Sweat is beginning to bead up on his forehead. His hands are trembling as his breathing is becoming somewhat restricted. The unruly mass of intoxicated men continues to move in closer to the house as Lot tries to speak.

"Boys! Hey, hold up! How's it go'n!? Is there a problem?"

A large man steps to the front of the pack and removes the cork of a whiskey bottle with his teeth. He spits the cork toward Lot and takes a long drink with much of the whiskey pouring down his neck onto his shirt. He shakes his head and belches.

"Where are they?" He yells

Lot steps back, "Where is who?"

The old drunk laughs, "Don't be stupid Lot. We know ya got them two cowboys in there. Bring 'em out! We got plans for 'em."

The crowd hears him and burst into corresponding yells and whistles. Some of the men begin jumping on each other, some even brake into a fight. More shots are fired into the air.

"Bring 'em out Lot!" they yell.

Lot holds up both his hands as a rock is hurled from the middle of the crowd and bursts through one of the windows in his house.

"These cowboys mean noth'n to you men! They're under my roof! What business you got with 'em?"

Lot can hear the screams of his daughters inside the house as a younger boy steps out of the crowd and flicks a cigarette into the air.

"We plan on have'n sex with 'em!" he screams with laughter.

Lot is taken back with fear. If his heart wasn't racing before it certainly is now. He's known for years that homosexuality is running rampant throughout both Sodom and Gomorrah but he never dreamed it would come to this.

"You're gonna what?"

Several of the crowd begins getting restless and yelling,

"Bring 'em out! Bring 'em out! Bring 'em out!"

A few whiskey bottles come crashing into the front yard and glass shatters at Lots feet. A piece of glass flies up and cuts him along his cheek. Once again the crowd moves in closer to the house pounding their fist in the air and forcing Lot up on to his porch. With his back against the door he makes another plea with an unexpected offer.

"Listen! . . . . Listen! . . . . I have two daughters inside that have never been with a man! If you leave these men alone I will let you have your way with my daughters."

Naturally his daughters and wife are astonished by his proposition. His wife grabs them both by the arm and runs them into the bedroom. She slams the door and props a chair against it in hopes of keeping everyone out. Together all three bundle up in a corner and cry. How could their own father offer them to an angry mob of bandits to be raped in place of some strangers that have just ridden into town?

"No! We want the men!" The crowd sporadically hollers.

The large drunken man steps forward once again.

"Lot, you ain't even from these parts! We let ya stay here cause ya got a little money. If you're think'n you're gonna start tell'n us what we can or cain't do you're bout to get it worst than those pretty boys you got in there! Now get outta the way, cause we're come'n in!"

For the third time the crowd presses against Lot and he is out of options. Suddenly the door swings open and the two cowboys grab Lot by the back of the shirt, pull him in the house, step outside and shut the door behind them. Lot tries to re-open the door but is unable. The lawless men of Sodom immediately start whooping, whistling and yelling with anticipation of what they think is about to happen.

Unfortunately, they are wrong.

Several of them suddenly attack the cowboys with intentions of dragging them back to town. Instead, the power of God is upon the two angels and they fight back against the mob with a force unknown to man. They have fury in their eyes and their hands are as quick as lightning. Instead of the crowd rushing them, they attack the crowd. Every man they strike fall to the ground blind with their eyes burning and bleeding. One by one they begin to fall over each other in their blinded drug inflamed rage of fear. No one has attacked the men of Sodom with so much force and power. Many of the men from Sodom are hurt just by being trampled in everyone's effort to get out of the way of the storm of physical punishment being inflicted on them. And after a time of fighting, a large number of Sodomites find themselves lying on the ground in pain. The cowboys, on the other hand, stand tall without a mark. Eventually the crowd loses interest and desire to be hurt. Though they continue to yell out threats they no longer have the courage to back them up. Finally Lot is able to open the door and join the cowboys outside. He stands on the porch starring at the angels who are standing victorious in the middle of his yard and watch as the cast of hell bound souls stagger back to town. *Once again the Lord has held victory in store for those he holds blameless.

Lot looks the cowboys over to see if they are injured.

"How did you keep from getting hurt, or even shot?"

Again the men just look at him with curious expression and shake their head. He's having a hard time remembering Who sent them. These cowboys had no fear of being injured.

When the noise of the rowdy drunks has subsided Lot's wife and daughters ease their way outside. Lot hears them as they gingerly make their way outside to the porch. Lot's wife pulls him to the side;

"Lot, who on earth are these men?"

Lot looks toward his wife and daughters. He can tell by the look on their faces that they are furious by what he told the crowd. He extends his arms toward them to embrace the girls.

"I would never offer ya like I did if I thought you were in danger. These men ain't just cowboys. These men are angels from God. I don't know why they're here, but whatever it is, we best listen."

One of the girls jerk her arm away from Lot.

"You offered us as meat! Like we were trash!" She cries.

Lot grabs her and hugs her tight in his arms and as she struggles to get away he begins to cry himself.

"I know, I know. But they really are from God. I had to believe that they would protect ya. I'm sorry."

They all huddle together and cry for a few minutes. In all honesty there has never been anything so dramatic, and especially in such a short time, that has ever happened to this family. After all the commotion has settled everyone ventures back in to Lots house and sits down.

"Lot, you need to take the rest of the night and gather a few things each of you need and get ready to leave in the morning. The Lord has looked down upon Sodom and Gomorrah and He's not pleased with what He sees. They've pushed His patience. He intends to destroy both towns and everyone in 'em."

"No!" both girls cry as they leap to their feet.

"What!? Why!?" his wife asks, "Who are you men? There is no way our God would destroy these people!"

Lot steps in front of her and extends his arm to move her back. He then looks desperately to the cowboys;

"Are you sure?"

One of the two move over and take the hand of Lot's wife to calm her. He looks her in the eye to make sure she will believe him.

"It's why we're here. Because of the Lord's heart for Abraham, you and your family will be spared if you do what we say. Otherwise, you're on your own."

He then looks back to Lot. "Have you got any other family you need to get?"

Lot moves toward his two girls who are dreadfully crying.

"I got two men in town who are fix'n to marry these girls. I need to go tell 'em and see if I can get 'em to go with us."

"Go now." One says, "We'll stay here and wait. But don't linger, time is short."

Lot kisses his girls on the forehead as they plead anxiously for him to make sure their fiancés come back with him. His wife seems distant and is struggling to understand all that is happening.

Lot replies, "Trust me, we have to believe 'em. Do as they tell ya and get some things ready to go. I'll be right back."

He takes another glance to the cowboys and hurries out the door. It's very dangerous for him to go after his soon to be son-in-laws because they are probably in the saloon along with several of the men who took a beating from the angels. He keeps himself hidden in the shadows of the buildings and makes his way down town.

When he gets to the saloon he sneaks into the back alley and looks through one of the smoke stained windows. He quickly spots them sitting at a table playing cards. It's as if they have no knowledge or concern for what his daughters have just experienced. He waits until one of them happens to look his direction and then motions him outside. The young man gives a slight nod of his head but acts like he didn't see him and continues to play. When the hand is over Lot sees him say something to the other man Lot needs to speak to. They finish a drink and get up to leave the table. In a few seconds they both ease out the back door to see Lot.

"Man are you crazy? These guys see ya out here you're good as dead!" The brown haired boy states.

"I know." answers Lot, "But I had to come get both of ya."

"Get us for what?" The other asks

"We're leave'n Sodom."

"Whose leave'n?" they interrupt.

"Me, my wife and the girls."

"Why?" they ask

Lot looks quickly behind him and leans against a log on the wall as they watch a drunk fall into the alley and pass out. He then steps in front of the young men.

"Those cowboys are from God. They came to get us out of here cause God is fix'n to destroy this place. We gotta go!"

Both the boys start laughing and pushing on Lot as if he were joking.

"What have you been drink'n?"

Lot shoves them away in anger;

"I'm not play'n! I'm serious! Ya gotta come with us or you'll die."

They quit laughing for a second and step back in surprise. Lot's emotions are getting the best of him.

"No disrespect Lot, but you're sound'n crazy. I ain't go'n no where."

"Me either!" The second follows up.

Lot throws his hands up, "I know ya don't believe me, but I ain't kid'n around. This ain't no joke. You need to come with me and ya need to come now!"

Both of them stand there shaking their heads in dismay.

"Sorry Lot, but I ain't go'n."

"Me either." Replies the brown haired man.

"Then you'll die."

Again the boys start laughing under their breath as they head back toward the back door of the saloon.

"Guess we'll die then. But if ya ain't careful bout get'n home, ya may beat us to it."

The first young man takes one last glance back to Lot before he enters the saloon and shakes his head. He then disappears into the smoke filled room. Lot stands for a second gazing through the window as he watches them order another drink and move to another table. His heart is broken and he has no idea how to tell his daughters that they wouldn't come. His main fear is that his daughters will try to stay. And he was right.

When he returns to the house without them the emotions run wild. It takes several hours of coaxing before he finally ends up slamming a chair against the wall and demanding that the girls stop arguing and be ready to leave in the morning.

His wife and daughters make their way into the bedroom and slam the door behind them. For the rest of the night the cowboys stand outside on the porch and Lot sits in the front room with a new awareness of the commotion that goes on down town. Over the years he has become used to his surroundings. It is not until this very night that he begins to see the mess he lives in. As the hours pass he fades to sleep in his chair.

In the early morning hours Lot is awakened by the cowboys shaking him on the shoulder. It alarms him and he jumps to his feet. His eyes are still blurred and he is not quite awake so he stumbles over a side table before getting his senses. Once he gathers himself he notices that the cowboys are moving about with certain urgency;

"Lot, it's time. Get your wife and daughters and get them out of here before you are killed."

Lot isn't quite ready to move a quick pace. He raises his arms and stretches his back. He walks across the front room and into the kitchen area to get a drink of water. One of the cowboys grabs him and spins him around;

"What are you doing?"

Surprised, Lot answers, "I'm get'n a drink of water and gonna wash my face off."

The cowboy slaps the cup from Lots hand and it clangs along the floor;

"There is not time for that! It is time to go now! Get your wife and daughters!"

He had no sooner said that when the three ladies come rushing out of the bedroom after hearing the cup banging around. Instead of discussing it further, one cowboy grabs Lot and his wife while the other grabs the daughters and takes them out the back door. They forcefully walk them across a field to the crest of a valley. At first they resist but it is to no avail. The cowboys push them ahead and release them;

"Go! Run for your lives! Don't look back and don't stop in the valley! Don't stop until you have reached the top of the hill!"

"Wait!" Lot interrupts, "We can't make it to the top of that hill. It's too far. Listen . . . . There's a little town a ways from here called Zoar. Let us go there."

The angels look around and then agree;

"Okay, but go now. God will not destroy that town and you will be safe. Go as quick as you can because we can't do anything until you are safe."

Lot and his family begin to leave. Since they delayed leaving and resisted the angels they weren't able to grab even a bag of clothing. Behind them the skies begin to darken and thunder is heard in the distance. The further they go from Sodom the darker the skies have gotten. Lightening begins to flare its way through the mountains of clouds like spears of fire from heaven. With every minute the storm becomes more intense. The lightening begins to touch its fingers to the ground causing anything around its point of contact to burst. The thunder rumbles and claps with a force that you can feel in your chest. And yet there is no rain. The temptation to look back at what they are leaving is too much for Lot's wife. As Lot and his daughters make their way ahead of her she pauses, and against the instructions of the cowboys, she turns and looks back toward Sodom and Gomorrah.

The very instant her eyes catch a glance of the towns she feels a pain so intense in her chest that it causes her muscles to cease. The pain runs through her entire body. Her throat cramps shut and her breathing is completely blocked. Her heart freezes, her eyes roll back in her head and she falls dead to the ground. As if her muscles have ceased, her body lies still and stiff. In the miracle of God's wrath her flesh turns to salt. It is said that we are made from the salt of the earth and the salt of the earth she became. Because of the noise of the storm and their concern for getting to safety, neither Lot nor the girls realize she has fallen to her death.

By this time the skies have begun to open with the fury of God the angels had warned Lot about. The towns are being ravaged by stones of fire. Flaming rocks of all shapes and sizes are pouring down on every town in the valley like a flood. They are crashing through buildings with no resistance. Everything they hit burst into fire. Within minutes people are running and screaming and seeking anything they can find to hide under. But they are not being protected. The rocks of fire are striking horses and cattle and literally slicing them in half. The people of Sodom and Gomorrah are being slaughtered by Heaven. Bodies lay bloodied, battered and burned in every part of town and in every home. The smoke of the fires create a canvas for more effects of the lightning in the storms. The screams and cursing of agony are drowned out by the constant explosions, strikes of lightening and claps of thunder. The raining of fire and brimstone continue constantly until every building becomes ash, every animal is killed, all the crops are destroyed and every citizen with exception of Lot and his daughters are dead. It takes a full day and into the night. When Lot finally reaches safety he realizes his wife is gone. It is too late, they can't go back. It is all they could do to take cover and survive.

Early the next morning Abraham returns to the tree line where he has made his plea with the Lord. As he looks down to the place where Sodom and Gomorrah once were, all he can see is smoke rising from the ground like a furnace. He is overwhelmed with emotion as he covers his face and turns his back to the view of hell on earth. He knows the Lord would not have gone back on His promise to save the towns if He could find at least ten people who were still trusting in God. But now, everything has been completely destroyed. He falls to his knees and cries out to God. He has no idea if his nephew Lot and Lot's family have been killed or have escaped. All he can do now is trust in God. It takes him a while to regain his composure but when he does he decides to go back to camp and have some of the men ride down to check things out. He can't go on his own for fear of finding Lot's family in the worst of conditions. It's going to take a few days for his men to ride down and return with word. And all Abraham can do is wait.

Several days pass as Lot and his daughters stay hidden and mourn the death of his wife, their fiancés and friends. In all their lives they could have never imagined seeing such destruction. Because of his association with town of Sodom, Lot is afraid to stay in Zoar and decides to take his daughters into the hills. He gathers up a few weeks of supplies and heads out. The girls are still struggling emotionally with everything that has happened. The reality sinks in that within two days they have lost their homes, friends, fiancés and mother. No one just moves on from that kind of catastrophe without some form of emotional backlash. Not to mention, the girls were raised around the lifestyles of Sodom and have developed a tolerance for the kind of behavior that caused the town to be destroyed. That tolerance will cause further problems.

They have been camping in the hills for a couple of weeks. The supplies had gotten low so the girls have return to Zoar for some groceries.

As they are walking back to camp they begin to talk.

"I hate camping out here." The eldest says

"Me too."

"How are we suppose to survive? How are we suppose to have a family? There is no man any where around that will marry us."

"So what do we do?" The youngest asks.

They stop along the trail to rest. They place their burlap bags down and sit on a rock.

"Look at us. We're not who we used to be. Our hair is dirty, our dresses are torn our shoes . . . . look at my shoes, the heel is coming off! I can only think of one way to have a family and I don't know if you're gonna be for it." The oldest replies as she removes her shoe.

The youngest sits there for a bit waiting on the rest of the story and finally asks,

"So what's your plan?"

The eldest stands up and walks over to the sacks. She unties the leather strap and reaches down into the groceries. When she pulls her hand out she is holding a bottle of whiskey.

"Where did you get that?" the youngest ask laughingly.

"In town." She answers.

"Is it part of the plan?"

The eldest took a deep breath, "Umm, yeah . . . . Okay, here it is. I wanna slip this whiskey in on Pa, get 'em drunk, and, ummm, . . . have a child with 'em."

The youngest stands to her feet with her mouth open and her eyes as big as silver dollars.

"Are ya kid'n?"

The eldest quickly puts her hand over her sister's mouth;

"Quiet. He'll hear ya. Look Sis, I cain't think of no other way and I want kids. So if ya don't wanna do it, then that's okay, but don't mess it up for me."

Her sister has her hands on her head as she is walking in circles.

"Oh my goodness! Seriously! This is our best plan!?

The eldest sister glares into the sky; "Ya got a better idea?"

They stand frozen in time. She finally answers,

"I reckon not."

That night the girls cook up an unusually elaborate dinner and convince Lot that they were putting out an effort to make things better. Lot is moving about the camp and stumbles over the bottle of whisky.

"You bought whisky?"

The girls were caught of guard.

"Well, its mainly for cook'n, but we are old enough to share a lil drink if we wanna."

They had no idea that Lot was as emotionally distraught over losing his wife and friends as they were. Being the father, he has withheld his emotions when around the girls. Even though it is God that spared their lives he has yet to get things right. *Though he knows better than to join others in drunkenness, he gives in to the temptation.

"Yeah, I reckon we can if we want." He says.

He opens the bottle and takes a swig much to the delight of his daughters. From here it only gets worse.

He picks up the bottle and in a weak time in his life, he gives in. One drink led to another and as the night passes, Lot has become drunk. The girls on the other hand have only sipped the whiskey and are still very sober. Eventually Lot has reached the point of no return and no longer has control of his own life. The eldest daughter walks over to Lot and motions for her sister to leave. That night she became pregnant by her father.

The next day Lot wakes up somewhere around mid-morning with a terrible head ache. Fortunately he has no recollection of the night before. He spends the rest of the day nursing his hangover as the girls conspire to get him drunk again for the oncoming night. As evening approaches the youngest daughter brings him some supper.

"Pa, brought ya someth'n to eat. Still gotta head ache?"

Lot slightly laughs. "Fraid so."

She hands him his plate and a cup;

"The cup's got whisky in it. They say the best way to get rid of a headache is to have another drink."

"Another drink?" Lot asks.

"Yeah, its what they say."

At first Lot shakes his head "no" and puts the cup on the ground. His youngest daughter thinks her plans will be put on hold. After his second bite of lunch he reaches down and picks up the alcohol.

"Don't see what is gonna hurt." He mumbles.

And once again they entice him into drinking until he was just short of passing out. And just as the elder sister had done the night before, the younger sister becomes pregnant by her father.

Once again Lot wakes up without any knowledge of what has happened. This time, there was no more Whisky to help the headache.

CHAPTER 11

The Birth of Isaac

Genesis 20 thru Genesis 21:8

Several weeks earlier Abraham had been to the top of the hills where he saw that God had destroyed Lots home. Abraham had returned to the ranch and told many of them about his conversation with the Lord and what had happen to Sodom and Gomorrah. He also sent a few of his best trusted men to go down to Sodom and look for Lot. For a few days while the hired hands were looking for Lot the entire ranch was in mourning and prayer. Three days later the men rode back into camp. They were discouraged and tired and without good news. The looks on their faces were almost enough said. Nevertheless they explained to everyone that they had witnessed some horrible sites.

Abraham walks out to meet them as they ride up to the ranch. He reaches out and gently takes hold of the bridle of one of their horses as he anticipates their response.

"I don't need to know everything ya saw. Just tell me if ya saw Lot or any of his family."

Both of the men shook their heads "no".

"We searched his house, his land, town, the trails, we looked everywhere Abe, and we didn't see anything. There ain't noth'n down there but ashes."

Again Abraham's heart is broken. He was sure that God would have protected Lot.

"Ya didn't see anything? Noth'n at all?" Abraham asks.

The two hands look to each other as if searching for some sort of agreement among themselves. Then one of them replies,

"We did see someth'n kinda strange."

Abraham looked up to him, "Like what?"

The hired hand shifts his weight and adjusts the saddle on his horse.

"In the distance we saw two riders. We couldn't see 'em very well, but they looked like they were ride'n those horses that were in the coral the other day . . . . they watched us as we rode around but never came up. . . . . we decided to go out and talk to 'em, but . . . . when we headed that way . . . "

He pauses and looks toward the other man and that man finishes the sentence;

"They rode about two steps and disappeared."

"Disappeared?" Abraham asks, "You mean like into the trees or what?"

"No" the first blurts out, "Like disappeared into thin air. They were just gone. We went ahead and rode out to where they were and found this."

He pulls an old leather woven hat band out of his saddle bag and hands it down to Abraham. Abraham's eyes well up with tears.

"It's Lot's." He says.

The hired hands are surprised. "Ya reckon it means anything?"

Abraham smiles, "I reckon it does. I reckon it means God kept His promise."

He steps away from the horse throws his hands into the air and screams, "WhoooHooo! Thank You God! Thank You God!"

He spooks the horses but its no concern to riders, they're just laughing at Abraham.

Abraham looks back to them, "I don't know where he is, boys, but he's alive! He's still alive!"

When Abraham realizes that everything, and by everything I mean everything, is burned to ashes, there would be only one reason for them to keep Lots hat band, and that is to let him know Lot has gotten out. Abraham hurries back to the ranch waving the hat band in the air and proclaiming the good news that God has kept his promise and Lot is still alive. The ranch hands are filled with elation.

"Sounds like a good reason for a party, Abe!" one exclaims.

"That it is!" Abraham agrees, *"Good news brings health to my weary bones and it is time to celebrate our joy!"

Well, this ranch has plenty of experience in celebrating the blessings of God and once again the women start cooking. That night there were smiles for all. The food is once again incredible, the children sing songs, the men have shooting, roping and knife throwing competitions and a few of the women even dare to enter the games. Mainly, it was just a good night of celebrating and fellowship. They end their night together as a ranch family by joining hands and thanking God for keeping his promise to protect Lot. No one has seen or heard from him but Abraham has faith and faith is being sure of what we hope for and certain of what we cannot see.

When these parties are over it has become customary for everyone of every age to help clean up. Otherwise, it will take forever and if it not cleaned wild dogs will be all over it during the middle of the night. One by one the tables and chairs are all carried back to the homes they came from and everyone is gathering their plates, pots and silverware. Abraham and Sarah are bringing their final load of leftovers back to their home. They carry everything into the kitchen area and place it on the coffee stained cabinets. As Sarah reaches up to place a cup on an upper shelf Abraham eases up behind her and wraps his arms around her waist.

"God is good isn't He?"

She turns within his arms and faces him;

"Yes He is. And some of it comes because of your faith. You have amazing trust in Him, Abe."

Abraham smiles, rubs his hand through her hair and gently kisses her.

"Well, you really are feeling blessed tonight aren't you?" she states.

Abraham laughs, "I guess so."

He reaches down and lifts her off her feet and into his arms. As she wraps her arms around his neck he carries her into the bedroom.

Even from the ashes of sin a rose can emerge. What an incredible example this is of the love and protection granted to those who trust in God as opposed to the wrath of God on those who rebuke Him. In one instance entire families, live stock, crops and towns are burned as the wasted coals of campfire; on the other hand, a new life is granted as a promise from God.

As Abraham lay with Sarah a light wind welcomes the essence of God. Tonight Sarah will receive the gift she has longed for since the day they were married. When she awakens in the morning she will be pregnant with child.

Three weeks or so pass and although no one has heard from Lot the ranch has returned to its normal everyday procedure. Normal that is, except for the morning sickness of Sarah. For the last five days she has woken up every morning rushing outside to throw up. At first she thinks she has simply caught a cold. Until, finally, it dawns on her. Early one morning, Abraham comes stumbling out of the bedroom to the echoes of her throwing up off the side of the porch. He hesitates to go check on her for fear that he may end up joining her. So, he stands in the front room waiting for her to get over it basically. Suddenly she appears in the doorway. She is standing straight backed as possible with a very strange and vomit speckled expression on her face. Abraham just stands there looking at her with no idea what she is doing or thinking.

"Oh my Lord." She softly expresses.

"Oh my Lord?" Abraham asks.

"It's happened." She states as she wipes her mouth with her skirt.

"It's happened?" Abraham asks.

She smiles and is ravished with tears of joy;

"I think I'm pregnant."

Abraham is speechless . . . .

She walks closer to him with wide eyes and a trembling chin;

"Abe, I think I'm pregnant."

Abraham is still speechless . . . .

"I have morning sickness. I've seen it with the other women a thousand times . . . . Oh my Lord, Abe . . . . I'm pregnant!!"

Though he is smiling like a possum caught in the light of a campfire, Abraham . . . . is still speechless.

Sarah jumps to him and kisses him several times on the face, screams and runs out of the house to wake up every woman in camp. Abraham, still standing in the middle of his house, is still speechless.

The news spreads like a wind driven brush fire and for several days, even weeks, she is fit to be tied with happiness. But even in the midst of the blessed promise from God, there is still a chance to mess things up.

Abraham has decided to take Sarah on a trip for just the two of them to a town called Gerard. They haven't gone off together for years and this should be a nice way of celebrating the addition to their family. Gerard is about a three day ride from the ranch. He plans on being there for several weeks and discussing the sale of cattle to some of the locals while he is there. It's a pretty easy ride even though he insists that they travel slower than normal in order to protect the child Sarah is carrying. They hitch a couple of the work horses up to a wagon, load it up with some pots and pans to cook on when they stop for the night and wrap several changes of clothing and other necessities for Sarah. The also agree to carry blankets with them that have been hand sewn by the ladies of the ranch. They will try to sell a few of them to the local stores and give many to the homeless. *They have found that their prosperity is blessed in great numbers often because of their generosity.

It would seem like this should be an easy and exciting little get away. But out here everyone knows that anything can happen at any given time. The women are very concerned about Sarah. She has waited so long to have this baby and now Abraham is putting her in an old roughed out wagon for a long three day ride across a fairly rough terrain. But even though Sarah and Abraham have gotten up in age they are by no means a stranger to the elements of the country and are more than capable of handling anything that comes their way. Thankfully, the trip to the town went smoothly with no issues from wild wranglers.

The town is as common as most towns in this area with the exception of the large mansion type home that houses the man who established the area. He owns practically every business around as well as most of the land. Every one in the town basically works for him. Abraham and Sarah are excited about getting to see a new place and be alone for a while and they can hardly wait to check in to the local hotel. Abraham guides the horses and wagon along the trench worn road that splits the town. One of the wagon wheels slips down into a ditch and almost tosses Sarah out on her head. She screams and grabs desperately at the air and thankfully Abraham catches a grip of her blouse and holds on while yelling "Whoa!"

to the horses. After she manages to catch her balance and sit back she gives him the "Are you crazy!" look and then they both laugh.

"Bout tossed that pretty woman right out on the ground didn't ya sir." A stranger states as he limps by with a cane in his hand.

"Bout did." Abraham answers with a smirk.

"Where ya folks from?" the grungy man asks

"A few days out." Abraham answers.

The man stands there staring at Sarah. She's not looking at him at first but gets that eerie feeling she's being stared at so she gives him a smile. After all these years she is still a beautiful woman and every man that passes by knows it.

"Best watch yourself, Mister," He says as he laughs and walks on,

"Abimelech might come call'n on this pretty woman."

"What's an Abimelech?" Abraham asks.

"It's Mr. Abimelech. The owner of ever thing you're look'n at. And what he wants he gets, one way or another."

The man holds up his hand and points it at Abraham as if he was holding a pistol and simulates a shot. Abraham doesn't find that to be funny. Flashes of Little Egypt suddenly come rushing to his memory. He doesn't mention anything to Sarah, but little does he know there is no need, she too is remembering what happened. Abraham climbs out of the wagon and walks around to help Sarah to the ground.

The town is crowded with more people than any place they have ever been, some polite, some not. The anxiety of being surrounded by the unknown is causing Abraham's temper to be a little short. He can't get them in a room quick enough. They make their way through the crowded lobby to the front desk to check in. A scrawny little desk clerk stands in front of the counter counting money and acting as if they don't exist. Abraham is a patient man, but there is really no need to push his limits.

He coughs and places his hand firmly on the top of the desk. The little man barely looks up. Quietly Sarah takes a step back. For some reason, that subtle move catches the little man's attention. He looks toward her and then moves his attention to the stern expression of Abraham;

"Ya need something?

Abraham places his other hand on the table.

"We need a room."

The little man sarcastically laughs, "Yeah, you and hundred others. We're sold out."

"Sold out?" Abraham asks

"That's what I said. Sold out!"

Abraham looks past the clerk and out a window behind him;

"Where else can we stay in this town?"

"Stay where ever ya want. I don't care. Ya just can't stay here."

He looks back up toward Abraham with an indifferent look of disdain.

"Anything else cowboy?"

As bad as Abraham would like to back hand him like a twelve year old boy who got caught stealing cookies, he chooses to stand in silence and breath. *A fool gives life to his anger but Abraham keeps himself under control. He and Sarah walk outside disgusted and with no place to sleep. They are standing at the edge of the porch looking up and down the crowded streets doing their best to figure out their next move. Across the street is the finest restaurant they have ever seen. As a matter of fact, other than a saloon, it's the only restaurant they have ever seen. As they decide whether to go over and look in, the doors burst open and a very well dressed elderly gentleman comes walking out. It's obvious by the reactions of everyone around him that he is Mr. Abimelech. People are swarming around him, some begging for money, some asking for work and some just to shake his hand. Strange as it may be, he doesn't seem to mind the attention and takes a few minutes to speak to them before he walks out into the road. He makes his way straight toward Abraham and Sarah as they are pushed aside from the crowd that surrounds him. Just as he is about to enter the hotel he catches sight of Sarah and stops.

Making his way toward her; "Well, who do we have here? You must be new to our area because I would already know ya if you weren't. What's your name pretty lady?"

Sarah moves toward Abraham and doesn't answer.

"I don't bite Mam." He looks toward Abraham, "I'm sorry, is this beautiful woman your wife?"

Abraham glances back and forth to all the faces that are suddenly staring right at him. Quietly he answers, "She's my sister."

Sarah didn't know whether to pass out, scream, hit him or perhaps all three. She can't believe he just said that. What causes this man of God to weaken when it comes to men approaching her? He turns to her and just as in Little Egypt she can see his concern written all over his face.

"Really?" Abimelech states as he grabs her hand. "I am Abimelech. I own this town. Come and have a drink with me."

He turns to make his way through the crowd with a strong grasp on her hand. She tries to resist and cuts her eyes to Abraham.

"Don't worry about your brother, he'll be fine. Come, let's talk."

For what ever reason, Abraham stands motionless and never says a word as Abimelech takes Sarah into the hotel. As the minutes pass Abraham makes his way to the porch but has not left the front of hotel. Finally, he decides to go inside and see what is going on, however, Sarah and Abimelech are no where to be found. The lobby of the hotel is filled with poker tables and people gathering around the open bar. Much of the crowd that has followed Abimelech inside is still there and just standing around. Abraham makes his way back to the front desk. The arrogant clerk glares up from his chair;

"Need someth'n? I done told ya we're sold out."

"Abimelech." Abraham says, "Where is he?"

"Don't know. Probably in his room. Don't matter though, you couldn't see 'em if ya wanted to. You'll have to wait with the rest of 'em."

He nods his head to a crowd standing in the lobby.

Aggravated at himself Abraham returns to his wagon and lies down in the back of it. Up stairs Sarah is sitting in a room fit for a king. Apparently furniture has been shipped in from all around the world as they know it. The bed is covered with sheets of multi-colored silks. There is a sitting area with a silver tea set and cookies. The room is immaculately clean and the chair she is sitting in is covered by foreign material and stitched with lace.

She sits without speaking and stares out the window. Abimelech goes straight into the other room and has not been out since they went up stairs. To Sarah's surprise, a housemaid comes walking out of the room Abimelech has been in the whole time. With tears in her eyes Sarah tries not to make contact with the Canaanite woman. Nevertheless, the woman comes to Sarah and places her hand on Sarah's shoulder.

"He's napping. He'll be that way for a while. I suggest you wait here."

Sarah nods her head and continues to glare out the window.

She has been there now for about three hours when the side door to the other room slowly opens and Abimelech comes staggering out of his room half dressed with his hair wadded from a pillow and his eyes glazed over. He looks like a demon right out of her worst nightmares. She jumps from the bed and runs to the far corner of the room. He wipes sleep from his eyes with the palm of his hands.

"You're married to that man!?" He exclaims with a raspy tone.

Sarah is surprised by his remarks. She can't imagine how he found out and can't think of what to say. She stands quietly afraid that any answer will only makes things worse. Abimelech begins moving about the room erratically. He grabs a vase of flowers from the table and throws it against the wall;

"You're married?! Why did he say you were his sister? Where is he?"

He grabs her by the arm and quickly leads her down the stairs. Shoving drunks and prostitutes out of his way he pulls her through the hotel lobby and out into the street. The needy crowd of homeless and beggars immediately push in around them. Abimelech is trying desperately to look over all of them for Abraham.

"Call for him!" He says, "Call for him!"

The mob of people are pushing and grabbing at Sarah. She begins to cry, "Abe! . . . . Abe!" She yells as she looks through the crowd that is now surrounding them in every direction.

The instant Abraham hears her cry his heart leaps into his throat as he leaps from the back of his wagon. He can barely see her image in the middle of the crowd as he rampages through them like a wild bull. Many of the by-standers will come out of the episode with busted lips or noses or blackened eyes and Abraham has know idea he has even hit them. As he fights his way closer to Abimelech he believes that he will be fighting for their lives. It's a fight he is ready to take. When or lose there will be no more lies. The real Abraham is awake. When he finally makes his way through the crowd he draws back a fist and heads straight for Abimelech who is still holding Sarah. When Abimelech sees him coming he releases Sarah and she runs to Abraham.

"Why did you tell me she was your sister? You almost got me killed." Abimelech yells.

Abraham grabs hold of Sarah; "What are you talking about?"

"I decided to lay down for a while and sleep. Your God came to me while I slept. He told me I was going to die if I didn't give you back your wife." He throws a handful of dirt at Abraham; "Why did you say she is your sister?"

Abraham hesitates, then releases Sarah and moves closer to Abimelech. Those at the center of the crowd begin pushing everyone back expecting a fight. That isn't what Abraham has on his mind;

"I didn't think anyone in this town would be hear'n from God."

Abraham looks around as the bewildered crowd quiets down by hearing Abimelech say he talked to God;

"There was a time when I woulda been killed for her. So she agreed to say she was my sister to protect me. To tell ya the truth, she really is my sister. My father is her father but we have different mothers. We were married a long time ago when we were very young."

He extends his hand to Abimelech;

"I'm sorry, I shoulda told ya the truth."

Abimelech just stood there shaking his head and twisting his fingers. Then he takes Abraham by the arm and pulls him close so the rest of the people can't here what he asks;

"Come here. God also told me you're a prophet, is that true?"

Once again Sarah wraps her arms around Abraham as she watches the deranged crowd.

"If it's what God told ya, then it's true." Abraham answers.

"Then we need your help." Abimelech states, "The women of my family are cursed and none of them have been able to have children. I want ya to pray for 'em and ask God to remove the curse."

Abraham takes a deep sigh. He really just wants to climb into his wagon with Sarah and get back to camp. Fortunately for the women, Sarah's heart understands their desire.

"Abe." She whispers, "Help 'em."

Abraham holds her understanding where she is coming from. He walks over and places his hand on the Abimelech's shoulder;

"I did ya wrong. I did Sarah wrong and my God wrong. Take me to each of your women and I'll pray for 'em."

The two of them walk back into the hotel. For several hours Abraham and Sarah walk through the upper rooms of the hotel and laying hands on the female members of Abimelech's family. Sarah is with him the entire time as he is asking God's blessings upon the women. Some of the women are very receptive and many are a bit skeptic. Either way they allow Abraham and Sarah to pray for them. When they have finished praying Abraham and Sarah are given a room in the hotel for the night. They were a little reluctant at first but eventually agree to stay. Sarah doesn't have much to say as they rest for the night. Abraham decides early the next morning to leave before anyone comes to them.

Needless to say the wagon ride back is not as exciting as they had hoped. But, time and prayer has a way smoothing things over, that, and the fact that Abraham promises her in front of God that he would never do that again.

As years pass the curse on Abimelech's family is lifted by God and the women are all blessed with children of their own.

Sarah and Abraham decide not to share all that happened in Gerard with the rest of the ranch. Instead they just say they had personal time and life moves on. Over the next several months Sarah's morning sickness goes away as her stomach begins to show the riches of a new life. It is hard to tell which grew quicker, her stomach or her desire to give birth to her baby.

And then, the day came.

Sarah is sitting outside with Hagar. Together they are sewing baby clothing when Sarah's stomach cramps. It catches her attention but just slightly. They continue talking and enjoying their time when about five minutes later it happens again. This time she reaches over and grabs Hagar's wrist.

"What is it?" Hagar asks.

Sarah pauses for a few seconds with a look of anticipation.

"Nothing."

They continue talking on and sewing but both are waiting to see if something is going to happen again. And in about four or five minutes, it does.

Sarah grabs her stomach. "It's a contraction." She says excitedly.

Hagar jumps to her feet and begins laughing like a teenage girl;

"C'mon, we need to get you to your house."

Sarah laughs as she waddles her way up and out of the chair;

"I'm sure I have time."

Hagar helps her to her feet as they both giggle at the effort. They make their way into the house without trying to bring any attention to themselves. Then in only a three minute span she has another contraction and this one is considerably stronger.

"Oh my!" Sarah states, "I may not have as much time as I thought."

She stands and begins moving about around the house in a bent over position like a crippled old woman.

"Maybe you should send Ishmael to get Abe." She groans.

As they are walking around in the house a couple of the other women are hanging clothes on the line and see them. They immediately run over to Sarah's;

"Hagar, why is she walking like that?" A healthy woman asks.

"Well she ain't constipated, if that's what you're think'n."

Between the occasional groan of pain there is still laughter and excitement. A few of the younger daughters run to tell others about Sarah and her house is quickly inundated with loving females. This is going to be a day of all days and everyone is excited. Ishmael runs out to the barn and tells Abraham that Sarah is cramping and his mom had to help her in the house. Abraham drops his tools and runs across the lane to see Sarah. One problem, the house is packed like a chicken coop. He can't get in and the women aren't moving.

"Just wait outside Abe. We'll let ya know when he's here." A friend states as she pushes Abraham out the door.

"When who gets here?" Abraham asks.

"Your son!" She answers.

Abraham almost falls off the porch as he backs away from the door. Sarah is about to finally give him a son. They have prayed for this day for too many years to count and now he is hours perhaps minutes from having those prayers answered.

A few of the older men of the ranch come around and sit with Abraham while the rest of the hands continue to work. Everyone thinks that she will have the baby quickly but to Abraham it is like watching a cow chew cud and it is going on and on and on. They whittle, play chicken with knives, toss horse shoes, pace back and forth, tell lies and jokes, and other than occasional laughter of the women or the timely groan from Sarah, still nothing happens. The front door cracks open and one of the ladies sticks her face out.

"It won't be long now." She smiles at Abraham, "Get ready."

He's not sure what that meant. How can he get ready? Did she mean clean up or stand up or wash his hands or simply be prepared to welcome his son into the world? A painful scream of Sarah's voice comes from inside the house with a loud roar of excitement and clapping of hands from the other women. Several of them come running out onto the porch to tell Abraham his boy had been born. Their faces are glowing with excitement and their eyes are as wide as the moon. A few of the men fire off some shots into the air to let the ranch know Sarah has given birth. And yet Abraham is still unable to get in and see his wife or his new son. Instead he jumps to his feet and hugs the men that are with him.

"God has made his promise true!"

"Abe! Abe!" Sarah cries out.

Abraham runs to the side of the house and sticks his head in the bedroom window beside the bed.

"Hey, I'm here." He says with excitement as he reaches through the window and places his hand on her cheek.

The ladies laugh out loud.

"We have a boy." She says exhaustedly.

Abraham looks and sees his son wrapped in a blanket and lying on Sarah's stomach. All he can do is stand there and smile. This strong brave leader of men is humbled and his eyes are overrun with tears of love. He moves away from the window and turns his back as his emotions have him completely overwhelmed. In time he returns to the window;

"Is the boy okay?"

"He's fine." One of the ladies answers.

"And Sarah?"

"I'm fine too." She answers.

A quiet peace enters the room as he takes the handkerchief from around his neck and wipes his eyes. For a minute he is completely inundated and can't make himself quit crying. He would try to laugh but then cry all over again. He has never felt this kind of emotion. All he can do is say, "Thank You Lord, thank You." After he fights through it, he blows his nose and looks back into the bedroom.

"So, Sarah, ... What did we name him? He asks with a crackling voice.

Sarah lifts the baby to her face and gently presses her cheek against his. She feels the smooth warm baby skin of the child God has given her. She closes her eyes;

"The Lord has brought me joy and laughter. And anyone that hears about this will laugh with me. Who would have thought that I would finally be able to give Abraham a son? And his name . . . . his name is Isaac.

CHAPTER 12

Hagar Leaves the Ranch

Genesis 21:9-21

It's been around two years since Isaac was born and he is indeed the prince of the ranch. He has all of Sarah's features and according to a few tantrums he has Abraham's temper. During his first several months of life he is never out of Sarah's sight. It is almost six months before she even lets Hagar take care of him. Around ten months he takes his first step and within thirteen months he is outside falling into cow manure.

Now Isaac is coming on a year and a half of age it is time for him to be weaned. Abraham has decided to throw a big party to celebrate his son's first step of independence. And naturally, being Abraham's youngest and first son by Sarah, the "shin dig" is going to be a good one. The ranch hands make whistles out of willow branches and flags out of old clothes. The women have gone crazy on cooking deserts and treats for all the kids, not to mention their normal ability to cook a dinner fit for a king. The work around the ranch, for the first time in years is stopping early in celebration of Isaac's weaning.

Around three O'clock in the afternoon everyone is beginning to shut down the work and get ready for an evening of celebration. The party will start earlier than most because the host of the party has to be in bed by 8:00 PM. Once again all the tables from each cabin are being brought together and put in a line in the lane between the houses to make one big festive place for all to eat and laugh. The party progresses with the kids blowing the whistles, waving the flags, hitting each other with the flags, getting a whipping for hitting each other with the flags and so forth and so on. Needless to say, it's a little noisier than normal. This time the children aren't separated from the parents at the table. This is a celebration of children so the families all sit together. After a great supper the kids are embellished with a rare sugar-fest that will most likely keep them up late into the night. About an hour in to the party Abraham stands to his feet at the end of the row of tables.

He bangs his metal mug on the wooden slat;

"Okay, okay! Let me have your attention! It's time to introduce the man of honor of our lil get-to-gather."

A small eruption of applause breaks out as Sarah stands and hands Isaac over to Abraham. Abraham lifts him high into the air above his head and tips him forward so that they are looking eye to eye.

The baby Isaac is laughing, squirming and yelling all at the same time until he finally has slobber drain out of his mouth and onto Abrahams face.

"Ohh!" everyone yells as they laugh and clap even louder.

Abraham quickly lowers him down, laughing himself. He stands Isaac on the table and takes a cloth to wipe the slobber from his own face.

"Okay, enough of the slobber showers." He says.

Isaac decides to run in place and rattles the dishes so Abraham lifts him back up to his chest.

"Today is a big day. Today my youngest boy takes his first step toward independence!"

"Thank the Lord!" Sarah says with laughter.

"Now ya'll have the honor of witnessing his first attempted at giving himself a drink of milk and moving into the next stage of his life.

"Are Ya Ready!!!"

Again the ranch families yell and laugh and clap their hands with anticipation of this major event, not to mention this first attempt is bound to be fun to watch. Sarah hands Abraham a small cup of lamb's milk. She would love to see Isaac be successful with his first drink being her son after all. But she also would kind of like to see him pour it on Abraham. Isaac is spun around to face the rest of the families. Abraham holds the cup in front of Isaac as Isaac takes his little hands and grabs the side of the cup pulling it to his mouth. At first Abraham tries to help but then releases the cup for Isaac to handle. The cup gets closer and closer and closer to Isaac's mouth and just as the first taste of milk hits his lip, ... he pours the rest of it straight down his chest. He laughs, cries and dances in one spot while eventually holding his breath until his face turns red, then, he lets out a hair curling scream. Naturally everyone is laughing and applauding his efforts. Isaac has no idea what is going on, all he knows is that he is wet and thirsty and it's a lot harder to quench your thirst than it used to be. Sarah moves up to be with Abraham and takes Isaac from him. She raises him again over her head for just a second giving him momma talk but that's not getting it done. They try to hand Isaac another cup of milk but he throws it in the dirt. This, I might add, gets him a little discipline. Abraham is a strong believer in the idea that *discipline can be used as a tool that would one day save a child's life.

"Well, looks like it's gonna be a long night tonight." Abraham laughs.

"And the party is officially over for me." Sarah says, "Good night all, thank ya'll for come'n."

She wraps up some supplies and takes the crying baby Isaac back into the house. As it turns out, he doesn't fight near as much as they were anticipating. Once in the house he settles in and drinks nicely out of the cup until he is full, with Sarah's assistance of course. Then after a sponge bath he is ready for bed. After he is fast asleep Sarah actually stands outside on the porch talking with other ladies as the party extends in to the night hours.

She is sitting in Abraham's chair on the porch listening to stories and watching the festivities with her ears locked keenly on any sound that might come from Isaac. To her left are a group of little boys who have been roping each others legs. As boys will do, they enter into their own little world never noticing that anyone is watching them. One of the boys happens to be Ishmael, Abraham's older son by Hagar. Sarah notices that he is doing something that causes all the other boys to laugh out loud but she can't tell exactly what he was doing. She can tell by the expressions of one the boys face that whatever Ishmael was doing, he shouldn't be, funny or not. Sarah knows his personality. *Even a child can be known by his actions. Sarah stands from Abraham's chair and nonchalantly makes her way to the end of the porch where Ishmael stands with his back to her.

Some of the other boys see her coming and are trying to give Ishmael a body signal to stop but he is way too far into his routine to notice their signs. As Sarah approaches close enough to see and hear him, she is about to get very upset.

Laughing and bouncing around Ishmael says,

"Did you see the stupid baby!? He cain't be no brother of mine!"

Jumping around like a monkey Ishmael pretends to be acting as if he were Isaac.

"I'm a stupid baby! I can't drink from a cup! I think I'll just pour this milk down my shirt and pee on myself. I need my mommy's milk! Waa! Waa! Waa!"

Ishmael was laughing the whole time until he notices that none of the others are laughing anymore.

"What's matter with ya'll? That's funny. Ya'll act like ya seen a ghost or someth'n!"

Then he sees one of the boys glance up toward Sarah and back away from him. He snappishly whirls his attention around and finds her staring down at him from the porch with a look of fuming fury.

"You best be glad I ain't your Mom right now boy, or I'd thrash you back side till blood filled your boots. Now get away from my porch!" Sarah yells.

The boys split out like a covey of quail. Sarah turns and stomps back into her house and sits down beside Isaac's bed. She rubs on his forehead as he lies there peacefully sleeping. Her hands are shaking with anger and her chest pounds as her blood pressure boils.

"I ain't have'n that. No one will mock this child of God." She whispers with a trembling voice.

It wasn't much longer until Abraham dismisses himself from the lingering hoopla of men who never sleep and comes in to be with his family. He's thinking Sarah will be asleep by now, boy is he wrong. There is never a better feeling for a man than to come in from a night of celebrating an event in your son's young life only to face the ranting and raving of a fired up wife. I say that sarcastically of course.

When Abraham enters the house Sarah has Isaac in her lap and is rocking him in the front room. He walks over to her and kisses both of them on the forehead.

"That was a fun night, huh?" He says.

She never answers and just keeps looking down at Isaac. At first her actions don't register to Abraham.

"Ya come'n to bed?" He asks.

Again no answer. He pulls off his boots and kicks them over by the wall, stands to his feet to remove his shirt;

"Hey, ya gonna rock that boy all night?"

"I might." She whispers.

He notices that she didn't say that as a means of "that's how much I love him" but more in reference to "what's it to ya". As he takes a deeper look toward her he finally realizes she mad.

"So now what?" He ponders. What could have possibly made her mad? Is she mad at someone, or did she get mad cause he stayed outside, did he say something he can't remember? Maybe he should just act like he doesn't realize she's mad and go to bed. And like most men who don't think as a woman, that's exactly what he chooses to do.

It doesn't work.

He has just manage to ease off into a comfortable state of mind when he feels her plop into bed and give a big *sigh*. Still, he pretends to sleep. She then grabs a hand full of covers turns to her side and . . . . *sigh*. He waits. It's quiet for a few minutes and then she finally breaks down and just starts crying.

Abraham turns over in bed and faces her.

"Okay, what is it?"

"Nothing." She answers, "Just go to sleep."

This of course means, "If you go to sleep I'll bust you with a frying pan".

"I'm not going to sleep. What's wrong?" He asks.

Sarah sits up on the side of the bed with her back to him.

"I want' Hagar and Ishmael to leave the ranch."

Abraham's thoughts whirl like dandelions in a gust of wind.

"What? Where did that come from?"

Sarah stands and walks to the window. Her nightgown floats in the night's breeze as the moonlight causes her silhouette to appear as an angel.

"I walked up on Ishmael mocking Isaac tonight. He is always making fun of him. He is jealous of our son and I don't think Hagar is do'n anything to discourage 'em. It's gonna always be a problem. I want'm to leave."

She turns to face Abraham and again she begins to cry.

"Sarah, Ishmael is my son. You want me just to kick'm out?" Abraham asks.

She angrily takes a few steps toward Abraham.

"He will NOT get any part of this inheritance. Isaac will get the inheritance and no one else! HE is our child!"

She storms out of the bedroom and into the kitchen. Abraham now sits up in bed wondering how he is going to handle this sudden and unexpected twist of fate. Not only did they practically raise Hagar and then ask her to do something so outlandish like have his son, now Sarah wants to kick them both out to the wilderness. He falls back onto his pillow with his arms crossed over his face. He closes his eyes and begins to pray.

"God, I know from the get go that this is all my fault. Had I just trusted Ya years ago, none of this would be happen'n. But I failed. Now, I'm in a bind and I need some help. How does a father kick his oldest son out of the house no matter who the mother is? I don't know how to keep everything good. I definitely need ya right about now."

He lay there in the dark for a few more minutes not realizing that he is falling asleep. While he rests God speaks to him and says,

"Don't be worried about the boy and Hagar. Do whatever Sarah tells you, because it is through Isaac that you will have the descendants I have promised. I will also give many children to the son of the Hagar. He too is your son."

The next morning Abraham wakes and finds that Sarah has never joined him in bed. He puts his clothes and boots on, grabs his hat and walks into the kitchen for a pot of coffee. Sarah is sitting on the porch with Isaac in her lap. Abraham pours himself a mug and walks out.

"I cain't say I understand. I don't know why we cain't all just live here and get along. But, it's whatever."

Sarah never looks his direction and never stops rocking.

"I'll tell Hagar that God has told me she needs to move on. But so you'll know, without God tell'n me to do it, it woulda never happened."

Without moving her head Sarah cuts her eyes toward Abraham and watches him walk down the steps and head toward Hagar's house. She's torn with a double edged knife of emotion. She too loves Hagar but will allow nothing to interfere with her expectations for Isaac.

Abraham enters Hagar's house and finds Ishmael asleep in the front room on a blanket. He stops for a few seconds and watches him sleep. He was so proud of him on the day he was born. Over the years he has been a pretty rowdy young man. He has had several fights with the other boys and is a constant handful to keep up with. As bad as he hates to admit it, Abraham can see where the boy will bother Isaac as they continued to grow. Abraham moves past Ishmael and walks into Hagar's room. She is still asleep when he sits down beside her on the bed. She feels the movement and opens her eyes;

"Abe? What are ya do'n?"

He leans forward resting his weight on one hand while he runs his other hand through her hair.

"We need to talk." He whispers.

Hagar pulls the covers up around her as she sits up in the bed;

"Okay, what's wrong?"

Abraham puts on a fake smile;

"Who said anything was wrong?"

She just sits there and looks at him as if to say "I'm not an idiot."

"Okay." He replies, "Something is wrong. I had a dream last night. God spoke to me while I was asleep."

"And?" She asks

"It looks like it's time for you and Ishmael to move out on your own. Go find what God has for you. Make a family away from the ranch."

Needless to say Hagar's eyes immediately fill with tears.

"You want me to leave? Ishmael is your son!"

"I know!" Abraham exclaims. "But God has assured me that there are great things for both of ya out there. Ya can't stay here. The boys aren't gonna get along."

Hagar pushes Abraham out of the way and gets out of bed;

"This is Sarah's do'n! She don't want Ishmael to get any of the inheritance!"

Abraham tries to grab her but she fights away.

"Listen to me. Even if it was someth'n Sarah wanted I wouldn't do it if God had not told me to. I wouldn't just kick you and Ishmael out of our ranch."

Hagar walks into the front room where Ishmael is asleep.

"So what are we suppose to do, Abe? We cain't take all this stuff with us! Ya want us just to grab a sandwich and start walk'n!" I can't believe you think God is tell'n ya this!"

The sarcasm against God does not set well with Abraham and his temper is tested.

"First of all, I might do a lot of stuff in my life and the Lord knows I've failed many times. But I ain't doubt'n what I know He said. Second, you ain't leave'n with noth'n. You'll get your clothes, some food and water. Long as you head to a town you'll be fine. I wanted this to be easy and excite'n for ya . . . "

"Exciting!" she interrupts.

"You're make'n it harder than it needs to be, Hagar."

She crosses her arms and stares at him;

"Well not everything Mr. Abraham does is always gonna be easy now is it?"

Her voice and attitude are filled with anger and sarcasm. She is very resentful at the circumstances Abraham is putting her in and she is reacting in a way that actually makes it a little easier for Abraham to handle.

"Get your stuff ready." He says as he walks out the front door, "I'll have a wagon ready for ya when you get outside."

Hagar grabs a plate from the kitchen table and throws it against the wall as she breaks down in tears. Ishmael is startled by the shattering of the dish and wakes up to see her distress.

Abraham continues across the lane to the barn grumbling to himself while he catches two of the best wagon horses he has and hitches them to the wagon. He gathers plenty of food and a small barrel full of water and puts it in the back of the wagon. His anger toward Hagar's reaction is keeping him from realizing how sad he will be to see Ishmael leave. He pulls the wagon around in front of her house. He has no sooner gotten out of it when Hagar throws a bundle of clothing into the back and lifts Ishmael into the seat. With moves of hurried resentment and disappointment she circles the wagon, climbs in and jerks the reins out of Abraham's hand. She sits there staring straight ahead for a few seconds.

"We'll always love you." Abraham says

She never looks at him;

"You sure have a funny way of show'n it."

She slaps the reins across the back of the horses and they saunter toward the end of the ranch.

Abraham stands in the middle of lane watching them rock from side to side as the wagon wheels climb over the roughness of the road. He can see Ishmael lean into Hagar's side. Then Ishmael straightens up and turns to look behind them and toward Abraham as they ride away. Even from a continuing distance Abraham can sense the emotion of his son as Ishmael realizes he will never have an honest father/son relationship. The boy raises his hand and begins to wave as they turn the corner and ride out of sight.

Now, and just now, the emotions of Abraham are slamming home. His oldest son is gone. It's overwhelming. He begins to choke, his face is red with agony, his entire body weakens and for as much man as he would like to pretend to be, he simply cannot hold back the tears. He bends over at the waist and places his hands on his knees and sobs. By now several families have seen what is happening and are standing on their porches watching him. His foreman walks out to join him in the lane. He has no idea what is happening between Abraham and Hagar, but honestly, it doesn't matter. All he knows is that Abraham needs someone to stand with.

Toward the end of the ranch they hear the rumbling of a horse tearing down the lane. When they look up it is Taylor Wilham racing out to catch Hagar. He has desired to be with her since before the night he saw Abraham come from Hagar's house. As far as he is concerned, now is his chance.

The foreman helps Abraham back to his house where Sarah is waiting. He sits in his chair on the porch with his face in his hands and in an uncommon scene to all who know him, he weeps with extreme emotion.

Outside the ranch Taylor catches up with Hagar about a half a mile down the road. At first he just rides behind her without her knowing he is there. In few minutes Ishmael sees him and tells her. She looks back at him and pulls the horses up to stop.

Taylor rides up beside her;

"So where ya headed with that boy?"

Her face is washed with tears.

"I don't know. Just go'n."

He nods his head and re-adjusts his hat.

"Mind if I ride with ya for awhile?"

She looks toward the ground and then slaps the reins across the horses.

"Do as ya please." She says.

Taylor lets the wagon pass him and then falls in behind them. It's not exactly the welcome he was looking for but he understands her mental status. For now he's just happy she didn't tell him to leave her alone. And although she didn't say it, she is glad he's there.

They ride on for days. The path to "nowhere" is a long hard ride. Eventually the food is scarce and the water barrel is getting dry. On their tenth day of hard travel they stop along a tree line for a break in the shade.

They are dirty, sweaty, hungry, thirsty and exhausted.

Taylor climbs off his lathered up horse and loosens the girth.

"We cain't travel like this much longer. We gotta find water."

"I know." Hagar replies.

"How much is in the barrel?" he asks

She shook her head in a tired and hopeless manner;

"We're out."

Neither of them has faced this situation before. Both have been provided for extremely well at the ranch.

"Okay then. I'm gonna ride ahead. You stay here with the boy. I'll find water and bring it back. Maybe that way we won't lose the horses."

Hagar knows her choices are limited and something has got to change.

"How long you be gone?"

As he looks for one more drip from his canteen he answers,

"Maybe a day or so at the most. I'll be back."

With that he tightens the girth and saddles up. There is no galloping off with heroism when you can barely walk to begin with. Instead he and his horse stumble off into the horizon.

The lack of water has been hardest on Ishmael. With hours passing Sarah does her best to keep him out of the heat but the boy has gotten incredibly sick and dehydrated. She can barely keep him awake and is afraid if he sleeps he will never wake up. Even in the hottest part of the day he has no water left within him to sweat. She holds him in her lap as they sit on the dried out dirt of the land and pray for help.

Her patience is weary and her thought process is as weak as her sleepy eyes. She decides to lay Ishmael's head on the ground and step away for a moment to look across the plains for Taylor. As Ishmael lays there in physical distress he whimpers softly through his dry throat. It is then that God hears his cry.

In mercy, God sends an angel to talk with Hagar. While she stands looking into the distance for any sign of Taylor returning with water, a voice in the wind speaks out.

"What are you worried about Hagar?"

She slowly turns but isn't sure what she heard.

"God has heard the cry of your child. Go get him, pick him up and comfort him."

"Who are you?" She cries out.

"You will be fine and he will have many children."

Hagar turns to see if she can tell where the voice was coming from or to see if she is hallucinating. There is no one to be seen. She rubs her face with both hands and lifts her hair to wipe the sweat off the back of her neck. She can hear Ishmael moaning as she walks toward him looking around in despair.

Behind a group of trees about twenty feet past Ishmael she notices a pile of rocks. They don't seem to be lying there randomly but appear as if they have been stacked. How has she not noticed them before? She walks to Ishmael and struggles to pick him up. She carries him toward the pile of rocks and as she gets closer she sees wooden slats that have been hidden in the weeds and realizes that this is an old home place. The rocks are the remnants of an old well. She quickly and yet gently lays Ishmael to the ground. She runs to the wagon and finds a leather bag. There is a rope under the seat that she gathers and wraps around the bag. She puts small rocks in the bag to give it a little weight. As she lowers the bag into the well just before she reaches the end of its length she hears it splash into water. With excitement racing through her veins she gives the bag a chance to fill up with water then hoists it back up. To her relief and disbelief it is filled with clear spring water. The first order of business is to get water down Ishmael. She lifts his head and helps him drink. He is drinking so hard and fast that he can't help but choke and occasionally spits up. She also pours water over his head and neck. When the bag is empty she repeats the process about three more times. With God's hand on both of them, it doesn't take long before they are getting color back in the skin and some form of conciseness. In a short time they are both sitting beside the well filled with water and alive. Hagar continues to dip the bag down into the well until she has completely filled the barrel in the back of the wagon and watered the horses. They are still in need of something solid to eat but for now they can make it.

She spends the rest of night and the next day watching and waiting for Taylor. The next morning while it is still at least a little cooler, she decides it is time to move on. She walks over to the well and kneels down. Looking into the well she can see her reflection deep in the sun lit hole. She takes time to pray and give thanks to God. Finally she helps Ishmael in to the wagon and moves on.

Miles away from the trail of Hagar and Ishmael in a place they will never venture, the body of Taylor lays pierced with arrows and without spirit. He was beaten, robbed and killed. The starving animals of the wild have left him unrecognizable. Hagar never finds out what happened to him. All she knows is that she never saw him again. As God assured her, both she and Ishmael were fine. They eventually venture into a town where people take them in and care for them. Ishmael grows to be a strong young man full of vim and vigor not afraid to stand toe to toe with anyone who dares challenge him. Over the years both Hagar and Ishmael become very well respected among the people. As it turns out Ishmael marries a woman of the same descent as Hagar and has many children.

CHAPTER 13

Abraham to Sacrifice Isaac

Genesis 21:22 thru Genesis 22:

The Ranch has been very successful and continues to grow. Abraham and Sarah have decided to build a new home outside the ranch along with a few of the foreman and their families. It's only a short ride away from the main lanes of the ranch but gives them a chance to have time on their own from all the hired hands that have come to work for him over the years.

Abraham's relationship with Abimelech has remained strong since his visit to Gerard. One day Abimelech and his Sheriff ride out to see Abraham. They ride up to his house late one afternoon while he and Sarah sat on their porch watching Isaac play with their old dog. This is the third old dog that has been raised by Abraham and constantly being hit by the last splashes of Abraham's coffee. Now it's all he can do to bark and run around Isaac about three times before he has to lie down and roll to his side for a breath of air.

"I cain't believe you still got that same ol dog, Abraham." Abimelech says as they ride up.

Abraham stands up from his rocking chair and leans up against the porch post.

"Yep, same ol dog. He can still bark at ya but now he tries to gum ya to death. What brings you boys out here?"

Abimelech takes off his hat. "Sorry Mrs. Sarah, I didn't see you sit'n up there. How are ya?"

Sarah smiles and nods her head. Even though he and Abraham have managed to get along over the years she is still not completely settled with him.

"I see ya'll are start'n to build a few more homes out this direction. Your ranch is quite a business."

He shifts to one hip in his saddle and looks around the place;

"Look, Abraham . . . . "

"You can call me Abe." Abraham interrupts.

"Abe. You and me been get'n along real good for quite a while and I wanna keep it that way. I wantcha to promise me that no matter how big your ranch gets, our families will always be able to live in peace. I'll respect you and you do the same for me."

Abraham walks down off the porch and along side Abimelech's horse. He reaches up to shake Abimelech's hand.

"I got no problem with that." He says.

Abimelech sits back up straight after shaking Abraham's hand;

"I'm glad to hear that. Is there anything ya need from us?"

Abraham takes Isaac by the hand and leads him out from behind the horses.

"Actually there is. I gotta water well that some of your men have taken over and won't let my men use."

"What men? Abimelech asks, "I didn't tell anyone to watch a well."

Abraham makes his way back up to the porch;

"Not a big deal. Just make sure they know I'm the one that dug it and it belongs to me."

Abimelech puts his hat on; "Consider it done."

A slight spur to shoulder of his mare and he slowly turns his horse and rides away.

"Sure is a nice place you're make'n here. Won't be long you'll have a big ranch here as well. We'll call this place Beersheba."

"Beersheba?" Abraham asks.

As the two men ride off Abimelech says, "It means 'Oath-Well'. We both made an oath around this well to take care of each other!"

He rides further into the distance; "Have a good night Mrs. Sarah!"

Abraham smiles at Sarah as Abimelech rides out of sight.

"I said I wouldn't bother them." Abraham laughs, "I don't remember say'n I'd take care of 'em."

As it turns out the name Beersheba caught on and that is exactly what people started calling it.

It's been well over ten years since their first visit to Gerard when Sarah was pregnant with Isaac. The boy has definitely had his growing spurts. Even at his early age many of the hands that have been with Abraham all these years see strong resemblances in the way they walk, talk, ride and even rope. *Abraham has made a point to teach young Isaac all his ways including his spiritual ways in hopes that Isaac will always make wise decisions. Isaac is like a shadow to his father and his trust in God at this young age is nurtured every chance Abraham gets. On occasion Abraham allows Isaac to go with him when he rides out to pray.

Abraham is riding back to his house one day on his new line back dun when the Spirit of God stirs him. Then the Lord speaks to him. The instant Abraham hears God speak to him he slides off the horse and kneels to pray;

"Here I am Lord."

For the most part, anytime God is speaking to Abraham it's been about encouraging matters or asking him to go somewhere or talking to him about the blessing God is promising. This time however is none of the sort.

"I want you to go get your son, Isaac. Take him to the mountains of Moriah and sacrifice him to me."

Abraham kneels there silently for a few minutes but there is nothing else said. It is a short request with no explanation and no discussion. Abraham stands to his feet and puts his hat back on. If anyone saw him right now he would appear to be strung out on some very bad whiskey. Through all the years that Abraham has been blessed with his relationship with God he has never doubted anything when God has spoken to him. But this is different. He trudges over to his horse and tightens the girth as he thinks about what he just heard. He rests his arms over the saddle and looks toward heaven. Did he really just hear God ask him to sacrifice Isaac or did he misunderstand Him? He climbs back on his horse and the horse just starts moving home without Abraham even noticing. This horse has made this trip so many times you can take a nap and wake up at home as long as you don't fall off. And other than the fact that he isn't really asleep that's exactly what happens. Abraham's mind is so far swallowed up in thought he barely notices when he rides through his gate. For as hard as he tries he just can't come up with a reason God would make such an outlandish request. So once again Abraham will have to do the only thing he's ever done that allows things to work out right, and that is trust in God. *Every time he has earnestly sought the wisdom of God he has been protected and found insight into the ways of the Lord. He may not understand it now, but trusting and seeking is the key.

The next morning Sarah is up bright and early to make coffee. She ties her hair in a knot behind her head and washes her face with some water from the bucket on the cabinet. As she walks past Isaac's room from the kitchen she finds an empty cup sitting on the table but can tell that Abraham is not on the porch. Pouring herself a cup of coffee she can hear the twisting of saddle leather and stomping of hooves as Abraham and two of his foremen ride up to the porch.

Sarah walks outside covering her eyes from the morning sun;

"Start'n pretty early this morning aren't ya Abe?"

Then she notices that Abraham is not only saddled with two other riders but he also has a couple of pack mules that are loaded with necessities for a couple of days ride.

"Where ya'll go'n?"

"Where's Isaac?" He asks

About that time the boy comes walking outside. He's dressed in his underwear and rubbing his eyes.

"Hey boy, Ya wanna go camping for a few days? Abraham asks.

Suddenly Isaac is much more awake than he was seconds before.

"Yes Sir." He answers, "I got to get my stuff."

"I got your stuff. Just get some clothes on and let's go." Abraham states.

Sarah unties her hair from a bun;

"So, again, where ya go'n?

"We're go'n to the mountains for a few days."

At this point Abraham has not felt the freedom to tell anyone what God has called him to do. So, that's all he has decided to tell her. He's not sure what's going to happen and if God requires him to kill Isaac there is no way he could come back home anyway. Sarah's intuition can sense that something is up. She steps down off the porch and walks to the side of the horse where the other two riders can't see her. She places her hand on Abraham's thigh.

"What's up? Why ya be'n so different?" she whispers.

He takes his hat off, leans over and kisses her;

"It's noth'n. Just got a lot on my mind. I need to get away for a bit."

She pats him on the leg as Isaac is crawling up on his own yellow mare.

"Okay . . . . well, ya best take care of that boy while your get'n away for a while." She says with a smile.

Abraham cues his horse and spins him around to the boy;

"Ya ready?"

Isaac raises his over sized hat up from his eyes, "See ya in a few days Mom."

Sarah smiles, "Okay son."

She turns her attention back to Abraham;

"Abe, you take care of him. He's still just a boy."

That's the second time she has said that and those words can't hit Abraham in the heart any harder if she had done it with a sledge hammer. Taking care of Isaac has been his exact thought all night. Why is God needing Abraham to sacrifice the only son of Sarah who is only ten years of age? He's just a boy. So far, it is making no sense. But, they're still going.

Along the ride most of the conversation is between the two hired hands and Isaac. They have notice that Abraham has little if nothing to say. Most of the time he has chosen to ride out front by himself. Every now and then Isaac trots up beside Abraham but shortly he is right back with the other two who will actually carry on a conversation. Before the sun rests for the night they pull up and make camp. The horses are tied to loose limbs and the saddles are once again back rests for the open air recliners. After a dinner of warmed up beans and wheat bread, Isaac can't stay hooked any longer and falls to sleep next to his dad. A hard day's ride, regardless of the speed can take a toll on a young body. Abraham is staying up with the other two for a while discussing ranch matters but eventually the other two find themselves fading and decide to call it a night.

Abraham is ambling around just outside the light of the fire gathering more wood. It's been a long time since he has had a hard time getting to sleep. But tonight is not any night. He just can't get settled in his mind what is going to happen. Ultimately, he knows he is going to do what he's been asked, but right now it's driving him insane. So he stokes up the fire and adds a few more sticks then shuffles his back around on his own saddle and falls asleep.

Early the next morning the sun casts its God blessed rays through the extended limbs of the trees and wakes everyone up. At their age you don't just jump up and get after it. There are joints to loosen, bones that need to crack, muscles to stretch and groans to make. And that takes a few minutes. Isaac, on the other hand, is up a hustling to the edge of the woods to water the shrubs in a way only young boys can do. The two foremen are used to getting up and getting around but today Abraham slows them down a little.

"You guys just relax here for the day. Enjoy the day off and take care of the mules. Me and Isaac are gonna walk up the mountain and we'll be back this afternoon."

That sits well with them. It's not often you get to just lie around the camp fire for a day and do nothing.

"Need us to saddle up your horses?" One asks.

"No, I think we'll walk."

Abraham gets an old cooking pan out of his saddle bag and scoops several piles of coals from the fire.

"Isaac, come here." He states.

Isaac goes to him and Abraham hands him several sticks of wood that he has gathered up.

"I want ya to carry these up the mountain for me." Abraham says as he watches his son drop the limbs.

Isaac, with an arm full of branches, looks up the side of the mountain;

"All the way?"

Abraham picks up Isaac's hat from the ground and places it on his head for him;

"You can handle it."

Together they begin to weave their way up the side of the mountain through briars and thickets over dead trees and ditches. It takes over an hour to make their way up to the top especially with Isaac tripping every fifty yards or so. Abraham has carried the pot of coals and Isaac manages to make it to the top with at least half of the sticks he was asked to carry. When they finally reach the pinnacle, Abraham sits the pot of coal down and begins to dig a hole. Isaac sits himself down and begins to rest.

After Abraham digs the ditch he pours the hot coals into the hole and stacks the sticks that Isaac has carried over them. He kneels down beside them and begins to blow on the coals. He can feel the anxiety of what he is doing building up inside of him. With a little assistance the sticks soon begin to smoke and eventually catch on fire. He struggles to stand to his feet and then begins to stack rocks on two sides of the hole and lays larger branches that he gathers from around the area over the top of the fire that made it look like a bed. Isaac sits quietly and watches while trying to learn from his father. Over the years he has learned that it is sometimes better just to wait and see what his dad was doing as opposed to constantly asking questions that ultimately get you whooped. After making the alter Abraham approaches Isaac.

He sits down beside his son and wraps his arm around Isaac's shoulders. They both sit and watch as the small fire continues to flicker and catch on to other twigs.

"Son, do you trust God?" Abraham asks.

Isaac picks up a rock and throws it into the woods; "Yep"

"Do you trust me?"

Isaac picks up another rock but Abraham grabs his arm and makes him sit down.

"Do you trust me?" He asks.

Isaac smiles; "Yeah."

"I need you to trust me and I need ya to do someth'n for me."

Isaac jumps up; "Okay Pa."

There are times in a father's life when their sons do something and it causes them to realize how much their son is just like them. This was one of those times. His heart is filled with affection. His hands began to sweat and his chin begins to quiver. Abraham pulls a handkerchief out of his back pocket and blindfolds Isaac.

"What's this for?" Isaac asks.

"Just trust me." Abraham answers.

He then lifts up Isaac carrying him to the altar where he places him on the bed of limbs that are lying over the small flame. Isaac realizes where his dad has placed him but he never removes the blind fold.

"I can feel that fire." The boy says.

Abraham's heart begins to race, his hands are trembling and he is finding it hard to swallow. The boy is getting restless and Abraham knows he will have to move quickly. Keeping one hand the Isaac's chest Abraham reaches down to the leather bag laying beside the fire and removes an eight inch hand crafted knife that he had made for skinning deer. Isaac begins to twist his body as the fire intensifies. Abraham struggles to hold him in place.

"It's starting to burn my back." The boy complains.

Trusting God now is reaching a level Abraham has never experienced. His hands are now shaking so hard he is forced to hold the knife with both hands to keep from dropping it. He looks toward the Heavens and raises the knife with both hands above his head. He can barely stand and tears are pouring from his eyes. His chest is pulsing as he tries to breathe. The time has come, he takes one last deep breath and with all the strength he can pull from within he prepares to thrust his knife through the chest of his son.

And . . . . in the perfect time . . . . a voice from the winds called out, *"Abraham! Abraham!"*

Overwhelmed by emotion he falls to his knees and rests his head on Isaac's chest.

Then he answers, "Here I am Lord."

"Don't hurt the boy. I see your heart. I know that you would have sacrificed your only son for your God."

Abraham quickly grabs Isaac and jerks him from the altar and carries him to where they have been sitting. He removes the blind fold and kisses Isaac on the face.

A few tears are on Isaac's face from the pain of the fire but he has not been burned.

"Are ya okay?" Abraham asks.

"Yeah, it was just get'n hot."

As those words pierced through the skies Abraham hears another noise and looks behind him. Entangled in a thicket is a mountain ram. Abraham laughs to himself. He turns the boy around and points out the ram. Abraham climbs through the briars with his knife and kills the animal. He cuts it loose from the thicket and carries it over to the altar.

Raising the ram above his head; "This is for You Lord."

He places the ram on the bed of limbs and stokes the fire. He sits down with Isaac in his lap and holds him like he would never let him go. They watch as the fire intensifies and consumes the dead ram. Abraham explains to Isaac that this was a symbol of what God means to them. It's important to be willing to sacrifice anything you have to God especially if God has provided it for you like He did this ram. *If we always do what is right and fair that will please God even more than a sacrifice. And if you do so, He will provide you with even more.

As they prepare to leave a breeze covers the top of the mountain and the voice of the Lord speaks.

"I vow in My own name that I will richly bless you because you did not keep your son from me."

Isaac yells and runs across the opening, grabs Abraham by the thigh and hides behind him. This is the first time he has heard the voice of the Lord. Abraham's chest swells with pride. To him he has trusted God beyond any measure he could have imagined. In all honesty, at that time Isaac never really understood why he had to lie on top of the fire before they burnt the ram. But at the age of ten, that's okay. He'll have a chance to get an understanding about it later in life. When the ram has completely burned Abraham puts the fire out and he and Isaac climb down the mountain. They meet up with the foremen who were doing exactly as Abraham instructed them, which was nothing. They gather all their belongings, saddled up and they returned to Beersheba. The ride back is much more pleasurable than the ride to the mountain.

Abraham knows that Sarah will be excited to see Isaac and will probably have a million questions for him about what they did. Isaac's answers are spiritually shocking.

"Mom," he says, "We sacrificed to God and God said thanks."

Other than that he has nothing to say.

CHAPTER 14

Sarah Dies

Genesis 22:20 thru Genesis 23

A small group of hired hands are gathering around the front corral whooping and whistling to the sounds of a three year old monstrous stud bucking and bawling as if he were being attacked by a den of lions. As it turns out it's Isaac on his back in saddle and doing all he can to hold on. The battle rages for about ten more seconds before a hard lunge to the left sends Isaac head over heels and slams him into a cloud of dust.

"Ahhh!!" They all yell.

Isaac groans his way up to his knees then stands and dusts himself off while laughing.

"Did I make the time?" He asks.

"Twenty-seven seconds!" One cowboy answers, "You owe us some deer jerky!"

Isaac is now a grown man and has assumed many of the responsibilities of running the ranch. Occasionally his physical abilities cause him to bet on something he isn't always capable of pulling off. He is very well liked and admired by everyone on the ranch because of his personality and that fact that he will get out and do anything he asks the others to do. Over the years God has held true to His word and the ranch has become the largest ranch in the land. It extends for miles in each direction. There are actually small communities of houses and families located in several different parts of the ranch in order to maintain its vast expansion. People from every direction known to man have heard of Abraham, Sarah and now Isaac.

Isaac has had several women of interest over the past thirty years, but none that have caught his attention long enough to get serious. He has grown to have many of the same characteristics of his father Abraham. He's long and tall, very distinguished and lives a life of honor and truth. Because of Abraham and Sarah he is exceptionally grounded in his relationship with the Lord. He and Abraham have moved through all phases of their relationship from the time Isaac was small enough to ride in front of Abraham on their horse through the time he first got his mare and learned to rope. Isaac's teenage years were filled with the same issues most teenagers have during this time such as testing the parents, finding the girls, fighting the boys and basically feeling his oats. He was pretty successful in all of it with the exception of testing his parents. *They were not guilty of sparing the rod. It is Abraham and Sarah after all. As a young man his maturity was incredible. Every woman within the distance of a cow's trail would accept the offer of marriage from him. But so far the main woman in his life is still his mother.

Abraham and Isaac are sitting on the top rail of the corral watching as some of the younger hands continue to try and break the big stud. From behind them a stranger hurriedly rides up casting a haze of dust on their backs;

"Mr. Abraham."

Abraham lifts his feet over the top rail and turns to face the young rider.

"Depends on whose ask'n." He answers.

The gentleman laughs. "I have a message from your brother Nahor."

Isaac looks to his father; "Seriously, who names their kid Nahor?"

Abraham laughs and slides down from the fence. He used to jump, those were younger days.

"Are ya from his ranch?" Abraham asks.

"Yes Sir." The rider answers, "When Mr. Nahor asked if anyone would bring ya a letter, I volunteered. I've heard a lot about ya. It's my pleasure to finally get to meet ya."

"Well, pleasure to meet you too." Abraham replies as he takes the message from his calloused hand.

"Ya stay'n for dinner?" Abraham asks.

"I appreciate it Sir, but actually I'm ride'n on in to town if it's the same to ya?"

Abraham nods his head, "Be safe and tell Nahor to come see me."

"Will do!" he states. Then he spurs up his horse and gallops off.

Isaac laughs out loud; "For someone that really wanted to meet ya it didn't take long for him to get enough!"

With a humorous grunt Abraham agrees;

"Sounds like town was more in his mind than me."

Abraham walks over to his front porch, opens the letter and sits on the steps. Sarah eases her way outside when she hears him walk up.

"Whatcha got there?" she asks.

"It's a letter from Nahor." Abraham answers and sits down.

"Seriously," She says, "Who names their child Nahor?"

Abraham pauses and looks toward Isaac. He smiles, shakes his head, and then continues to read.

"What's it say?" She asks.

From what I can tell he's been as busy make'n a family as he has run'n that ranch. Him and Milcah have eight boys. Some of 'em old enough to have kids Isaac's age.

"Lord, they started early, huh!" She remarks

"I reckon so. Good for 'em though. I'm proud to hear it."

He hands the message to Sarah and returns to the coral with Isaac. Sarah sits down in Abraham's chair and reads through the letter that has all the children's names. She too is proud to hear that Nahor has been blessed with a large family. She looks out toward Isaac and smiles. Her family is not as large, but to her, every bit as blessed.

Sarah loves Isaac more than life itself. With every day of his life she has found something different in her child to admire. Not a day has passed that she has not asked the Lord to forgive her for doubting and then thanking him for the gift of Isaac. That love goes both ways. Isaac would definitely stand up for and protect his dad, but his mother is a whole different level of life. Just a thought of doing wrong toward Sarah and you would provoke an experience that entails of a dreadful quantity of pain. He is a true athlete in every sense of the word and in many occasions he has been more than happy to prove it at the expense of someone who was seriously wishing they had chosen their words with a little more consideration. Isaac, in the essence of a true cowboy is constantly going out of his way to honor his mother. *A wise parent will always stray from spoiling their child, but a smart child will strive to spoil their parents. If anything were to happen to her, he would be devastated.

Since birth Sarah has been blessed with an incredible physical beauty. In the jealousy of every woman she has ever met, her beauty continued throughout all her years. Even now at such an old age people are still amazed at the sophisticated appearance of her natural beauty. The only difference now is that she has reached an age where getting around isn't as easy as it use to be. After reading the letter from Abraham's brother Nahor, she has been sitting in her house sewing on one of Abraham's shirts. Isaac jumps the porch and flies in to the house through front door.

"Hey Ma!" he says hoping he startles her just a bit.

She didn't jump much, just slightly looks up and shakes her head. He walks over and kisses her on the forehead.

"Whatcha do'n?"

She shakes her head slightly, "Just sewing on your Pa's shirt."

Isaac notices that her voice seems a little weak and it seems as if she has slurred her speech. He dips himself a cup of water from the kitchen and walks back into the front room.

"Ya okay, Ma? Ya sound a little frail." He asks.

This time she doesn't acknowledge him.

Isaac stands and looks at her for a few seconds. He notices that she is sitting and holding the needle in the same spot and has not moved. She is looking down at the needle as if she is sewing but she is sitting perfectly still.

So he asks again, "Ma . . . . ya okay?"

She never moves. It is as if she never hears a word he says. She is still sitting there holding that needle but her mind is not responding to anything around her. Isaac gently removes the needle from her hand and sits Abraham's shirt on another chair. She keeps her hands in her lap and her face focuses down where the shirt used to be. She tries to speak but it is just a slur. Isaac places his hand under her chin and raises her head. The left side of her face is drooping and seems to be paralyzed. Her left hand falls out of her lap and hangs as if it is asleep. Isaac's heart races and his mouth drops in fear. He runs out to the porch to find help. Next door working in the garden is one of Sarah's close friends.

"Mrs. Slater! Mrs. Slater!" he says frantically, "I need your help."

Mrs. Slater drops her clothes back into her basket and rushes to Abraham's house. She runs right past Isaac and straight to Sarah.

Catching a quick glimpse at Sarah's glazed eyes and paralyzed muscles;

"Oh my Lord! Help me get her to the bed!"

Isaac quickly lifts her up and carries her to the bed.

Mrs. Slater runs in behind him with a pan of warm water and rags.

"Isaac, go get your father!" she exclaims.

Isaac's face is showing expressions of stress and worry as he stands their gawking at his mother who seems to be gazing mindlessly in to space.

"Isaac! Go get your father!" she yells.

He runs out to the front door, leaps over the porch and in to the middle of the lane. He stumbles almost all the way down to his knees. Spinning in circles with his arms outstretched;

"Pa! Pa!" He yells

Abraham is standing by the barn when he sees Isaac come running out and he knows immediately that something is wrong. Abraham is not capable of a full out run anymore but he hurries to the best of his ability to get there. When Isaac sees Abraham heading that way, he quickly returns to his mother's bedroom. Mrs. Slater is sitting beside her wiping her forehead with a warm rag and praying. Sarah is staring toward the ceiling on her left. Her face has lost all expression and her breathing is very light and sporadic.

Abraham comes into the room and almost knocks Isaac over as he rushes to the side of the bed. He kneels down beside the bed and looks deep into Sarah's eyes.

She never looks into his.

"Sarah." He whispers.

No response.

"Sarah." He whispers again.

Still nothing.

He reaches down and takes her by the hand. She had no grip. Her breathing is suddenly becoming a deeper strangled effort and still sporadic.

Seconds will pass with no effort to breath and then she will gasp for a few short breaths. Abraham looks to Mrs. Slater;

"What happen to her?"

Mrs. Slater shakes her head;

"I don't know. It's the same thing that happened to Mrs. Belier years ago. Somth'n happen inside that paralyzed her and took her home."

"What do ya mean, 'took her home'?" Isaac asks, "She cain't die! It ain't time! Pa, it ain't time!"

Abraham stands to his feet and backs away from the bed. His eyes fill with tears.

"We can pray son, but time ain't about us, it's about God. Everything happens in God's time. All we can do is pray."

Mrs. Slater begins crying as she places one of her hands over her mouth and releases Sarah's hand with her other.

"It's her time." She softly cries.

At first neither Abraham nor Isaac realize what she says until she glances at them and then returns her attention back to Sarah. When Abraham and Isaac look at Sarah, they realize what Mrs. Slater means.

Sarah was gone.

A few seconds pass as they stand in shock and disbelief. Sarah's eyes have closed, her mouth is slightly open and her chest lies motionless. Abraham slowly makes his way back to the side of her bed as Isaac moves to the other. Abraham kneels down beside her, takes her by the hand and kisses her on the forehead before the pain of his broken heart resounds through his cries. Isaac wraps his arm across his mother's lifeless waist and weeps like a lost child. Mrs. Slater can't stand the crush of mournful emotions and quietly makes her way outside. She sits on the steps of the porch with her face buried in her hands as she weeps. It doesn't take but a second for others to see her distress. Within minutes the word is spreading and the entire ranch is rushing to Abraham's house. Out of respect, no one enters. Instead they stand quietly outside. The house is completely surrounded with family and friends all in disbelief. The Spirit of the Lord encompasses the house and not a word is heard. Even the children stand in silence. There have been many deaths on the ranch over the years, but this is Sarah. This is different. No one escapes the feeling of loss, no one.

Inside, Isaac walks around to the other side of the bed and embraces his father. They stay there beside Sarah's body for quite some time. When they have cried themselves down, Abraham begins to pray.

*Never before has he felt like he needed God more than now but in his righteousness he knows that even in death there is refuge. His head falls back and his face lifts toward Heaven. His arms stretch as far as he can reach as if he is trying desperately to be wrapped in the arms of the Lord. Then, with the frail voice of an aged and broken man, he gives thanks. He thanks the Lord for everything he can think of in reference to Sarah's life. But more than anything he thanks Him for taking her into His arms. After he has prayed Isaac helps him stand. Isaac takes a cover from the closet and covers Sarah's body so that she looks as if she is simply sleeping.

Coolness makes its way through the front door and begins to swallow every part of the room. There is a different Spirit in the house.

"Can you feel it Pa?" Isaac asks.

"Feel what?"

"The Spirit of God." Isaac answers. "It's the Spirit of God. He's still here. I can feel 'em."

Abraham pauses with his eyes closed. He wants so badly to be happy for Sarah but right now he just really misses his wife. Once again he rises up to his knees and leans in toward Sarah's face. He gently kisses her several times on the cheek and forehead and with one last embrace he stands to his feet.

In time Abraham makes his way outside onto the porch. With tears still streaming down his face there is nothing that he needs to say. The entire ranch is weeping. He tries to speak but can not find the words. He weakly makes his way to his old rocking chair and sits down. Sensing that something is amiss, the old dog rests his head in Abraham's lap and whimpers. Isaac places his hand on Abraham's shoulder and addresses the families.

"Mom is gone . . . Today . . . God called her home." He pauses as his emotions overtake him;

"I need some ladies to help with her body and some men to help with a casket."

He pauses while trying to maintain his emotions. He wipes his eyes several times and finally just gives up trying to fight pain.

"Thank you for love'n her. You know how much she loved everyone of you. I think we owe it to her to show our respect in a special way."

He brakes.

Immediately many of the elderly ladies make their way into the house and into Sarah's room. You can hear them weeping as they gather together around her bed.

A few men step up to the steps of the porch.

"Abraham, we'll make a really nice casket." One mentions.

Abraham is wiping his eyes as he nods his head.

"Pa, do ya have any idea where ya want to bury her?" Isaac asks.

Again Abraham nods his head but this time he stands and grabs his hat. His emotions change like the movement of wind and his focus becomes very direct.

"Get my horse; I need to go to town." Abraham commands.

"What's in town Pa?"

"I know where your mom would wanna be. I need to go buy the land." Abraham answers as he makes his way down the stairs.

"Why don't we take care of things here today and go to town tomorrow." Isaac suggests.

Abraham is having no part of it. He makes his way out to the barn and saddles up. So, Isaac follows suit. Together they ride to the gates of the town where they find a young man by the name of Ephron. Ephron, like everyone else in town knows who Abraham and Isaac are and is surprised to find out they were looking for him.

Abraham rides up and steps down from his horse.

"Are you Ephron?"

"Yes Sir," Ephron answers.

Abraham extends his hand.

"My wife, Sarah, has been with me since before the day I left my father's ranch to come and live among your people. Today she went home to be with the Lord."

"I'm sorry to hear that." Ephron offers.

"Thank you. Earlier this year we was ride'n the country and came across a place you call 'Double Cave'. We went inside the cave and rested. Sarah loved the quiet. I was hope'n you'd consider sell'n me the cave and allowing me to bury her body there."

Ephron shook his head "no".

"Abraham, we all know that you are a mighty man of God. You've brought great things to this land even though you weren't from here. If you want to bury her there, go ahead and I'll give ya the cave. But you don't need to buy it from me."

Abraham is touched but doesn't waver from his request.

"I appreciate that, but if it's the same to ya, I'd rather buy it out right." He offers.

Ephron continues to try to persuade Abraham to accept it as a gift but he can see the old man isn't feeling it.

"Okay Sir, what is money between us. If ya want it I'll sell it to ya so it will be yours outright." Ephron agrees.

They agree to an amount and Abraham pays him on the spot. More importantly they shake hands and finalize the deal in front of several of Ephron's friends and family. Now they will all know that Double Cave is the property of Abraham. After the deal is made he is anxious to get back to his home where Sarah's body lays waiting.

By the time he and Isaac return to the ranch the women have bathed Sarah's body and dressed her in her favorite dress. When Abraham walks into the room all he can think about is how beautiful she is even now. Every day his love for her has continued to grow stronger and stronger; he has no idea how to handle tomorrow. As he stands at the foot of the bed looking at her, one of his foremen comes in and wraps his arm around Abraham's shoulders.

"We have her casket ready." He says respectfully.

Abraham looks to Isaac, "When would you wanna take her to the cave?"

Isaac stands wiping tears from his cheek; "First thing in the morn'n."

The foreman pats Abraham on the back; "I'm sorry Abe."

Abraham nods his head.

"I'll get everything ready for in the morn'n." The foreman states, "Don't worry about anything."

Isaac reaches over and shakes his hand; "Thanks."

Without having to be told everyone makes their way out of the house and leave Abraham and Isaac alone for the night with Sarah's body. As one would expect, the entire night is spent sitting and looking at Sarah, sitting in the kitchen and crying, reminiscing with each other about things she had said and done, laughing and crying again, dozing for short periods of time and then staring into the night.

Early that morning Abraham and Isaac are once again sitting in the bedroom with Sarah's body when the foreman comes in.

"Abraham, when you're ready . . . " he offers.

Abraham turns and looks to him; "I think we're ready."

The three of them walk outside. In front of Abraham's house sits a horse drawn buggy that is covered in wild flowers and plants. A couple of the original ranch hands sit in the buggy seat dressed in the best clothes they can find. Even the horses are washed up. Behind the buggy are every grown man and women of the ranch in their own buggies or on their horses. Behind the adults the teenagers are driving several buggies full of kids. All are dressed in the best they have. All sit there quietly waiting on Abraham.

Four of the elderly men have gone in and place Sarah's body in the casket. They carry it outside and lift it in to the back of front buggy. Isaac rides up beside the buggy leading Abraham's horse.

"Ya ready Pa?" he asks.

Abraham stands on the porch taking the time to look at each individual of the parade of families that are taking Sarah to her final resting spot. He tries hard to look each one of them in the eyes and even though he never speaks a word, every one of them knows his heart.

He walks around the buggy and saddles up on his horse. He and Isaac lead the way to the Double Cave. Other than Abraham and Isaac no one else from the ranch even knows where they are going. It takes about an hour to ride to the cave. Most everyone is surprised when they stop. They have no idea Abraham has bought the property for Sarah.

The buggies surround the cave and everyone gathers around the entry. When Abraham is ready the four men slide the casket out of the wagon and carry it into the belly of the cave. Those closest to her follow the casket into the cave for a short prayer and word in remembrance of Sarah. When they are finished they return to the rest of the families outside the cave. Abraham stands in the opening of the cave for a moment with his head bowed. Eventually he looks to his right and sees a pile of rocks lying on the ground. He walks to the side of the cave and picks one up, carries it over to the entry of the cave and lays it on the ground. Isaac watches his father and does the same. As if it were an old ritual, every one that has followed behind them makes their way to the side of the cave and gathers a rock to place in the opening of the cave. When every man, woman, boy and girl has stacked a rock the entry is completely enclosed.

Abraham speaks to the families;

"I hope you will take the rest of the day and remember everything you can about Sarah. I hope that in the future you'll share your stories with your children and your children's children and continue it for generations to come. Sarah was a woman of God, the mother of our ranch. She'll be the mother of many generations. All of us have been blessed by God Himself for having the chance to be a part of her life. Especially me and Isaac. Now, she's with God and I cain't wait to see her again."

Isaac steps forward and prays.

"God, I ain't got a lot to say except, thanks. Thanks for bless'n me with a mother so great as she was. Thanks for help'n her teach me how important it is for me to know You. Thanks for help'n me and Pa know that we can see her again when we come to live with You. Allow us the same heart for everyone in this ranch as Mom had."

He pauses for a moment with his head bowed and then looks up to the crowd. Everyone quietly mumbles,

"Amen."

CHAPTER 15

A wife for Isaac

Genesis 24

One day Abraham is sitting in his rustic ranch house forcing down an extra strong cup of coffee that he had made himself when his head foreman comes in to visit.

Abraham looks to the front door as the foreman comes in;

"Micah!" he says with a smile.

"Hey Abe. Got any ah that coffee left?"

Abraham nods his head toward the cabinet where the metal coffee pot was sitting and burning a ring on the counter top.

"You're gonna need to have a lil muster about ya if you're gonna drink it." Abraham laughs, "It ain't Sara's coffee."

Micah walks over to the pot with a cup and sees the smoke coming from the top of the cabinet. He starts to say something but skips it and just sits the pot down in the sink after pouring himself a cup of coffee sludge.

He takes a sip; "Wheh! That's stout!" he says while grimacing

Abraham just laughs; "Cowboy up a lil Micah, somebody's gonna hear ya whine'n."

"I don't know if I can be this much cowboy." He snorts, "Whatcha been do'n anyway Abe.?"

Abraham smiles a crooked old smile with a look that tells Micah something is up.

"Actually, I been think'n bout Isaac. I'm think'n its get'n close to time for him to be get'n married."

"Oh really!" Micah spouts.

"Yep. But here's the deal. I don't want 'em marry'n some woman from these parts. I want 'em to marry some one from back where we come from. So, ... *he smiles again* . . . . I want cha to do someth'n for me."

"I figured as much." Micah says

Again Abraham chokes down a sip of coffee.

"I want cha to go back to the area where my brother Nahor lives and see if you can find Isaac a wife."

Micah just sits there with a funny look on his face.

"What?" Abraham asks.

"Let me get this straight." Micah interjects, "You want me to go back to your brother's land and see if I can find a woman that I think is right for Isaac? What if Isaac already has someone? What if he don't want anyone? What if he don't like who I pick? Then what?"

"Then you've done all ya can and that's all I'm ask'n." Abraham answers as he stirs a clump out of his coffee. "I'll tell ya though, I think it'll be good. I believe God will take care of it. He'll show ya which one is right if ya let Him. Then Isaac will like her too. Just trust yourself with God."

Micah still thinks the idea is crazy. But, it wouldn't be the first crazy thing he has ever done for Abraham. Not by far. So when the chores are done for the day Abraham gives him plenty of supplies and some pack mules and sends him off on his journey. I should say secret journey because they didn't tell anyone else where he was going.

The ride to Nahor would not be easy. Abraham has been gone for many years and a lot of things have changed. The wilderness has gotten more dangerous with rebels and animals. Riding on your own would be one thing, but riding with a line of pack mules slows you down quite a bit. He'll have to pay attention every step of the way for many days. The first night he makes his way to the top of the mountain where he will have a good view of anything or anyone who might try to approach him. Micah is no stranger to living among the mountains and trees. Over half his life he has herded cattle and protected the ranch from anyone who might mean to bring harm. The only thing catching his attention tonight is a senseless jackrabbit that will soon be his dinner.

By himself Micah will travel many hours of the day and push his horse and mules to their limit. He has great knowledge of the lay of the land and that will allow him to find watering holes to keep his animals from being too thirsty. A portion of the packs the mules are carrying are feed to get them through the trip. He stops only for a chance to fix a sandwich, drink a little water and feed the horse and mules. At night he lays on the ground with his saddle at his head and a single blanket to cover him from the insects. The Lord has told Abraham that He will send an angel out in front of Micah to guide him and that is definitely the reason he has no problems with thieves or wild dogs. After many days of riding, Micah finds himself in the land of Mesopotamia where Nahor lives.

Outside Nahor's ranch with a large well that many of the women still use to carry water to their houses. Micah stops at the well to rest for a while before he enters the ranch. He is sitting underneath the trees trying to decide how to go about approaching Nahor and asking him to help with the mission for Abraham. It will not be long before the sun sets behind the mountains. He notices in the distance that several women were starting to make their way out to the well. He takes off his hat and begins to pray.

"God, the God of Abraham, help me be successful today. These women will come to the well and will see me. I'll ask 'em to share their water with me. Which ever one offers to water my horse as well, let that be the gal I'm posed to take back for Isaac."

Before Micah has finished his prayer one of the ladies has already made it to the water well. It is a beautiful young virgin woman by the name of Rebecca who happens to be the granddaughter of Nahor. Micah pauses for a few minutes and then approaches her as she is dipping water from the well.

"Excuse me, Mam." He states, "Is there anyway you might be able to share a drink of that water with me?"

Rebecca continues pulling the bucket from the deep of the well and then turns to face him. He is taken back by her beauty. He has not seen anyone with physical characteristics so outstanding since Sarah was a young women. She smiles at him in a pleasant way and answers,

"I'd be happy to share this water. Why don't you come and drink from this bucket while I pour some out more for your horse and mules?"

Micah is without doubt one of the toughest and hardest headed men that has ever worked for or traveled with Abraham, but when God proves Himself in such a way it's hard to maintain your composure. He fights the lump in his throat and thanks her for her hospitality. As she walks past him he slightly pats his chest and points to Heaven. It's his way of telling God "thank You."

In his pocket is a sheep skin cloth that is bound together by leather strapping. He unties a leather strap and removes a gift that Abraham has sent with him. He sits quietly for about ten minutes and watches as she dips water from the well and makes sure every horse and mule has plenty to drink. Other than God, he cannot imagine what would cause a woman to go to that measure for a stranger. As she finishes he stands to talk to her beside the well.

As she walks toward him after watering his last mule he speaks to her;

"I have something I'd like to give you."

"You don't owe me anything sir. I was glad to help you." She replies

"Its not pay Mam. It's a gift."

She smiles. "A gift? Why would you give me a gift?" She asks.

He pulls out several bracelets that Abraham has sent with him and places them on her wrist.

"Let me ask ya someth'n. Who's your Dad?" Micah asks.

While she is admiring the bracelets she answers, "My Dad is Bethuel and my Grandpa is Nahor. He is the brother of the one famous Abraham."

Micah grins from ear to ear.

"You reckon he'd have any place I might be able to rest tonight?"

"I'm sure he does." She says quietly.

Micah steps back a few steps and bows to the Lord.

"My God, the Father of Abraham. Thank You for keeping Your promise to him and for bringing me to his relatives."

At first Rebecca steps back not realizing what he is doing. Then she bows her head for a second. As he continues to pray Rebecca decides to run home to her mother's house at the ranch of Nahor with her jewelry. She is telling her family what has happened at the well and what Micah has said. Her brother is there to hear the entire story. Her brother's name is Labon. He also knows of the history of Abraham and knows that Abraham was his grandfather's brother. When he sees the bracelets on Rebecca's wrist he gets excited about the man by the well.

"Get a nice place ready for him to sleep and have the women cook up the best of meals." Labon says to Rebecca. "I'll ride out to get him."

He then rides out to the well as hard and fast as he can go. When he gets to Micah he finds him brushing out the horse's tail.

"Sir, I know you are a man blessed by God. Why are you still standing out here? Come with me. We got ya a place to sleep, some good food and good place to rest your horse and mules."

Micah spits a mouth of water to the ground and wipes his face with his sleeve;

"That would be good, I'd appreciate it."

Micah ties all his mules together on a long rope and saddles up on his horse. He dallies the rope around his saddle horn and begins following Labon down the hill toward Nahor's ranch. As they enter the gates of the ranch it is refreshing for him to see men working the cattle, women doing chores and kids running through the houses just like they would be doing at home. Labon leads him to a cabin just to the side of Nahor's house.

"This is where ya sleep. Go on in and I'll take care of the horse and mules." Labon suggests.

Micah slides slowly off his horse and hands the reins over to Labon. He grabs a tied roll of clothes from behind the saddle and makes his way to the cabin door. Labon takes his horse and mules to the barn and feeds them fresh hay and grain while Micah goes into his cabin. On the bed inside the cabin is a bar of handmade soap and a towel. Lying on the floor is a pan of water. Micah tosses his bags into the corner beside a rocking chair and falls back on the bed. It has been a long hard ride. He lays there for a few minutes admiring the carpenter work of the cabin before sitting up on the edge of the bed.

"Wheh, what a day." He thinks to himself.

He pulls off his boots and begins removing his clothes. He hasn't had a bath since he left Abraham. The water is still warm which helps to ease the scratching of the home made soap. He scrubs his entire body with the exception of his hair. Sometimes men just don't seem to remember everything. After he has bathed himself he puts on a pair of cleaner jeans and a shirt from his pack, cleaner, not clean.

There is a knock on the door.

"Sir, Sir." A voice calls.

Micah opens the door and finds a young girl standing in front of him.

"Are you ready for dinner?" She asks

"I am indeed." He answers.

He follows her past a few other cabins and into the house of Bethuel. He is welcomed in by Bethuel, Rebecca's father and Labon, her brother. Together the family sits around a large oak dinner table that appears to have enough food for a banquet when compared to what he has eaten for the last several days. It is a little awkward at first as he waits for all the others to find their seat. Though no one speaks a word he is welcomed with many smiles.

"We're pleased to have ya join us, Mr.?"

"Micah." He interrupts.

"Micah." Bethuel continues, "It's good to meet someone from the families of Abraham. Please, eat all you can eat."

It is obvious to Micah that many of the teachings of Abraham were being taught to this part of his family. *Only those who are gifted with the righteousness of God are willing to give when others are craving. Everyone but Micah begins to dip food and pass bowls around in order to fill their plate. Micah sits still and watches.

"Is there a problem?" Labon asks.

Micah takes a deep breath and stands at the end of the table;

"I'm sorry, but, I just cain't eat until I tell ya why I'm here."

With that everyone puts down their bowls and plates to listen to what he has to say.

"Go on, speak." Labon says.

Micah wipes his mouth with his sleeve and runs his fingers through his greasy hair. It was just then that he realizes he has not washed his head. He wipes his hands on his jeans and begins to speak.

"The good Lord has blessed Abraham. He's blessed 'em with a lot of land, livestock, money, friends, everthing you can imagine except a wife for his son, Isaac. Years ago Abraham's wife, Sarah, passed away. Now, all he's got left at the ranch is Isaac. Abraham asked me to do a favor for 'em cause I'm who he trusts most. He told me he didn't want Isaac marry'n a woman from the land of the Canaanites. So he ask me to ride to ya'lls ranch and . . . . well . . . . strange as it may sound, he wanted me to find a wife for Isaac."

The family snickers.

"I know! That's what I thought! But here's the deal, I told 'em I'd try. So I loaded up and rode to your ranch. Then, I was sit'n out by the well try'n to figure out what to do when I saw the women start to head that way. So, I prayed. I told God I was gonna ask 'em to give a drink of water and which ever one offered to water my horse and mules would be the one I was suppose to pick. And, well . . . . I ain't even hardly finished pray'n when Rebecca is dip'n from the well. I asked her for a drink . . . . .she gave me one . . . . then offered to not only water my horse but all my mules as well."

Rebecca's eye brows raise and her chin drops. It didn't take a genius to realize what he is about to suggest.

"Wait just a second," Labon says, "You tell'n us you wanna take Rebecca back to marry Abraham's son?"

Sweat begins to bead up on Micah's forehead as he stands in front of all the family while they are staring a hole through him

"Umm . . . .yeah . . . . I guess that's what I'm say'n."

He's figuring this was probably going to do away with this supper they laid out . . . . *his stomach grumbles*

Everyone looks to Rebecca as she stares in shock at Micah. Micah smiles back at her like a scared little kid.

"He's a really nice guy." He mutters.

One of the brothers snickers. Rebecca lowers and shakes her head in amazement.

"Can I ask you someth'n Sir, what is it that made you think I would even consider your offer?" she asks.

Micah walks around the table to her chair.

"It ain't about what I thought Mam. It's about me trust'n God. And God told Abraham He would send a wife back for Isaac. If ya don't think it's you, that's okay. I'm just do'n what Abe asked me to do."

Bethuel speaks up, "If it's really a God thing, then you best give it some thought Rebecca. But for now, its still good to see someone from Abraham's ranch. I say we let this lie for a bit. Let's eat before this good food gets cold."

"I agree." Labon says.

Micah nods his head in agreement and returns to his chair. They all resume filling their plates and passing bowls around the table. Not a word is spoken as the food is spread about. Occasionally Micah catches Rebecca looking at him. They smile somewhat uncomfortably and continue eating. The conversation for the rest of dinner is mainly about Abraham but as often as possible Micah turns it to include Isaac. He makes sure that everyone knows that Isaac is a good man, a leader, a man of God. When dinner is over they sit in the front room for about an hour telling stories and enjoying each others company. Rebecca hardly speaks. Finally Micah decides it was time for rest.

"Well, I best be get'n to bed. I'll be leave'n early in the morn'n."

He looks to Rebecca;

"If you're ready to go you can load up and go. If you ain't, I understand. No hard feel'ns."

Micah returns to his room with no idea what the outcome will be tomorrow. But, he has convinced himself that he did what Abraham has asked him to do.

On the other side of the street, Rebecca has spent several more hours in the house hashing this out with her family. They have no idea what to think of such a wild episode of events. When it all comes down to it, they agree on one thing, Abraham is a good man, surely his son is raised to be one as well, but most importantly, Rebecca needs to go pray and allow God to help her decide what is right for her life.

Late that night Micah is lying in bed staring at the ceiling when he hears a soft knock at the door. He rises from the bed and slides his britches back on. He pulls on an old T-Shirt and opens the door. To his surprise Rebecca stands outside clasping a shawl around her shoulders. Her expression tells Micah that she is scared.

"Sir, do you really think God intends for me to marry Isaac?"

"I do." He answers.

She takes a deep breath, looks up to the right as if she is thinking and says,

"I'll be ready at sun up."

Then she turns and walks away with a quick brisk step. Micah is ecstatic. He waits calmly until he gets the door shut and then does the worst rendition of a celebration dance by an old, white, un-coordinated man that you can imagine. He lies in bed for hours and could hardly sleep. He is dressed and packed before sunrise and is sure he will be outside waiting for her for quite a while when morning comes, but he is about to be surprised.

When he awakes from a short rest he gathers up his clothes and goes outside to get his horse and mules. To his amazement he is actually the last to join the party. Outside his cabin are all of Bethuel's family and several families of the Ranch. All of Micah's mules are packed with fresh supplies, more than enough for the trip. His horse are saddled and tied to the back of new wagon being pulled by two more mules. In the wagon sits Rebecca and another young lady with bags of their clothing.

Micah hesitates in his doorway for a second smiling at everyone who is standing around waiting on him. He is twisting on the brim of his hat and everyone can tell he has finally taken the time to wash his hair.

"Micah you guys must sleep in a lot where you're from." Labon says jokingly.

"I guess so." Micah says as he climbs into the wagon.

"Who is she?" he asks as he looks at the strange young woman.

"A friend of mine." Rebecca answers.

Rebecca's family gathers around to tell her goodbye. They shed tears of sadness because she is leaving but they are also crying tears of joy because they understand that she is being blessed. With a slap of the reins and quick whistle from Micah the team of mules heads off. Rebecca actually does pretty well until just before they were going out of sight then she cries. Hence the good reason for the friend that will be traveling with her.

It takes three days to get back to the land of Abraham's ranch. During the nights on the trail Micah does everything he can think of to be a gentleman to the girls. But you just don't change personalities that quick. Try as he may the girls are still surprised sometimes by his mannerisms. After the first night of Micah's cooking it becomes obvious they should take over that portion of the chores. While making the trip Micah has a chance to get to know more about Rebecca. They have plenty of time to share stories, discuss things they like and don't like and simply get to know one another. With each hour they spent together Micah receives a deeper confirmation in his heart that she is a God send for Isaac.

Meanwhile back by Abraham's ranch, Isaac has gone out by the well where Hagar had once heard from God. He has been camping there for a few days. He still has no idea what Micah has been doing. As he sits on a large moss covered rock chewing on a twig he notices a cloud of dust rising through the air. He stands to his feet and looks over the ridge. He can see the wagon with horses following but has no idea who it is. He puts on his holster and gathered his rifle. He slips into the edge of the woods and hides himself for protection. When Micah gets close enough for Isaac to recognize him, he steps out of shade and in to the open range waving his hat. He is the image of cowboy. He is a tall, strong, young man whose eyes are shaded by the brim of his worn out hat. A five o'clock shade of whiskers outlines his face. His sun darkened neck is being protected by a sweat covered handkerchief. His shirt is tucked half in and half out. His jeans are dirty, worn and tucked into his dark leather boots. His holster is wrapped around his hips with a 45 Cal tied to his thigh and single shot rifle draped over his shoulders.

Rebecca straightens up as she reaches a point where she can get a good look at him.

"Who is that?" She asks.

She's hoping and praying that Micah says Isaac.

Micah brings the wagon to a stop. Smiles and says, "That's Abraham's son."

Rebecca lifts an eyebrow waiting for further explanation.

Again Micah smiles, "Yep, that's Isaac"

It is obvious that, to this point anyway, Rebecca is pleased. He's fairly rugged looking right now but she's liking what she's seeing.

"You should probably wait here while I tell him what's go'n on."

Rebecca quickly looks toward Micah. "What? Are you tell'n me he didn't know you were bringing me?"

Micah crawls off the wagon grinning and without answering. He walks up to Isaac and gives him a hug. While Rebecca sits in the wagon with her friend she watches the body motions as Micah is explaining to Isaac what he has done. She watches Isaac throw his arms in the air and place his hands on top of his hat. She can tell that Micah is talking hard and fast. Isaac turns his back to Micah and walks in a circle. Then he looks to the ground and shakes his head from side to side as if to say he can't believe Micah would try that. Isaac takes a quick look around Micah toward Rebecca. Seeing that she is staring right at him, he tips his hat then hides behind Micah again. Eventually Micah moves out of the way and holds his hand out to Rebecca in the wagon. She takes that as her hint and climbs down to go see him.

"Wait here." She tells her friend, "We may have to make a quick get away!"

They both laugh and she climbs out of the wagon. Isaac is still spinning in circles with amazement that someone would try to find him a wife without telling him when Rebecca walks up.

It's funny how beauty can replace aggravation.

When his eyes behold her immaculate beauty his anger with Micah shrinks. Rebecca has been wearing a veil to protect her face from the wind and sand. She is removing it from her face as Isaac first lays eyes on her. *It is always Gods will that a man's wife bring him joy and her charms keep him happy. It is His will that she surround her husband with her love. These God guided connections sometimes have a strange way of making things better.

"I'm Rebecca. I think they intend for you to marry me." She says with a smile.

"So I've been told." Isaac states as he glares at Micah.

Micah just shrugs his shoulders, laughs and walks to the wagon.

Isaac stands admiring Rebecca's beauty; "I'm sorry, I don't know what to say."

Rebecca takes him by the hand;

"I didn't know until we just rode up that you didn't know I was coming. I thought you knew. So . . . . who knows what will happen. But, Micah told my father and brother the story of his prayer to God. If he is telling the truth then we'll let God work it out."

"What story are you talking about?" He asks.

"The story of Micah praying outside our ranch by the well," she states, "The prayer that allowed God to choose me as your wife."

"Oh, that story." Isaac laughs with no clue what she was talking about, "Well, you're here, it was a long ride, we might as well get to know each other at least."

He moves the saddle bags from the back of the saddle and wraps them around the saddle horn. He jumps into the stirrup and swings his leg over saddle while his horse saunters in a circle. After gathering up his reins he reaches out to Rebecca.

"Ya go'n?"

She laughs and reaches up to take his hand. He pulls her up to back of the saddle and motions for Micah to follow along with the wagon, mules and, oh yes, the extra woman. Micah is somewhat proud of himself at this point and is quietly laughing as he climbs back into the wagon with the other young lady.

"I guess you think you pulled this off?" she asks.

"Well, he didn't beat me down." Micah laughs.

The young lady smiles; "Isaac got any brothers?"

They both laugh out loud as Micah whips the mules and moves out. They are only about an hours ride out so Isaac doesn't have much time and Rebecca does the best she can to tell him the story of how she got there. The main thing Isaac discovers is that his dad is the one that sent Micah. They rode back to the ranch and straight to Abraham's house.

Abraham is sitting on the porch telling stories to the kids when Isaac lopes the horse up with Rebecca riding behind him. Abraham's story is immediately interrupted. Abraham grabs an old oak stick he has been using to help him get around and walks to the edge of the porch. He can tell that Isaac is waiting on an explanation.

"Who ya got with ya Isaac?" Abraham asks.

"I think you know who she is." Isaac answers.

"He doesn't know me." Rebecca whispers.

Isaac was thinking that Micah went to pick up a girl that Abraham has sent for.

"You sent Micah to find a woman for me to marry and he didn't even know her?"

Abraham laughs to himself; "He didn't need to know her. God knows her."

"So you think she is my God sent wife to be?" Isaac asks

Abraham walks off the porch and beside the horse. He leans his stick on the porch rail then helps her off the horse and down to the ground.

"She's perty as an angel." He replies, "Should I have Micah take her back?"

Everyone looked to Isaac. "Well . . . . I reckon I could at least get to know her."

That brings laughter from everyone. Isaac has waited many years to try and find a love for his heart that could heal the wound of his passing mother. His Father leads Rebecca into his house. They seem to immediately connect. He doesn't know why, but he knows that he can feel the Spirit of God within him. Even though it has come about in probably one of the most unusual manners something tells him Rebecca will soon be his wife. He shakes his head and smiles with anticipation then joins them in Abraham's house for dinner.

She ends up sleeping in a house next to Abraham's. For the next several weeks she and Isaac spend many hours together. It is hard at first as Isaac tries to juggle his work load with his romance. Rebecca actually makes it easier by falling in to the routine with several of the other ladies. In time, she has become part of the family whether she is to marry Isaac or not.

As it turns out they do fall in love. Every day they become more and more attracted to each other. There are a few times when they even try to resist it and fight, but that never works out. Six weeks almost to the day Isaac and Rebecca are wed.

The wedding is held on the mountain outside the ranch. They have decided to make it a small wedding. To them this is showing respect to their mothers. Had their mothers been there, they would have surely thrown a big event. Since Rebecca's mother is still at home and Sarah has passed, the wedding is small and respectful. The two of them spend the next several days camping by themselves. The day before they decide to return to the camp Isaac takes Rebecca down a trail to a place he feels she needs to see.

The sun is casting brilliant colors of red, orange and yellow across the tops of the purple mountains as the silhouette of birds fly through the last hours of the day. Together they stand embraced in each others arms.

Isaac kisses his new bride and looks to the side of the hill in front of them.

"This place is called 'Double Cave'". Isaac says as he removes his hat, "My mother would have loved you."

She looks to the cave not understanding at first what he means. Then she sees all the rocks that cover one side of the opening and she realizes they were standing at the burial place of Sarah. Rebecca moves closer into his arms and hugs him a little deeper. Isaac is reaching a new place in his life. It is time to move on. These two young children of God stand embracing each other and cleaving to life as the night wraps them in its spirit.

CHAPTER 16

Abraham Goes Home

Genesis 25:7-11

Many years pass and Abraham cannot have been happier to see Isaac and Rebecca enjoying life together. As far as Abraham is concerned God is good, life is good. It is still a habit of his, just as he has always done, to get up before the rest of the families and sit on his porch with a cup of coffee. And yes, there's still a dog sitting with him. As a matter of fact there have been several dogs over the years. And every dog that has ever slept on the porch beside Abraham's chair has experienced the last bit of hot coffee being tossed across his back.

Isaac is beginning to adhere to Abraham's long lasting tradition. Generally Isaac shows up around ten minutes after Abraham has the coffee made. A year or so ago Isaac drug his own chair over to Abraham's porch and day after day they sit together and watch the ranch come to life. It would probably be impossible for Abraham to tell about all the wonders of God that he has experienced just by sitting in that chair.

The first crow of the rooster is yet to be heard as Isaac sits on the side of his bed slipping on his boots. Rebecca is lying asleep in the pleasantness of God's grace. Isaac pulls his shirt over his head, tucks it in and buckles his belt. On his way out the door he grabs his hat and yawns like a lion.

It's time for some coffee.

He makes his way through the moon lit morning stepping over the cow manure, around some chickens, past a few horses, around piles of fire wood, over the dog and around the corner of Abraham's house only to find out that Abraham is not on the porch. He walks up the steps and glances in the window to see if he can see his father in the kitchen making coffee. He sees nothing. Perhaps Abraham has just decided to sleep in. He is quite old now and maybe this enjoyable process isn't so enjoyable anymore. Isaac sits down in his chair and decides to wait for a few minutes. He's petting the old dog on the belly for a while but is getting a little impatient about his coffee. In a few minutes he is just sitting there wondering about his father. Soon enough he can't take it any longer and he goes into the house.

"Pa!" he says as he entered the door.

"Pa! You in here?"

There is no reply. He eases his way through the darkness of the house and in to the bedroom. He can tell that his father is still lying in bed. He finds the lantern on the nightstand and lights it up. The flickering of that small fire casts light on the peaceful resting expression of his father. Abraham's eyes are closed and there is a slight smile on his face as he lies on his back. Isaac shakes him a little to wake him up.

"Pa, better get up. It's time for coffee."

Abraham does not respond.

Isaac shakes him again. "Pa, it's time for coffee."

"Pa . . . . Pa . . . . "

Isaac steps away from the bed. His eyes are filling with tears, his hands begin to shake and his heart begins to race. His face fills with the sadness of a man who just lost his father. He can't hold it back and his emotions take him to his knees. He kneels crumpled beside his father's bed with his hands across Abraham's lifeless chest and cries out to God. Time is of no essence as he lies over Abraham's body holding to his Pa.

He is literally broken at heart.

This is the extreme overwhelming feeling of loss, sadness and loneliness that he has never experienced. He can't pull himself out of it. Ultimately his grief makes him sick and he is forced back out to the porch to vomit. When he is able to regain his composure he raises his head, leaves Abraham's house and walks back home, lost.

His occasional break down of crying as he sits on the edge of his own bed eventually wakes Rebecca. She sits up in the bed wrapped in blankets and unaware of what Isaac has found.

"Isaac . . . .what is it?" she asks as she begins to rub his back.

The touch of her hand causes him to break down and weep. His body pulses as he struggles to breath. Rebecca climbs out of the blankets and sits beside him doing all she can to comfort him without knowing what is wrong. Then it dawns on her. She realizes he is dressed. She realizes this is the time he should be drinking coffee with Abraham.

"Oh my Lord!" she gasps, "Is it Abe?"

Isaac nods his head but is unable to speak. She wraps her arms around his neck and together they morn with great emotion.

"Where is he?" she cries.

"In his bed." Isaac whispers.

"I should go over there." She says as she nervously puts on her clothes and shoes.

By now a few of the families have begun to wake up and stir around. As Rebecca runs from her house one of men is outside getting a bucket of water. He can see that Rebecca is crying as she runs into Abraham's house. In a few seconds he notices Isaac standing on his porch and looking toward Heaven as he sheds tears. He knows in an instant what has happened. He runs back into his house and gets his wife. Together they run to Abraham's house and find Rebecca kneeling down beside Abraham's bed and crying.

When Rebecca hears them come in she stands up to speak to them.

"Is he gone?" The man asks.

"I'm afraid so." She answers.

"When did . . . . "

"Last night." She interrupts, "Isaac found him this morning. There's no need to rush everyone out of bed. But as they wake up, I'd appreciate if you help me let everyone know."

"We will." They agree as the woman places her hand over her mouth and begins to cry.

Rebecca ushers them out of the house. The man makes his way to Isaac and reaches out to shake Isaac's hand.

"He's the greatest man I ever knew." He offers.

Isaac shakes his hand; "Thank you."

"You rest for now, we'll take care of ya." The man suggests.

Isaac nods his head in agreement.

As the lights of each family's houses began to flicker the word of Abraham's passing quickly spreads. In each house you can hear the cries of the unexpected news. Even before the sun has welcomed the day the families are standing around Abraham's house holding candles and lanterns and in complete silence. The cows are unattended, the horses are not fed, the eggs are not gathered, the garden is empty, chores will wait and breakfast will be passed. The visual will last until mid morning. Several times Isaac steps out of his father's house to encourage the families to go ahead with their daily routine, but it falls on deaf ears.

Inside the house of Abraham is the man that had given them the life they enjoy.

Because of Abraham's faith in God, he had the courage to walk away from the security of his father's ranch with a small heard of livestock and some daring families. Because of his faith in God, this man was blessed with a ranch that gave life to hundreds of families. Because of his faith in God, children have been born to couples that may have never known each other had Abraham not followed Gods call. And because of Abraham's faith in God, people have passed away throughout the years knowing that there family was safe in the protection of the man God loves. Generations will be created because of the man in the house the people are circling. More importantly, and most importantly, Abraham's faith has taught the families of this ranch what it means to trust God. And because of that, they are in no hurry to walk away.

In the front of the line a little girl bows to her knees and places her hands together to pray. Another little girl sees her and joins her, then another child and another and another. Finally, one of the ladies kneels down beside the children. One by one each person kneels to God around the house of Abraham and prays. They pray for Isaac, they pray for Rebecca, they pray for the ranch and they give thanks for Abraham.

"Mommy, I'm hungry." A child says

Isaac hears what he says and walks over to him. He rubs the boys head and smiles.

Looking to his mother; "Take him home."

She nods and lifts him up to go home.

"Everyone, it's time. Go home. Get your chores done. Give us a chance to get things ready to pay gratitude and respects. I promise, I'll give ya plenty of notice before we go."

One by one the families come by Isaac and hug him and Rebecca and basically tell them they are loved.

Isaac turns to Rebecca; "Do ya think you can handle this for a bit?"

"I can.", She answers, "What are you fix'n to do?"

"I got to go find Ishmael." He answers.

"Good. Abe would like that." She stated as she hugged him around the waist.

Isaac saddles up, but not on his own horse, this time he takes his fathers. He finds Ishmael about a half day away. Even though Ishmael and Hagar haven't been around the ranch they are still in an area where Abraham was able to keep up with Ishmael's life. Ishmael is still very much loved by Abraham. Together Isaac and Ishmael tell Hagar of Abraham's death. In the town where they live many people know of Abraham and the relationship between him and Hagar and Ishmael. Abraham is very well respected by them all.

A day later Isaac sits on the porch of his father's house. He sits there drinking a cup of coffee and waiting for God to give him a sign that it is time to bury Abraham. In the distant east the mountain gives a color of deep purple until the very tip of Gods created light glances over the horizon. Isaac sits there for several more minutes and watches the sunrise just as he had done for several years with Abraham. *For Isaac and his father their road to righteousness is like the sunrise that continues to get brighter and brighter until daylight comes. This time, however, he isn't waiting on the rest of the families to wake up and join him, they were already up and lined down the lane on horses and wagons waiting on Isaac. On the porch Abraham's dog is asleep beside the old broke down rocking chair. In the chair sits Abraham's boots with his hat hanging on the back. Isaac steps off the porch and saddles up on his horse. Behind Isaac is Ishmael on his horse. Following behind him would be Rebecca and Micah in a wagon that is carrying Abraham's casket. And as you can imagine, behind them is every member of the entire ranch.

From top his horse Isaac takes one last sip of the coffee and then tosses the rest of it toward the porch and onto the back of that old dog. The dog yelps and jumps and then makes its way to the wagon. Without being called, it jumps into the back of the wagon and lies down beside the casket.

Smiling at Ishmael, Isaac gently spurs his horse and the procession heads out of the ranch. It's a slow meticulous ride that will take several hours to get where they were going. They take a trail that leads them past all the areas that Abraham has enjoyed living around. Many of which only Isaac knows about. Many are places where Abraham has gone quietly to spend time talking to God. In due course, they make their way over a ridge that opens up to the Double Cave. When Isaac tops the ridge he is shaken by what he sees. As far as the eye can see, in a distant half circle, people from neighboring towns that have either met Abraham on occasion, heard of Abraham and many that have never seen him, have come to pay their respect. Not hundreds, thousands. As Micah pulls the wagon up beside the cave where Sarah is buried the multitude begins to move in. Isaac sits and waits for over thirty minutes as the crowd gathers. Then he and Ishmael lead the way as four other men slide Abraham's casket out of the wagon and carry him into the open portion of the cave. Inside the cave, Isaac, Rebecca, Ishmael and Hagar stand together and pray. The multitude outside the cave wait patiently until Isaac steps out. He lifts his hands and offers a prayer of thanks on their behalf. It is a prayer that expresses his sincere appreciation for allowing him and Ishmael to be children of such wonderful people and his promise to carry on his father's dedication to God. He thanks God for all the blessings that the families have received because of the faith that Abraham had in God. He thanks God for all the blessings that are yet to come because of his father's faith.

When Isaac finishes his prayer they stand in complete silence for several more minutes.

Everyone has made their way back to their horses and wagons except Isaac. He stands alone in front of the multitude of people staring at the resting place of his parents. Their historic lives tell a story that many will never believe.

Many times as his parents have aged he has tried to convince himself that he is ready for their death. He is not. If it were not for his unwavering trust in God and the truth that he will one day see them again he would be forever lost.

From behind the wagons that have carried the casket two strong slender young cowboys slide down from their horses and walk up beside their father. One is a red headed brawn of a young man and the other a humbled and quiet nature. They are third generation cowboys that are already learning the *wisdom that has been passed from generation to generation. Fighting back the tears from their eyes and the lump in their throats, they walk over to the opening of the cave, remove their hats and quietly say good bye. Their chaps whisper in the silence of the day as they walk toward the pile of rocks that had enclosed the side of the cave housing Sarah's body. They each take a rock and place it on the ground in front of the opening on Abraham's side of the cave. The eldest then picks up another small rock and places it in his pocket for a keepsake as a tear wash's a trail down the redness of his cheek. Together, the young men stand beside their father and watch in amazement as the multitude of people began to make their way toward the cave to pay respect to their grandfather. Even late into the evening the parade of people who have been blessed by Isaac's father continues to pass and place rocks at the opening of the cave of Sarah and Abraham's final place of rest.

On the ridge above the valley of the Double Cave Isaac sits upon his father's horse and watches as God begins painting the western skies with magnificent colors. As the sun begins to take rest behind the horizon, the final light of the day outlines the silhouettes of three sad cowboys.

Isaac and his sons, Esau and Jacob, sit proudly upon their horses in the land God has promised them as Godly examples of what Abraham's faith was all about.

The legacy continues . . . .

"HOPE"

Hope, Hope is the name of my travel'n mare.
I ride her around on days that I dare.

And up the road is a town called "Doubt".
I've wandered its roads go'n here and about.

Doubt can be dangerous if I didn't have Hope.
What with all the temptation, man can barely cope.

On the other side of Doubt there's a fence and a gate.
I'd like to go through it if it's not too late.

Though the gate has me locked out by chain and key,
The presence on the other side keeps beckoning me.

And then I remembered as I was going through strife,
That God had given me the key to life.

So I opened the gate and we traveled on through,
Seems like Hope knew just what to do.

Now I leave Doubt behind and forget what I lack.
I keep riding Hope and never . . . . .ever . . . . look back.

Sonny Jacks

About the Author

Though Sonny was born in Oklahoma City, Oklahoma, he grew up in the small town of Antlers, Oklahoma. He was raised by what he calls, "The strongest prayer warrior in the world", his mother, Shirley Jacks. While growing up with two sisters, Teresa, the oldest, (she'll love that) and Ginger, his younger sister, he had the pleasure of sampling all that country life had to offer. He graduated from Antlers High School and received his graduate degree from East Central Oklahoma State University in Ada, Oklahoma. He has been married to his High School Sweetheart, Jennifer for thirty two years. After graduating from college he and Jennifer moved back to Antlers, Oklahoma. Together they have a son, Josh and a daughter, Jayci. Sonny has been writing devotions, commentaries, poetry, music and manuscripts for the past six years. He is a licensed minister and has traveled for years speaking on the excitement of being a Christian. His presentations are filled with laughter, encouragement and most of all, truth.

"I am not a 'name it and claim it' kinda guy, but I also don't see the need in be'n a soured up Christian."

Sonny believes that humor and laughter is the key to . . . . well, a bunch of stuff! He has been blessed through the years to participate in all areas of ministry. When asked how he would like for others to describe him, Sonny replied,

"I'm a humbled man who serves a great God."

Glossary

Chapter 1 Proverbs

*Prov 14:29, A patient man has great understanding, but a quick-tempered man displays folly.
NIV

*Prov 10:26, Never get a lazy man to do something for you; he will be as irritating as vinegar on your teeth or smoke in your eyes.
TEV

*Prov 16:9, You may make your plans, but God directs your actions.
TEV

*Prov 21:9, Better to live on a corner of the roof
than share a house with a quarrelsome wife.
NIV

Chapter 2 Proverbs

Prov 20:11, Even a child is known by his actions,
by whether his conduct is pure and right.
NIV

Prov 2:6, It is the LORD who gives wisdom; from him come knowledge and understanding.
TEV

Prov 18:22, He who finds a wife finds what is good and receives favor from the LORD.
NIV

Prov 21:31 You can get horses ready for battle, but it is the LORD who gives victory.
TEV

Chapter 3 Proverbs

Prov 21:5, Plan carefully and you will have plenty; if you act too quickly, you will never have enough.
TEV

Prov 25:14, People who promise things that they never give are like clouds and wind that bring no rain.
TEV

Prov 12:4, A good wife is her husband's pride and joy; but a wife who brings shame on her husband is like a cancer in his bones.
TEV

Chapter 4 Proverbs

Prov 29:20, There is more hope for a stupid fool than for someone who speaks without thinking.
TEV

Prov 16:32, Better a patient man than a warrior, a man who controls his temper than one who takes a city.
NIV

Prov 29:25, Fear of man will prove to be a snare, but whoever trusts in the LORD is kept safe.
NIV

Prov 24:10, 10 If you are weak in a crisis, you are weak indeed.
TEV

Chapter 5 Proverbs

Prov 28:20, A faithful man will be richly blessed, but one eager to get rich will not go unpunished.
NIV

Prov 10:5, He who gathers crops in summer is a wise son, but he who sleeps during harvest is a disgraceful son. NIV

Prov 12:24, Hard work will give you power; being lazy will make you a slave.
TEV

Prov 13:20, Keep company with the wise and you will become wise. If you make friends with stupid people, you will be ruined.
TEV

Chapter 6 Proverbs

Prov 10:14, The wise get all the knowledge they can, but when fools speak, trouble is not far off.
TEV

Prov 21:16, A man who strays from the path of understanding comes to rest in the company of the dead.
NIV

Prov 24:24-25, Whoever says to the guilty, "You are innocent" — peoples will curse him and nations denounce him. 25 But it will go well with those who convict the guilty, and rich blessing will come upon them.
NIV

Chapter 7 Proverbs

Prov 12:20, Those who plan evil are in for a rude surprise, but those who work for good will find happiness.
TEV

Prov 14:8, The wisdom of the prudent is to give thought to their ways, but the folly of fools is deception.
NIV

Prov 15:29, When good people pray, the LORD listens, but he ignores those who are evil.
TEV

Prov 12:25, Worry can rob you of happiness, but kind words will cheer you up.
TEV

Prov 3:5-6, Trust in the LORD with all your heart and lean not on your own understanding; 6 in all your ways acknowledge him, and he will make your paths
NIV

Chapter 8 Proverbs

Prov 26:15, Some people are too lazy to put food in their own mouths.
TEV

Prov 23:12, apply your heart to instruction and your ears to words of knowledge.
NIV

Prov 23:23, Truth, wisdom, learning, and good sense — these are worth paying for, but too valuable for you to sell.
TEV

Chapter 9 Proverbs

Prov 30:4, Who has gone up to heaven and come down? Who has gathered up the wind in the hollow of his hands? Who has wrapped up the waters in his cloak? Who has established all the ends of the earth? What is his name, and the name of his son? Tell me if you know!
NIV

Prov 27:18, Take care of a fig tree and you will have figs to eat. A servant who takes care of his master will be honored.
TEV

Prov 31:30, Charm is deceptive, and beauty is fleeting; but a woman who fears the LORD is to be praised.
NIV

Prov 24:19-20, Don't let evil people worry you; don't be envious of them. 20 A wicked person has no future — nothing to look forward to.
TEV

Chapter 10 Proverbs

Prov 6:26, A man can hire a prostitute for the price of a loaf of bread, but adultery will cost him all he has. TEV

Prov 10:4, Being lazy will make you poor, but hard work will make you rich.
TEV

Prov 2:7-8, He holds victory in store for the upright, he is a shield to those whose walk is blameless, 8 for he guards the course of the just and protects the way of his faithful ones.
NIV

Prov 23:20-21, Do not join those who drink too much wine or gorge themselves on meat, 21 for drunkards and gluttons become poor, and drowsiness clothes them in rags.
NIV

Chapter 11 Proverbs

Prov 15:30, A cheerful look brings joy to the heart, and good news gives health to the bones.
NIV

Prov 11:25, Be generous, and you will be prosperous. Help others, and you will be helped.
TEV

Prov 29:11, A fool gives full vent to his anger, but a wise man keeps himself under control.
NIV

Chapter 12 Proverbs

Prov 23:13-14, Don't hesitate to discipline a child. A good spanking won't kill him. 14 As a matter of fact, it may save his life.
TEV

Prov 20:11, Even a child shows what he is by what he does; you can tell if he is honest and good.
TEV

Chapter 13 Proverbs

Prov 9:9, Instruct a wise man and he will be wiser still; teach a righteous man and he will add to his learning.
NIV

Prov 2:1-8, Son, learn what I teach you and never forget what I tell you to do. 2 Listen to what is wise and try to understand it. 3 Yes, beg for knowledge; plead for insight. 4 Look for it as hard as you would for silver or some hidden treasure. 5 If you do, you will know what it means to fear the LORD and you will succeed in learning about God. 6 It is the LORD who gives wisdom; from him come knowledge and understanding. 7 He provides help and protection for righteous, honest men. 8 He protects those who treat others fairly, and guards those who are devoted to him. TEV
Prov 21:5, Do what is right and fair; that pleases the LORD more than bringing him sacrifices.
TEV

Chapter 14 Proverbs

Prov 13:24, He who spares the rod hates his son, but he who loves him is careful to discipline him.
NIV

Prov 14:32, When calamity comes, the wicked are brought down, but even in death the righteous have a refuge.
NIV

Chapter 15 Proverbs

Prov 21:27, All day long he craves for more, but the righteous give without sparing.
NIV

Prov 5:18-19, So be happy with your wife and find your joy with the girl you married — 19 pretty and graceful as a deer. Let her charms keep you happy; let her surround you with her love. TEV

Chapter 16 Proverbs

Prov 4:18, The road the righteous travel is like the sunrise, getting brighter and brighter until daylight has come.
TEV

Prov 4:1-9, Sons, listen to what your father teaches you. Pay attention, and you will have understanding. 2 What I am teaching you is good, so remember it all. 3 When I was only a little boy, my parents' only son, 4 my father would teach me. He would say, "Remember what I say and never forget it. Do as I tell you, and you will live. 5 Get wisdom and insight! Do not forget or ignore what I say. 6 Do not abandon wisdom, and she will protect you; love her, and she will keep you safe. 7 Getting wisdom is the most important thing you can do. Whatever else you get, get insight. 8 Love wisdom, and she will make you great. Embrace her, and she will bring you honor. 9 She will be your crowning glory."
TEV

CPSIA information can be obtained at www.ICGtesting.com
Printed in the USA
LVOW111032091111

253918LV00001BB/1/P

9 781462 706754